THE TELEPATH

BY BRYAN COHEN
&
CASEY LANE

The Telepath

ISBN-13: 978-1547281404
ISBN-10: 1547281405

First Edition

Printed in the U.S.A

ACKNOWLEDGEMENTS

Thank you to everybody who made this book possible. Our beta readers Julianne Clancy, Tim Matson, Barbara Pohland and Torsten Spooner made a difficult project much easier with their notes. Damonza & James Olsen did a great cover, and Oomphotography did an amazing job with the key art. Thanks to Alisa Rosenthal for helping out and to Michael Silberblatt and Cordelia Dewdney for bringing the characters to life. Ashley Gainer & Abigail Dunard went so far above and beyond this time. Craziness. Lastly, thanks to Amy for everything.

Prologue

A man wearing sunglasses and a bulky coat that hid his build walked through the abandoned parking lot at Page's Diner attempting to sense any power Ted Finley may have left behind. He was a stranger to Treasure, though he'd forced himself to become more integrated after he saw the news reports of Ted's heroic exploits. Most of the glass had been cleared from the lot after the neighborhood chipped in to cut down on cleanup costs for the diner's owner, Debra Page. A few shards glistened in the bushes as the man looked up at the broken building. His mind turned to his childhood home, which had been similarly ravaged the last time he'd seen it. The pit in his stomach ached as he opened the half-cracked front door. A hint of power was left in the room, as a fire might leave a burnt carbon aroma.

"It's not here anymore. But it was."

Aside from the broken windows, the diner looked like it could have been ready to open the next morning. The stranger understood why when the realtor walked in.

"Hello?" The woman sported a big smile, as if she could sense a hefty commission. "I saw you walk in. Are you interested in hearing about the building?"

The man rested his hands against the wall and felt something seep into his body. For him, it was like the odor of a cigarette to a former smoker a few months after quitting. His mouth watered.

"I'm very interested," he said. "What happened here?"

The woman's face brightened as she went into salesman mode.

"Local hero – no, national hero – Ted Finley saved over a dozen patrons from a gang of thugs here not three months ago. If it weren't for him, this would be a spot of tragedy, but he made it a triumph."

"It looks a little tragic." He kicked a piece of glass from under one of the booths toward the wall. It ricocheted against a blue piece of tile, making a pinging sound before it caromed to the woman's feet. "I'd heard something about classic literature on the walls. Are those books still here?"

The woman carefully picked up the glass and placed it in a wastebasket. "The former owner actually donated those books to the local library. They were put into a special collection."

As he walked over to the woman, she straightened her spine. The corners of his mouth turned upward.

"Thank you." The man laid a hand on her shoulder. "I was never here – and you can't see me now."

The realtor flinched and put her hand up to her forehead. A few seconds later, she recovered and began tidying the diner up for her first appointment of the day. When she looked in the stranger's direction, her eyes moved through him as if he were transparent. The stranger placed his hand against the wall once again as he walked toward the exit.

Like many buildings on the upscale side of town, the Treasure Library was new. The fresh smell of air conditioners and Lysol covered up any evidence that there were books inside. The stranger would have taken the musty odor of old paper any day.

It only took a few minutes for him to find the right librarian.

"How may I help you, sir?" The woman didn't look up from her computer.

"I'd like to see the special stacks."

"Do you have a library card?"

When the stranger said he didn't and wasn't a town resident, the librarian pointed to a placard displaying the policy for viewing the special stacks.

He could accompany a town resident with a library card, but the man had no desire to bring anybody else into this situation. At least, not yet.

"Would you mind letting a fellow book-lover see a few first-edition classics? I've been tracking these down for weeks."

His explanation was a half-truth. Seeing the original print of Moby Dick mattered less to him than what might lie between the lines. The librarian's monotone seemed pulled straight from a computerized voicemail system.

"We appreciate your commitment to the arts, but a policy is a policy."

The stranger rubbed the back of his head. "It was worth a shot to do it the old-fashioned way. I figured a little charm never hurt."

"What do you mean the old-fashioned way?"

The stranger reached toward the librarian and spoke as if he were chanting. "Take me to the special stacks. Nonchalantly, if you please."

The librarian closed her eyes for a second before standing up and grabbing the key beside her. "Right this way."

She was no perkier than before.

They passed through several doors on the way to the stacks. While many of the rooms were visible through glass walls, the hand-carved door to the stacks was opaque and heavy. The librarian opened the door and led the man in before locking them inside.

The smell of crumbling paper and stitched covers sat in the room like a cloud. He felt like he'd left a world made of plastic to enter a truer reality.

Beyond his five senses, he felt a powerful force drawing him closer. If Page's was the smoke, this room was a blazing fire.

He tried to sense the source with his eyes. "I need to see the books from Page's."

With every step the librarian took, the man felt a stronger pulse of energy. She laid a few books on top of a table, and the stranger swore he could hear a faint hum emanating from them. One in particular began to call to him without words, and he touched it.

A flash of blue electricity shot through the room, the lights dimmed and the stranger flew backwards into the wall. The man squinted to cope with the pain and pulled himself back up. He rubbed the spot on his shoulder where he'd made an impact.

"I think it's fair to say that wasn't the right one."

The librarian remained stoic beside the table as the man chuckled to himself.

"Thanks for your concern."

This time, he concentrated more carefully on the book he should choose. When it became clear that a first edition of the book *Of Mice and Men* was the right fit, he opened it to the first page and put his finger on the text. His body vibrated with the first wave of energy.

The man flipped through the first few pages of the book and felt his mental powers increase with every passing second.

"While you play, it's time for me to get to work."

Chapter 1

Erica LaPlante sipped her coffee as she watched the living soul, Ted Finley, attempt to arrange a series of objects five feet off the ground in the form of a word. She gave him the option of using anything in the lair, as long as none of the items he chose were the same weight as one another. Ted had finished the E and the R of her name when she started to take in their surroundings.

She didn't believe Dhiraj at first when he said he'd cobbled together the funds for a secret hideout. A small staircase beneath a closed-down bakery led to a massive space that must have connected the basements of almost every storefront on the entire underdeveloped block. The subcontractors had outfitted the formerly abandoned space with the latest technology: 50-inch touchscreen monitors, holographic simulators and even a state-of-the-art fitness center.

A five-pound weight from the letter I tumbled to the ground, and Erica noticed the rest of the word start to falter.

"Concentrate." Erica took another drink, the warm beverage tickling her throat on the way down. "Just because one thing falls, doesn't mean the other ones have to."

Ted sneered at Erica before turning his attention back to the word. His gym shirt was covered in sweat, the result of a two-mile jog at 4 a.m. fol-

Bryan Cohen & Casey Lane

lowed by hand-to-hand combat training. Erica liked to do the mental work last, because a living soul needed to be prepared for the most difficult of circumstances. She'd seen multiple living souls fall prey to a failed effort to use their powers when they were exhausted. She'd also seen one die because of his inability to balance physical and mental energy.

She didn't enjoy thinking back on that moment. After all, she was the one who'd had to kill him.

"That looks good."

Erica was startled to hear Ted speak. He'd been completely silent for the previous few minutes as he arranged the letters.

"It is." She took an exaggerated sip and licked her lips.

Every time she got too focused on training him, Ted would do or say something that reminded her they were dating.

Ted's face turned up into a grin. "I think I know a good place for that."

Erica felt the half-full cup of coffee zip out of her hands. "Hey!"

The beverage stayed completely upright and undisturbed as it moved across the room and formed the last part of the word.

"I think you mean 'A.'" Ted beamed at his joke and his three-dimensional word.

Erica already felt the absence of the warm cup against her hands. "There were less delicious objects you could have picked."

Ted raised his chin in air. "I just wanted to make sure you were paying attention."

She wanted to be angry, but her name was spelled out so expertly that she let pride bubble to the top instead.

Erica put her hands together. "Good work. It really is something."

When Ted looked up at the word to admire it, Erica struck. She dashed in with lightning speed and tried to catch him in the back with a jump kick. He turned to block the blow with his elbow, though the objects from the E and the R toppled to the ground. She swung at him with a left and a right punch, but he feinted both before pushing Erica's chest to knock her backward.

He crouched down into a fighting stance. "So that's how it is." Ted looked down at the fallen objects.

"You dropped your E." She mimicked his stance.

"Maybe I did it on purpose." With that, Ted put out his right hand and started shooting the items in Erica's direction.

She kicked a trashcan to the side and let several crumpled pieces of paper and pencils zip past her. "Gotta aim better than that."

When a medicine ball came right for her midsection, Erica caught it in one hand, spun around and threw it right back toward Ted. The ball shot at him with such speed, he didn't have time to react before it knocked into his thighs and sent him face-first to the ground. The dumbbell from the I made a clanging sound as it hit the ground; the C and the A were the only letters that remained hovering.

Ted coughed. "Good toss. Almost de-manned me." He rolled onto his back, did a kick flip onto his feet and turned back toward his protector. "Now it's time for a little offense."

Ted came running at Erica. She sighed as she easily sidestepped his attack, got underneath his arm and used his momentum to flip him onto his back. As the thud echoed throughout the room, Erica watched the items from the C and the A start to waver and fall. She made a mad dash for the A and flipped through the air, catching her coffee before it reached the ground and landing on her feet.

She took a sip and shook her head. "Here's a tip: when you're tired and floating something, stay on the defensive."

Erica offered Ted a hand and easily pulled him back up to a standing position.

He dusted off his shirt. "Good to know."

After Ted took a quick shower in the lair's full-service bathroom, they packed up Erica's car in the back alley. Ted looked at his watch and back at Erica multiple times.

"Yes?" Erica finished loading the car and shut the door.

"I noticed that its 6:30."

"Mmmhmm."

Ted put his hands on his hips. "So that means we're getting out early."

Erica nodded. "Mmmhmm."

Ted rolled his eyes and took Erica around the waist. "You're driving me crazy! I wanted to see if we could do less training and get up later."

Erica brushed away a strand of hair that was getting in the way of his eyes. "No. I just have somewhere to go before school."

She started to turn toward the car, but Ted pulled her back toward himself.

"You said you haven't felt any dark souls cross over since Sandra, right?"

Erica could tell where Ted was going with this. She slumped against the car. "Correct."

"And there's been no evidence of any otherworldly activity."

Erica nodded.

Ted inched himself closer to Erica. "Then maybe." A few inches closer. "Maybe." Even closer. "We could scale things back a little bit."

Erica gave Ted a quick peck on the lips. "Not gonna happen." She pulled herself away from Ted and walked around to the driver's side.

"But–"

"Sorry, Ted. No buts. You've got to be ready for anything at all times." Erica got inside and started the car.

Ted walked around to her side, and she rolled down the window to accommodate.

"Will you at least consider going to three days a week?" Ted sported a pair of puppy dog eyes that had more of an effect on Erica than she'd wanted. Unfortunately for Ted, it wasn't enough.

"Goodbye, Ted."

Ted squinted at Erica. "Wait, we're not going to school?"

Her lips twitched. "We are going to school. But I've got somewhere to go first. Alone."

"But what am I going to do?"

"You're a superhero. Take your wings and fly away."

Erica took the car out of park and left Ted standing in the alley. She wasn't quite sure what he'd said as she drove away, but she swore she heard the words, "But I'm tired!"

The musty air of the cave was thicker than usual that morning. Even though it had been three months, Erica couldn't help but picture the battle pitting Ted and herself against the dark souls. Erica looked up at the walls, which were still covered in ancient writing. Nigel and his gang had foolishly told her that the dark souls were using the wall to communicate between the Realm of Souls and Earth. It had taken a little bit of work, but Erica was able to reconfigure the communication device to send a secure message to Gan and Reena, the commanders of the light soul army. Erica traced the stone wall with her fingers and found her way back to the latest conversation they'd been having. The chat reminded her of a long-distance chess match, with each side taking a week to reply to the other. She typically went on weekend mornings to hide her communications from Ted, but she felt particularly anxious this week to see how her superiors would respond. She looked up at the last few inter-dimensional messages.

"He's stronger than I thought. The training is going well and I'm pleased with his progress."

"You said the same about Adam. Should we be worried?"

"Ted isn't like that. He doesn't crave power. He's of great service to this mission."

The latest response from Gan and Reena was written right next to the room's entrance. "Does he suspect that there are other powers he can tap into? Is he aware of them?"

Erica gripped the rock and thought up her response. As she conjured words in her mind, the words transposed themselves in the ancient script on the wall.

"He's only been able to use the one power. He doesn't suspect a thing. Our secret is safe."

CHAPTER 2

Ted traced the length of Erica's hair with his eyes. He didn't care that she'd made him fly to school when he was dead-tired. Ted tended to get over any of Erica's so-called transgressions the next moment he saw her.

She was focused straight ahead on Mr. Redican, their long-term English substitute, who was discussing one of Shakespeare's Henry plays. Ted couldn't have told you which one as he contemplated the beauty of Erica's wide, deep eyes.

"Hal was the son of King Henry IV, so he could have had any friends he wanted in the entire kingdom." Mr. Redican took a few paces before stopping just ahead of the front row of desks. "Why on Earth would he hang out with Falstaff?"

Travis, a confident jock, piped up from the back of the room.

"Because he was his dealer?"

Even Erica laughed at that one. Ted got her attention with an exaggerated frown. As Travis high-fived the person at the desk next to him, Erica shrugged her shoulders and mouthed the words, "What? It was funny."

Travis had been friends with the Torello twins before they died, turned evil and were killed again by Ted. While most of the town was on the hero's side in the conflict, Travis was firmly part of the opposition. Travis was part of the popular crowd now, but Ted remembered a time when he would stand

11

next to him at science fair competitions.

Mr. Redican cleared his throat, and most of the students turned their attention back to the front.

Redican was younger than most of the other teachers, which made Ted feel like he could relate to him more. As a sub, he'd gotten stuck with one of the oldest rooms in their school. The tiles on the floor needed to be replaced. Unlike most of the rooms, it still had a dark, green blackboard instead of a whiteboard. A square of the ceiling right above the instructor was missing, which allowed Ted to see a copper pipe and a thick, black cord.

Redican took the beat-up room in stride, using his energy and enthusiasm to keep Ted and the others invested. At least, Ted was engaged whenever he didn't have the urge to stare at Erica, which he continued to do after a few moments of paying attention.

"For all we know, he may have been Prince Hal's dealer," Redican said. "They were drinking buddies. But how would it make you feel if you saw the Vice President, the next person in line, getting drunk at a bar down the street from your house? Ted?"

Ted turned his glance away from Erica for just the second time in at least five minutes. Mr. Redican may have been one of the cool teachers, but his patience for ogling could only be stretched so thin.

"I might worry he'd suck at his job, but at least I'd think he was a cool guy."

Several students laughed politely, though it wasn't quite the ovation Travis had gotten for his joke. Ted didn't mind. After all, the slight chuckling beat the usual silence his comments received before he became a celebrity.

"Great point, Ted," Redican marched the length of his desk. "The people who see Hal drinking with his buddies think he's a cool guy. He's out with the commoners. He's not sitting on some throne somewhere. He's with the people." Redican came to a stop. "Now here's the big question. Is he doing this as a political tactic or because it's fun?"

Erica raised her hand.

"Ms. LaPlante?"

She turned her head to the side and pursed her lips together. "A little from column A and a little from column B."

The class really got behind that one. Even though Erica was dating a former loser, her popularity stock couldn't be higher. The bell rang and Mr. Redican called out the assignment to read through the end of Act IV.

Before Ted could pack up his things, Erica's buxom friend Beth had reached his girlfriend's side. While he had every morning to train with Erica and most evenings to talk hero business, he was still jealous to cede any of his Erica time.

"I can't handle it." Beth tucked her long, red curls behind one ear. "Mr. Redican is too hot for words."

Beth wasn't a quiet girl. Ted figured that Mr. Redican heard every word she'd ever said about his body and his mind, but he appeared to ignore every last one.

As Beth and Erica walked out of class, Ted followed closely behind.

"I see the goods." Erica tossed her hair. "I'm mostly in agreement."

Beth rolled her eyes. "Would you be 100% in agreement if you weren't in love with Captain Eavesdrop?"

Ted cleared his throat. "I'm not eavesdropping."

Beth and Erica stopped and turned around. Ted's girlfriend and protector put her arms around his neck and pulled him toward her. The combination of the sweet smell of her shampoo and the spritz of rich perfume she wore made his heart pump just a little bit faster. She only met his eyes for a second before she looked back at her friend.

"He can listen in on whatever conversations he wants to, as long as I get to kiss him at the end of it."

The words rang true enough, but ever since Erica returned from the dead with a whole new bag of personality, Ted wondered if lines like these were more theatre than reality.

Beth made a gagging sound. "I've officially choked on my own vomit and died." She imitated a corpse. "Can you see if Mr. Redican will come to my funeral and weep over my grave?"

"I'm sure everyone will, Beth." Ted tightened the grip around his girlfriend.

Beth gave Ted a minor death glare and turned back to Erica. "I'll see you in sixth period." Beth gestured at Ted. "Maybe you'll have this out of your system by then."

Beth gave a strained smile and left.

"It's not likely." Erica pulled Ted toward her once again and kissed him on the cheek. She lingered there for a moment. "You need to stop staring at me in class."

Ted's mouth opened wide. "Staring? I would never stare. There's a very interesting poster about Charles Dickens right over your shoulder. I'm sure you just saw me reading that."

Erica took her hands off of Ted's neck and let one hand brush the side of his arm before grasping his hand. Ted interlocked his fingers with hers.

"I'm sure that's the explanation," she said. "You're making it hard for me to concentrate. You've been in school for the last 12 years. I'm trying to get the hang of it again."

Erica looked 17 years old, but Ted needed to remind himself from time to time that she'd been around a lot closer to 17 generations.

"I figured you'd have this stuff down pat." Ted grinned. "Didn't you pal around with Willy Shakes?"

Erica dug her nails into Ted's palm. "You see one play in the 1590s and everybody thinks you're some kind of expert."

Ted knew there was a lot about Erica he'd never know. When would there be time to go over several hundred years of history? But he had a strange feeling about the morning's training session.

"So, where did you have to go today?"

Erica stopped to get a drink at the water fountain and pretended not to hear. "Hmm?"

"Where'd you drive off to? Does it have something to do with the sword?"

After Ted had taken out Nigel and the Torello twins with the other-worldly sword, he suggested that he should walk around with it at all times. Erica had said it was too dangerous and she needed to put it somewhere safe. Not even Dhiraj knew where Erica's secret hiding space was.

"Ted, you need to trust me." She reached up and kissed him on the cheek. "I only hide things when it's for your own good." Erica took Ted's hand and continued to lead him toward her locker.

Ted trusted Erica, but there was something strange about the way she said "your own good" that gave him pause. He made a mental note to run the conversation past Dhiraj and moved forward.

As they got close to Erica's locker, Ted felt his free hand dig into his pocket. He looked over at the large poster on the wall. It read:

"I Can Be Your Hero, Baby.

Get Your Tickets for Junior Prom."

They were dating, but aside from occasional hangouts with Beth, Winny, Jennifer and Dhiraj, it'd been mostly a private affair. He wasn't sure how Erica would react to being asked out to prom, so he'd put it off. After weeks of being dogged by Dhiraj, he broke into Erica's locker using his powers and placed a "Will You Go to Prom with Me" sign inside. Even though Erica wasn't the same person he'd grown up with, it would still fulfill a lifetime goal if she said yes.

When Erica reached her locker, she gave him a probing glance. "What is it?"

Ted looked up at the ceiling and then the walls. "Oh, nothing. Nothing."

Erica laughed. "You are too strange."

When she reached for her lock, both of their phones buzzed at the exact same time. Ted's heart sank when she put down the lock to check the message.

"It's Sheriff Norris." Erica's popular-girl grin was gone. She'd gone right into game face mode. "There's a robbery and hostage situation downtown."

Ted felt like he'd just heard Erica speak Greek. "In Treasure?"

She nodded. "We better go."

As Erica turned, Ted grabbed her hand. "But, what about sixth and seventh period?"

"Sheriff Norris'll write you a note."

She tried to leave again, but Ted held her firm. He looked back at the locker and wondered if he should just ask her right then and there. "Wait!"

Erica rolled her eyes. "What is it, Ted?"

For a moment, Ted couldn't help but see the old Erica in his girlfriend. The one who'd be willing to end their relationship in a heartbeat. "I... I was wondering if—"

"Whatever it is, we'll talk about it after. Duty calls."

Erica took Ted's hand again and began leading him in a fast-paced walk toward the parking lot. He looked at Erica's locker.

Then Ted used his powers to move the card under a stack of books inside. "You know, sometimes I kind of hate duty."

CHAPTER 3

Dhiraj knew he had checked the PayPal balance of Super Ted Finley LLC about 20 minutes ago, but he felt the need to check it again. The numbers were clear: Ted's superhero practice was a million-dollar enterprise. The crowdfunding campaigns came fast and furiously after Ted's heroics at the diner. There were endeavors to create a costume for Ted, a lair for him to plot against villains, and even a comic book featuring his exploits. Dhiraj corralled every single one, and the end result was seven figures in the account, even after the construction of the lair.

As Dhiraj leaned back in the white, plastic chair, he remembered how he'd dreamed of the day he could manage a million bucks. Soon enough, he'd be able to do his thinking in a high-rent office with glass walls like his father's practice. He figured it would put the study hall room with its boring, taupe paint and its short, green carpet to shame. As the daydream continued, Dhiraj tapped his pencil against his desk so loudly, his neighbor had to catch the pencil in mid-air to stop him. Dhiraj nodded and moved his thought process back to the inside.

What the hell am I going to do with this money?

When the study hall proctor came around to check on computer screens, Dhiraj quickly switched to a decoy paper in a writing program. He sighed as the beep from a text caught his attention. The proctor was about to admon-

17

ish him when he showed her the text.

"Official hero business." Dhiraj puffed out his chest. "Check the five o'clock news for more info."

Less than a minute later, Dhiraj had packed up and spun his blue sub-compact car around to pick up Ted and Erica. He laughed at the rows of luxury vehicles that would need to remain in the lot past three o'clock.

"Suckers."

His passengers were waiting under a red metal awning just outside of Hall B. The three of them had run multiple drills to exit school in an orderly fashion, but this would be the first one with real crime on the other end. Erica sat shotgun while Ted took the back.

"Everybody buckle up." Dhiraj clicked his belt into place. "It's going to be a bumpy ride."

"Why?" Erica followed his advice. "Do you need to get your shocks fixed?"

Ted did the same. "Are we going off-roading?"

Dhiraj glowered. "I just wanted to say something cool." Dhiraj pulled out of the Lexus showroom-like parking lot and gave the gas pedal a push. "Let's be the superhero team that has fun."

Dhiraj merged onto the highway and got into the fast lane.

"Actually, Ted and I are the superhero team." Erica typed a few words into her phone.

"What does that make me?"

Ted chuckled. "The superhero team's driver?"

Dhiraj changed lanes and took the curve of an exit a lot faster than he should have. The tires made a skidding sound. The car was about to spin out of control when Ted steadied it with his powers. Dhiraj could feel the tires moving into the right position without his steering command.

When they'd stopped skidding, Ted returned control to the driver. "Careful there, buddy."

"Just warming you up." Dhiraj put on a fake smile. "Nobody should superhero cold."

"Uh huh." Erica pointed toward the sign outside the shopping complex.

"Pull in over here."

Dhiraj parked and scampered around the car to open the door for Erica. She stuck out her tongue at him and exited. Ted followed, and they were about to dash away before Dhiraj held up his hand.

"Guys! Don't forget the gear."

"Oh yeah." Ted rubbed his hands together. "All the secret agent stuff. Did you ever have this as a kid?"

Erica raised her eyebrows. "Sorry, we didn't have plastic yet when I was growing up."

Dhiraj opened the trunk to reveal some of their crowdfunded goodies, including night vision goggles, bulletproof vests and fiberoptic cameras. Dhiraj grabbed the cameras and locked the car.

Sheriff Norris and the rest of his squad were camped outside the jewelry store where the situation was taking place. The shopping center consisted of a chain Thai restaurant, an ice cream parlor, the jewelry store and a couple of knick-knack shops Dhiraj had never entered.

When the three of them walked in, Sheriff Norris and the rest of the department parted like the Red Sea. Ted was in front, with Erica and Dhiraj flanking him. Dhiraj imagined the trio looked pretty awesome; that is, until Ted tripped on a power cord that led into one of the department's vans. He fell forward so quickly that the hero didn't even have time to deploy his powers, landing face-first on the ground. There was a gasp from the onlookers. Dhiraj saw Erica shake her head as the sheriff ran over to help Ted to his feet.

"I'm okay." Ted brushed some dirt from his face. "I'm good."

Sheriff Norris chuckled. "You three sure know how to make an entrance."

"Once we're done learning how to walk"—Erica glared at Ted—"how about you tell us what we've got, sheriff?"

Ted nudged Erica.

"Shouldn't I take the lead on this in public?"

Erica put up both her hands and smirked before taking a step back.

Ted took her place. "What've we got, sheriff?"

"It's a robbery gone bad. Six hostages, one of whom has a potentially serious injury. At least three kidnappers. All of them armed."

Ted squinted. "I don't remember the last time there was a robbery—"

"Four years." Sheriff Norris looked past the three of them to the jewelry store. "Discounting the occasional house burglary, it's been four years since anything like this."

Dhiraj presented the cameras. "You want some eyes on the inside?"

The sheriff's eyes twinkled. "And it isn't even my birthday yet."

Dhiraj set up the equipment as the sheriff and his men guided two of the cameras in through an air conditioning vent on the back of the building. They flipped the devices on and Ted used his powers to maneuver them through two storage closets and into the jewelry store. Before long, they could all survey the scene. Dhiraj flipped a switch, and the sound from inside the store played through a speaker.

"Will you stop crying?!" A scrawny kidnapper stood over the body of an injured hostage.

There was a puddle of blood beside her, and Dhiraj wondered if it was from a knife or a glass wound – shards of glass from the jewelry cases were spread throughout the room.

"Stop looking at her!" The scrawny man gestured to his fellow robbers. "Get the cops back on the phone."

Judging by the way he gave orders, the man seemed to be in charge. That didn't seem to stop him from nervously pacing back and forth.

Ted cleared his throat. "What's the play here?"

Before Erica could say a word, a noise came from the other side of the parking lot. There were voices, one of which echoed louder than the others through a bullhorn. A group of about 50 people marched in unison and began to surround the sheriff's forces.

"Here they are." The sheriff looked over at his squad. "Set up the barricades, boys."

Erica placed her hands on her hips. "Do they have a permit?"

The sheriff nodded. "It just came in before you got here. I was hoping we'd be through already, but they work quickly."

Dhiraj marveled at the growing crowd. He recognized some of them from outside the school parking lot. Most of them were middle-aged or older and carried signs. Dhiraj wondered how any of these folks could maintain a day job while harassing Ted. He looked through the crowd to see if any of their slogans were clever. Most of them said one thing and one thing only.

"Go Home Alien!"

The Go Home Alien movement had grown from a hashtag into something much more annoying.

Dhiraj shrugged. "If only they were protesting robberies."

Nobody laughed at the joke. Erica looked angry enough to punch somebody.

CHAPTER 4

Erica watched Ted as he reacted to the arrival of the GHA movement. She'd seen him grow in a lot of ways over the last few months, but this was always going to be the toughest part.

How are you supposed to feel like a hero when it seems like everyone is out to get you?

Erica leaned in toward Ted. "Are you alright?"

Ted squirmed and gave the crowd a final glance before turning to her. She could already see the sweat starting to bead on his forehead.

"Never been better." Ted's voice cracked. "I'm glad all my fans are here to see it."

Erica put her hand on his back and took a soothing tone. "Hey, it's okay. It's just like the lair. Just you and me."

"And a hundred protestors." Dhiraj looked around. "Oh, and the local news just got here."

Erica moved her hand from Ted's back to the base of Dhiraj's neck. When she squeezed, he yelped from the pressure. "We're coddling now, Dhiraj. We're not writing the screenplay."

Dhiraj shrank from the challenge and nodded. Erica watched Ted as he stared into the camera monitors. She saw a silver necklace on the far wall of the store begin to move as Ted tried to get his bearings.

"You're doing great, Ted." Erica could hear Ted's breathing grow faster. "One step at a time, okay?"

"Sheriff!" Erica waved the lawman over to her. "Can you quiet down the crowd and get your men in position?"

The sheriff returned a dubious look. "We'll do our best. Tell me when he's ready."

Ted let out a huff. "Oh, you'll know." He looked back at the camera and pointed his hands forward.

In the background, Erica heard one of the sheriff's deputies attempt to silence the crowd with a megaphone. Meanwhile, Ted had zeroed in on the weapon of the kidnappers' leader. The gun was in a holster on the side of his black trunks. Through the camera monitor, Erica could see the gun begin to shake.

"Almost got it." Ted was focusing so hard, his eyes could have burned a hole in the monitor. "Almost got it."

"Boo!" A single voice from the crowd bellowed, causing the rest of the mob to join in.

The noise startled Ted, and instead of removing the gun from the man's holster, he unfastened and removed the belt. The kidnapper's black pants, gun and all, dropped to the floor, revealing boxers with pink and red hearts on a white background. While the other kidnappers laughed at their cohort, he seemed poised to kill.

"What the heck is going on!?" His face turned bright red as he fumbled for his gun.

Ted looked back to Erica eyes wide. "What do I do?"

"Improvise!"

Ted looked back at the monitors and used his powers to wrench the leader's belt around his ankles. With a yanking motion, he tripped the robber and let his face hit the carpet. Before the other two kidnappers could realize this was no laughing matter, Ted had undone their belts and let their trousers hit the floor as well. When they tried to reach for their pants and their weapons, Ted swept their legs with a flourish of his arm and watched as they tumbled to the ground.

Dhiraj snorted. "It's a good thing they were all wearing underwear."

Erica couldn't help but grin as Ted pulled all three guns away from the half-naked men and sent them flying to the far end of the store.

One of the kidnappers unknowingly whined right into the camera. "I feel so exposed!"

The sheriff and his men cheered. Dhiraj hugged his friend around the waist. "You're amazing, Ted!"

Erica felt a sense of pride as she gave a nod to Sheriff Norris.

He smiled in response. "Alright men, go in on my mark."

"Wait!" Ted closed his eyes. "Something's not right."

The cheering halted as everyone focused back on the hero of the hour. Erica saw something happen within Ted. For a moment, he reminded her of a different living soul entirely. The admiration Erica felt started to drain out of her.

A fourth kidnapper came out of the back room with his gun pointed directly at the hostages. "We said no heroes!"

The man was about to shoot the injured hostage when Ted made a gripping motion with his hands and lifted the man into the air. The gun went off, though the bullet landed harmlessly in the wall. Ted tossed the man from one end of the store to the other, and his gun fell to the ground. Ted removed the clip from the weapon and placed it in the corner of the room with the other weapons.

"Now you can go."

The sheriff waved in his men. Ted put his hand up for a high five. Dhiraj and several of the sheriff's men obliged.

Erica did her best to hide the feeling of fear that was building up inside her.

He used another power. This is not good.

Ted noticed her lack of cheer. "You alright?"

She nodded and searched for an answer that would change the subject immediately. "Sorry, it's just that time of the month."

Ted appeared to short-circuit for a moment before forcing a smile. "Oh."

Erica turned away. "Great job, though. Looks like all the training I made you do paid off. Though we probably could have done without the hairy legs and boxer briefs."

She walked up beside him and reached out to shake his hand. Ted took her offering and squeezed.

"Wait. Are you taking credit for me saving the day?"

Erica bit her lip. "I would never. I'm just saying you shouldn't get 100% of the credit."

Ted moved from Erica's hand and put his arms around her waist. "How much credit do you want?"

Erica moved closer. She could feel his heart pulse through his skin. "I'll take 11%."

"Just 11?" Ted grinned.

Dhiraj cleared his throat.

Erica cocked her head to the side. "Yes?"

"As long as you give me some credit for getting the cameras, you two can make out on the news as much as you want."

Erica spied the Channel 5 news van and gave Ted a quick kiss on the cheek before pulling herself away.

"Couldn't have done it without you, Dhiraj."

Dhiraj flashed his newly updated smile, courtesy of a tooth whitening regimen.

Erica looked around to take in the scene. The four kidnappers were cuffed, and the sheriff's men were pushing them into the back of a couple of squad cars. Several members of the GHA movement couldn't help but give their enemy a clap of respect. Dhiraj began to give a TV interview. Ted shook the hands of one of the hostages and received a bear hug in return.

Erica tried to absorb the happiness of the moment as much as she could. But as she looked at Ted, the anxiety built in her stomach. Memories from another lifetime began to stream back without her control.

I won't let this happen again. I can't.

CHAPTER 5

Ted felt his chest puff out a bit as the final kidnapper was loaded into the squad car. As far as he could see in front of him, the scene was one of victory. Even the jewelry store's owner had praised Ted's actions, despite him causing a little extra damage when he'd tossed the fourth kidnapper across the room. Ted dared not look behind him as the chanting continued from the Go Home Alien contingent.

They'd feel differently if I were saving them.

A hand touched the back of his neck and moved down his spine. When Ted spun toward Erica, she wasn't looking at him. She wasn't even looking at the mob. Wherever she was mentally, it wasn't anywhere near a strip mall parking lot.

"We trained, we saw, we conquered." He put his hand around her midsection. "Don't look so glum."

Erica looked back at Ted. Her beautiful smile almost hid the feelings underneath. Almost.

"Sorry. You're right, but it looks like we've got some other fish to fry."

Ted allowed himself to look back at the mob. He couldn't believe that so many people would come out just to yell at him.

Didn't they see me save people's lives?

As Sheriff Norris walked over, Ted could tell the intensity of the situation hadn't left him. He wondered how much longer the hostage negotiation would have gone on without his powers.

"Thank you, guys," the sheriff said. "We're really lucky you could get over here. Once again, the city is in your debt."

"How much debt?" Dhiraj appeared on the opposite side of Ted. He gave the hero a similar pat.

"He's kidding, Sheriff." Ted wrinkled his forehead at Dhiraj.

"I am," he said. "Just write us the excuse note for school and we'll be all settled up."

Sheriff Norris smiled as he chewed a piece of gum.

"You've got it." The sheriff looked at the growing crowd behind the trio. "Need any help navigating out of here?"

Ted took a deep breath. The initial several dozen GHA protestors had grown into more than 100.

"Thanks, Sheriff." Ted extended his hand to Sheriff Norris. "I think we'll be fine."

The sheriff shook all their hands before he walked back over to supervise his staff. After Dhiraj packed up the gear, they considered the path to his vehicle.

"The bastards." Dhiraj pointed straight ahead. "They set up right between us and my car."

Erica took Ted's hand, which caused him to jump.

"Let's just get the escort. Dhiraj can come back and get his car later."

Ted squeezed Erica's hand and let it go. He'd just stopped a robbery. It didn't make sense that they should have to run away afterward. Especially from a bunch of people who called him a murderer and a freak.

"I'm not just going to let them win." Ted tried to build the courage inside himself. "I'm in the right, here. It's only fair we should be able to leave without being hassled."

Ted took a step toward the crowd. Even that tiny movement caused the crowd to get louder. Part of him wanted to take Erica's advice and run away. The nervousness grew in his stomach like a balloon. Ted inhaled deeply as his feet moved even closer to the mob.

"Life isn't always fair, Ted." Erica hesitated for a moment before joining

Ted's side.

Dhiraj struggled with the equipment behind them. "Sure, take your stand. Life would be a lot more fair if I had a hand truck. Or a wheelbarrow."

The three of them reached the edge of the crowd. Ted's pulse quickened and the crowd's chanting transitioned into more of a roar. Most of the GHAers were middle-aged. Some wore special shirts and brandished homemade posters with anti-Ted slogans. Ted noticed a little girl sitting on her father's shoulders. He caught her eye, and the girl's face scrunched up in anger.

"Excuse me." Ted waded into the mob, which parted enough to fit someone half of Ted's size.

He considered using his powers to spread them further, but he resisted the urge. When Ted paused for a moment, Erica pressed her hand against his back.

"You're the one who got us into this." Erica's voice was barely audible over the buzz of the crowd. "Just keep moving."

Ted complied and doubled his pace. As he held Dhiraj's car in sight, the mob started to press in around him. He smelled breath and sweat and looked around for a possible opening. There was none.

This was a bad idea.

Ted felt his throat close up.

"Now!" The shout came from far off to his left.

By the time he looked toward the noise, a projectile had already struck Ted in the head from the other direction. The balloon stunned Ted momentarily as it unloaded its contents of green paint and water onto him, Erica and several nearby GHAers. In addition to the painful ringing on the side of his head, Ted got the worst of the splatter. Half of his face and most of his clothing was dripping with green paint.

As if it were second nature, Ted used his powers to push the mob backward, creating a circle of space around the three of them. The GHAers who felt the unseen force pushing into them began to scream, while those outside Ted's range jeered at the hero with all their might.

"Ted, don't." Erica did her best to settle Ted, but his head was throbbing. The fear was gone. It had been replaced by focus and anger.

Another balloon flew through the air toward them. Ted crushed it from afar before it could get halfway to him. A half-dozen people were drenched with the paint and flaps of balloon. Ted zeroed in on the source of the projectiles and was about to float the thrower up into the air when a voice burst through the shopping center on a bullhorn.

"This is the Department of Homeland Security." Agent Vott's voice rang loud and clear through the shopping center. "You are in violation of your permit and all of you are subject to arrest. Disburse immediately… or else."

If the mob had been in a city, the participants might not have listened, but the suburbanites quickly walked in the direction of their cars and vans. Ted recognized Agents Vott and Harding in the front seat of the black SUV. Vott stowed his bullhorn and motioned for the three of them to approach. Ted looked back at the two green paint stains in the middle of the lot. His pulse continued to race.

"Get in." Black sunglasses covered up Vott's eyes. "Stay on the towels."

Ted glanced at Erica for approval. When she nodded, he wiped his hand on the clean side of his shirt and opened the door. As soon as Dhiraj secured the gear in the back, the SUV pulled around the dissipating crowd and out of the lot. Ted watched as Erica attempted to assert her popular airhead persona.

"I'm like, literally overjoyed you came to get us." Erica twirled a strand of hair. "Green paint is so tacky."

Agent Harding looked at the three of them through matching shades. "Save it, LaPlante." He removed the glasses. "We know you're the brains of this operation. You can stop playing dumb."

Erica let out a gasp of air. "Good. That made me feel like taking a hammer to my skull."

Agent Harding smiled before his partner hit him with a sharp slap in the shoulder. The grin faded. He threw them a couple more DHS-embroidered towels.

"If she's the brains…" Dhiraj leaned forward in his seat. "What does that make me?"

Harding looked at his partner and then back at Dhiraj.

"It makes you the capital." Vott dismissed the question with his hand

and looked back at Ted. "You did good work at the jewelry store. The three of you should be proud of yourselves."

The SUV had gotten far enough away from the lot to resume normal suburban driving speeds.

"Thanks." Ted wiped the side of his face with the towel. "But it sounds like you're trying to butter us up."

Vott and Harding exchanged another glance.

"Ted, we've been monitoring you for the last few months. Originally, we were sent to make sure that you weren't a threat to homeland security."

"And what was your assessment?" Erica crossed her legs and glared at the agents.

"We determined that you could do more good than harm." Vott ignored Erica's body language. "We can make this GHA problem go away pretty quickly for you."

Dhiraj cleared his throat. "All of a sudden, this is sounding a lot like a negotiation." Dhiraj turned on one of the cameras. "Don't mind me. Just recording this to make sure you don't kill us if we refuse."

"This isn't a movie." Harding's face tightened. "It's business. Ted, we want your help in the fight against terrorism."

Ted scratched his head. "I'm 17 years old, guys. I still haven't finished high school."

"We've had operatives younger than you, but none of them had the promise that you have," Vott said. "You could easily blow up a cruise missile before it kills innocent people, float a suicide bomber up into the air or disarm an entire militia before they can fire a single shot."

"Plus, we'd get a bonus for recruiting you." Harding grinned. "And I've got this eye on a great condo in the city."

Vott slapped Harding again.

"At least you're being honest." Erica focused her attention on Vott. "Ted can't really make that kind of commitment. He needs to be ready to save the world."

Erica looked at Ted to indicate that he was supposed to agree with her. He'd never thought that he could save people worldwide. Three months ago, he wasn't sure he'd be able to save himself in that diner. The idea of making people's lives better throughout the world intrigued him.

When a few seconds of silence went by, Erica pinched the skin on his thigh. The pain brought him back to the moment at hand.

"Erica's right, guys." He rubbed at the red skin on his leg. "If I'd been off fighting terrorists when Nigel and his gang attacked the school, things could've been much worse."

Vott pulled onto a side street and put the car in park. "You're right." He turned to face Ted. "But you stopped Nigel, and if another challenge comes, you can face that, too. But if you want protection from the GHA and you want to be a true hero, you should consider our offer."

Erica opened her door. "Thanks for the towels. We can walk from here."

Before Ted could form a cohesive thought, Erica was already out of the vehicle. Dhiraj followed suit.

Vott tilted his head forward, peeking out over his shades to get a better look at Ted. "What do you say, Ted?"

Ted felt the leather seat through the towels with his fingers. He wondered if he'd get a car like this if he joined the department. Ted took a deep breath. "Let me think on it." He glanced at Agent Harding. "Good luck with the condo."

When Ted stepped out onto the curb, Vott restarted the engine.

"We'll be in touch." Vott rolled the window up and drove away.

Ted felt his stomach churn and wondered if he should have let them drive away so easily.

"You should've said no," Dhiraj said. "Haven't you seen the X-Files? Trust no one." He pushed a camera into Ted's chest. "Now help me with this."

Ted floated all the camera equipment into the air.

Dhiraj stomped his foot. "Couldn't you have just done that the whole time?"

Ted ignored him and tried to read Erica's mood.

"What is it?" he asked.

"Just thinking about the pre-social media days. Secret identities made things a lot easier."

Erica started to walk toward her house. Dhiraj and Ted followed.

"There's nothing wrong with wanting to be a hero."

Erica looked out toward the horizon. "Do you want to help a few people here and there or keep the entire world safe?"

Ted hadn't asked for either. But he supposed he'd have to choose one way or the other.

CHAPTER 6

Natalie sat on the edge of her bed and dribbled a basketball between her legs. When the doorbell rang, Natalie thought it was her phone buzzing for a fourth time. She continued dribbling until she heard another ring. She caught the ball in one hand, palmed it and laid it on her bedspread. After a few bounds down the stairs, she looked out the small window to the side of the door. The close-up of Dhiraj's face would have frightened her if he didn't do the same thing every time he came over. Natalie opened up the door and put her hands on her hips.

"Now that looks like someone who's happy to see me." Dhiraj scooted around Natalie and into the foyer.

"You know, when someone doesn't answer your texts, they're usually busy." Natalie swatted a bug back outside and closed the front door.

"You don't look busy."

"And when people who don't answer your texts aren't busy, what do you think that means?"

Dhiraj pulled at an imaginary chin beard. "It means they want to talk to someone, but they have some kind of psychological block that prevents it?"

Natalie grumbled and headed toward the kitchen.

"What do I get for being right?" he asked.

Natalie poured the two of them some juice and sat at the kitchen table.

"A glass of juice and a one-way ticket home." Natalie sipped the beverage.

Dhiraj nearly spilled his glass as he joined her. "So, my cameras worked today and helped Ted to disarm—"

"I saw the news."

Natalie knew she was being snippy, but Dhiraj was preventing her from ignoring the world around her – from ignoring Ted.

"You should've been there, Nat." Dhiraj inched his chair closer to hers. "You're part of this."

Natalie looked upward and back at Dhiraj.

"I didn't sign up to be a part of a crime-fighting team, Dhiraj." She chugged the rest of the juice. "I'm getting recruited by schools. I could get a full ride somewhere. That's a little less likely if I'm recovering from stab wounds all the time."

Dhiraj took a small sip. "When you broke things off with Ted, you said you'd try to stay friends with him. Instead, you're pushing both of us away."

Natalie walked away from the table and rinsed her glass. "Don't you mean all three of you?"

Dhiraj shook his head.

"You could be friends with all of us, but you're choosing to have nobody. Were you happier before you met any of us? When you just kept to yourself and had no support whatsoever?"

Natalie glowered at Dhiraj. "Why do my choices have to be fight evil or have no friends?"

Dhiraj took another sip of his drink and moved closer to Natalie. She couldn't help but feel like she wanted him to hug her. She also sort of wanted to throw him through the glass sliding door behind them.

"We want to see you, Nat." He put his hand on her shoulder. "If you don't want to help us, that's fine. But life is better with good friends in it. Please keep that in mind."

Natalie was silent, which Dhiraj took as a cue to leave. She wanted to stop him. Instead, she simply watched him go.

To clear her head, Natalie did a pyramid set of pushups, starting with five and working her way up to 10 with short breaks in between. Each time she lowered her body to the floor, she tried to eradicate her anger. It didn't work.

"I just want all of them to leave me alone. Don't they understand that?"

As she moved her body up and down, an idea came to mind. She never would have even considered it if it hadn't been for the endorphins.

It's what I have to do.

When she finished her set, Natalie reached for her phone and searched for one number in particular. She was hyperaware of her heavy breathing as she dialed.

"Hey, this is Natalie Dormer. I know you might not be expecting this, but I want to know how I can help."

CHAPTER 7

Dhiraj pulled his car up to Jennifer's house at daybreak. He placed a mouthwash strip on his tongue as he saw Sheriff Norris exit the front door. The lawman's face looked tired and strained.

"Top of the morning to you, sheriff." Dhiraj grinned and walked up the driveway.

"Hey, Dhiraj." Sheriff Norris' voice was a hair lower than usual. "You looking for Jennifer?"

Dhiraj doubled his grin, attempting to snap the sheriff out of whatever funk had settled over him. "I am. She's still here, right?"

The sheriff stepped into his car, propping the door open with his foot. "If she had her way, she'd be here till noon. Maybe you'll have better luck."

"I'll do my best, sir."

The sheriff tipped his cap and backed his truck into the street. Dhiraj waved in his direction, but the sheriff looked straight ahead with vacant, emotionless eyes.

Dhiraj had been over at the Norris house for dinner twice, so his first glance past the front door was familiar. The dinner invitations had both come from the sheriff himself, but Jennifer always seemed happy to see him. He wondered if she'd be as enthusiastic at this early hour. Dhiraj glanced at the family pictures on the way up the stairs. Jennifer had gone from cute to full-on beautiful as a teen, and Dhiraj remained as spellbound by her as he was the day they met.

Dhiraj took a guess with the only closed door upstairs and knocked. He heard a groan on the other end and the sound of Jennifer shifting in the bed.

"Hey Jen, it's Dhiraj. You know, that cute Indian you're always thinking about."

There was a moment of silence from the sleeping beauty. Dhiraj felt his fight-or-flight instinct kick in and he considered dashing down the stairs.

"Hey, Dhiraj." Jennifer's unsuppressed yawn could be heard through the entire house. "You can come in."

Dhiraj opened the door. A quick scan of the room revealed the pink paint, white, frilly curtains and dozens of photographs framed and unframed that were placed like punctuation on the walls. It was a tribute to childhood and innocence.

Jen's face emerged from the comforter, her hair tousled and uneven, a few uncovered blemishes on the side of her cheek. Dhiraj couldn't help but see the flaw-free woman of his dreams before him.

"Isn't it time for school?" Dhiraj internally kicked himself for sounding like a mom.

"As I was telling my dad"—Jennifer threw the sheets off, revealing a tiny shirt and even shorter boxers underneath—"today didn't feel like a school kind of day. You know what I mean?"

Dhiraj was no peeping Tom, but he felt like one seeing Jennifer in such skimpy clothes. He did his best to avert his eyes while still paying attention to her.

"You might as well go." Dhiraj watched Jennifer's face contort into a dreamy smile. "There's nothing good on TV during the day anyway."

Jennifer's smile grew and she stood up.

"I could never say no to you, Dhiraj." She brushed his shoulder with her hand as she passed by him. "I'll get ready."

Jennifer took the first items she could reach from her hangers and walked into the bathroom. She left the door open and began to change. For a split second, Dhiraj saw her bare back and turned red. He turned away from her and felt his face grow hot.

What in the hell?

The Jennifer he'd grown to love was sweet above anything else. She was the kind of person who would not only remember your birthday but make you a birthday card by hand. She took photographs and knitted socks. The girl he knew was sentimental and caring, and someone who looked just like her was naked 10 feet to his right.

He nearly jumped when she tapped him on the shoulder. She was now fully clothed.

"Are you sure you don't want to skip with me?" she asked. "The two of us could spend the entire day together doing whatever you want."

He'd chatted with Jennifer in the hallways of school and after field hockey games on many occasions, but Dhiraj had never been this close to Jennifer's face and body before. His attention went to her lips.

"It sounds like a dream, Jen, but I think I should just drive us to school." Dhiraj did everything he could to suppress the bodily excitement he felt. It was not working.

Jennifer laughed. She placed both her hands on his shirt. "Alright, but you're driving." She released her grip and left the room.

Am I in the right dimension?

It only took a few minutes for them to get to school. When they arrived in Dhiraj's parking space, he clicked the unlock button. Jennifer immediately countered by locking the doors with the button on her side. She leaned over, and Dhiraj could feel her breath blowing into his ear.

Dhiraj felt ecstasy and anxiety in equal measure. When he tried to speak, the words lodged themselves in his throat.

"Thanks for the ride." Jennifer kissed him on the cheek. For some reason, his mind went back to several months earlier when Erica had done exactly the same thing.

He remained frozen.

Say something!

"You're welcome." Dhiraj tried to keep still and calm.

"Why do you still like me, Dhiraj?"

Dhiraj wasn't sure he got the gist of the question right away. He'd been trying to face forward, but one look to the side put him two inches from

Jennifer's eyes.

"I've... I've always liked the kind of person you are. Beautiful inside and out."

Jennifer remained there for a moment, fixed on Dhiraj's eyes. Then she sat back in her seat.

"I'm not sure who I am inside anymore."

As Jennifer relaxed into the passenger side, Dhiraj recognized the familiar posture and tone of voice he'd admired for nearly half a decade. He let out a long breath and rotated to face her.

"Even if you don't know, I know who you are. And that person is amazing."

She turned toward him and forced a smile before unlocking the car doors. She grabbed her backpack, pulled the handle and began walking to the school.

Dhiraj let a minute of silence pass.

Would she have let me kiss her?

By the time Dhiraj had pulled himself together, he was already a few minutes late for homeroom. The hallways were empty, aside from a few stragglers, and his sneakers echoed against the hard floors. When he stepped into the bathroom to prepare his reasoning for the principal's office, he didn't notice three guys slip in behind him all at once. Dhiraj reached down into the sink to splash some water on his face. When he looked back up into the mirror, the three upperclassmen had surrounded him. Dhiraj stood still.

"Need to borrow a comb, gentlemen?"

Dhiraj recognized one of the teens as Travis, the pal of the deceased Torellos and one of the main GHAers at school. He reached out and pushed Dhiraj into the gray marble wall.

"Where's your alien friend when you need him?" Travis cracked his knuckles as close to Dhiraj's face as he could.

The other two moved into position on either side of Dhiraj.

"If you mean Ted, he's getting ready for a day of first-class education. Something you three seem to have ignored for the last 12 years or so."

Travis grinned. The bully's teeth were whiter than Dhiraj expected.

"I probably have a higher GPA than you, moneybags. Plus, I know how to break a bone." Travis put his hand on Dhiraj's chest and pressed him against the unforgiving wall. "Wanna see?"

Dhiraj reached into his wallet pocket and opened up the change container. His fingers sought out the only way he could think to escape.

"How can you call Ted an alien?" Dhiraj did his best to stall and feel for his escape tactic at the same time. "Ted was in the same class as you when you wet your pants in second grade, Travis."

One of the other GHAers laughed until Travis gave him a violent glance.

"I had a bladder infection." Travis' voice echoed in the confined space. "Besides, who's to say Ted hasn't been replaced by an alien?"

Dhiraj leaned in toward the bullies. "Me. You. Everyone. If we stop all this nonsense—"

As Travis pushed Dhiraj backward once again, Dhiraj found what he was looking for in his pocket.

"You know, I think you'd look better without a few teeth." Travis popped his knuckles again.

"I hear differently." Dhiraj clapped his ears over his hands as he triggered the loudest portable alarm on the market.

The noise rocked the bathroom and the eardrums of Dhiraj's attackers. The decibel level was higher than most airplanes taking off and had two of the teens on their knees in seconds. Travis grimaced but swung for Dhiraj anyway. His eyes gave away the punch and Dhiraj shifted to the side. Travis' fist missed Dhiraj and made a cracking noise against the marble. At least, Dhiraj assumed that's the noise it made, given the overwhelming alarm noise that was beginning to get to Dhiraj as well. As Travis held his now-broken right hand with his left, two janitors unlocked the door and entered the bathroom. Dhiraj switched off the alarm.

"What's going on in here?"

Dhiraj walked toward the door. "Just giving these gentlemen some sound advice." He smiled at Travis. "Team Ted doesn't go down easy."

As Dhiraj exited the bathroom, the adrenaline that had been keeping him up crashed at once. He walked to his first period desk as quickly as he could and collapsed into it as the bell rang.

CHAPTER 8

Albert Redican could hear himself speaking the words to his class, but he wondered if anyone was listening at all. There were five or six faces making eye contact with him, though he knew that two of them had the worst grades in class. The majority of the students were either looking down at the book or pretending to take notes. Albert could easily tell the difference between drawing a doodle and writing down a cohesive thought – he didn't need to spend several months getting a substitute certificate to figure that one out. Another three of the students were using their classroom time to stare at the opposite sex. He wasn't surprised to see that Ted Finley was one of the three.

In his decades on this world, Mr. Redican had rarely seen a living soul he felt was worthy of the challenge.

The bell rang. Much to their credit, the students didn't rush out the door as quickly as usual. Redican smiled to himself.

"Don't forget to do the handout tonight." Redican watched as the students whispered to each other while packing. "And remember that your outline for the 10-page essay is due on Tuesday."

Redican estimated the reminder only elicited half as many groans as usual. He caught Erica and Ted holding hands on the way out the door when he felt a tap on his shoulder.

"Mr. Redican, do you have a minute to talk?" Beth's eyelashes fluttered as she opened her eyes wide.

Redican stifled a laugh. "I have a free period now. Why don't you shut the door and hang for a minute?"

Beth shimmied across the room and closed the door before sitting down in the center seat of the front row. Redican noticed her legs shake as she crossed them.

"How can I help you, Ms. Lynch?" Redican leaned back against the desk.

"I'm having some trouble with my outline. I was wondering if we could schedule a couple of one-on-one sessions."

Redican let out a shallow breath before walking around behind his desk. "Beth, you're friends with Erica LaPlante, am I right?"

Beth nodded.

"Good." Redican pulled out a weathered book from deep within his desk. "I think I have something here that can help the both of us."

Redican opened to a page with a bookmark from the Treasure Public Library and touched the ink. Several extra handouts flew off the desk as if a gust of wind had blown in.

"Mr. Redican, I–"

Redican pointed his hand toward Beth, and the words went out of her. The girl's eyes narrowed and moved off of her instructor. She stared straight ahead at the blackboard.

"Beth, I have a very important mission for you." Redican felt inside her mind for any resistance. There was none.

"Yes, Mr. Redican." Beth's eyes remained focus straight ahead.

Redican took his hand off the book and leaned over in front of his student. "Can I trust you to do whatever I ask of you?"

Beth nodded three times, each one slower than the last.

"I'm afraid this is like an airplane emergency exit, dear. I'm going to need a verbal confirmation."

Beth's eyes moved away from the board and focused on Redican. "Yes. I'll give you my life if you need it."

Redican's cheekbones rose with a wide grin. "Good. I just might."

CHAPTER 9

Natalie had re-worked her day to avoid seeing Ted ever since he'd asked her to join "the team." Gym was the only class they shared, but she made a deal with Coach Fowler to spend the entire class training for next basketball season. Natalie had enjoyed beating up on the less athletically gifted, but with Ted's powers becoming more and more of a participation requirement, she didn't mind staring at a motivational poster while doing barbell squats.

After gym, they used to meet up to walk over to Hall C. To take away the chance they might bump into each other, she went out and around the opposite side of the building. Instead of going to the cafeteria near her fourth period math class, she took a 10-minute stroll to eat at the freshman cafeteria. The plan had worked for almost a solid month, until Ted went out of his way to follow her. She was eating alone at a small table in the corner when he sat down across from her.

"I have a sneaking suspicion that you've been avoiding me." Ted's grin was just a shade shy of cocksure.

"Did you pick up mind-reading during your morning training sessions?"

"All that time working out alone has made you snippy."

Natalie attempted to shoot laser beams out of her eyes and into Ted's face. It didn't work, but the glare was enough to take his grin away.

Ted changed his approach. He looked down at his tray and started to eat.

Natalie watched him open up the plastic container and chow down on the same chicken salad his mother had always packed him. All the little tics that used to make him seem endearing were getting on her nerves. She'd seen him chew with his mouth open nearly a hundred times, but a part of her wanted this to be the last.

"Close your damn mouth."

Ted, along with several students at the nearest table, stopped what they were doing to look at Natalie. She came off angrier than she intended, but maybe that was the tone she had to take. Maybe it would get Ted to leave her alone.

"Sorry." He made sure to chew the next bite of chicken salad with his mouth as closed as could be.

Natalie dropped her fork and let it clack against her plate. "What are you doing here, Ted?"

He looked up at her with his big, round eyes. "Checking on you."

Natalie wished he were lying. "I don't need anyone to check on me. I'm doing great, actually."

Ted smiled. "Really? Did you hear from one of your top five choices?"

Natalie growled. "Why do you care, Ted? You've got someone else now. You can finally leave me alone!" She stood up and began to walk away. Natalie felt herself being turned around as if hand grabbed her shoulder. But it wasn't a hand. Ted had used his powers on her.

"Natalie!" Ted hopped up from the table and followed after her.

She felt her fists clench tight. "Did you just use your powers on me? Did you just turn me around against my will? You're walking a fine line, Finley."

Natalie realized that everyone in the freshman cafeteria had their eyes and phones trained on her.

Let them watch.

Ted's eyes held nothing but fear. "I'm sorry. I'm just trying to say I still care about you."

Natalie pushed the center of Ted's chest. Her ex-boyfriend went flying to the ground, back first. The crowd of freshman gaped in horror.

"You care about me, Ted?" Natalie tried to approach him, but she could feel herself being restrained by the lunch aid and Principal Stoll. "You care about me? If this it what it feels like to be loved by Ted Finley, I think I'd rather get stabbed in the heart this time."

Principal Stoll tried and failed to get a hold of the strongest girl in school. "That's enough, Ms. Dormer."

Ted's eyes were as wide as she'd ever seen them. "I was just hoping we could–"

Natalie lowered her voice. "There's no we. Not as friends. Not as more. We're done, Finley."

With that, Natalie let herself be led out of the lunchroom.

She ignored most of what Principal Stoll told her during the next 15 minutes of lecturing. The end result was three weeks of before-school detention, a cruel trick Stoll had devised to hit his students where it hurt: in their number of hours slept. Natalie ignored two calls from Ted and a call from Dhiraj after she got home from school. When a different number came up, she let herself answer.

"Hello?"

"Few people go viral as often as you, Ms. Dormer," an unfamiliar voice said.

"What can I say? I have a talent for yelling at superheroes. Who is this?"

"Someone who wants to have you for an ally. You asked if you could help. And we're interested."

When Natalie parked her car outside the abandoned factory, she didn't expect to see the lot as full as it was. Three people smiled at her and wished her a good evening as she walked past the other. She returned the gestures with more of a happy grimace than a smile and walked onward. A makeshift sign above the front door pointed out her destination and she willed her legs to move forward. She knew that what could be found beyond that sign was exactly what she needed.

Natalie walked through the door and waited in a line of three. To her left, she saw several classmates laughing together as they built up a true story into fiction. A group of moms to her right were showing either baby or cat pictures to each other on their phones. There was even a group of elderly folks playing checkers in the corner. Natalie was too busy checking out the variety to notice she was the next in line.

"Welcome to Go Home Alien's Treasure Chapter." The perky woman at the table looked proud of every word she'd uttered. "How can I help you, young lady?"

Natalie stood up straight. "I'm Natalie Dormer. I believe you guys are expecting me."

CHAPTER 10

Natalie realized she must have been a little early to the GHA meeting, as at least a hundred more members showed up to the abandoned factory after she had. She probably couldn't even call it an abandoned factory anymore – after all, the inside looked more like a posh country club than a dilapidated example of the state's crumbling industrial work. The massive space had been broken down into expansive rooms with white walls and chandeliers. She expected the facility would see more wedding guests than factory workers, going forward.

A crowd of parents with their young children gathered around a video monitor. Natalie adjusted her trial member's badge and walked over. The screen showed two teenagers laughing with an upbeat, excessively happy song playing in the background. Natalie recognized them immediately. A graphic on the screen memorialized the Torellos' deaths and intercut a touched-up photograph with the security footage of Ted throwing one of Nigel's goons through the jukebox.

They're teaching everybody to hate Ted, she thought.

Natalie felt a hand on her back. After suppressing her instinct to punch whoever it was, she turned to find herself face-to-face with Travis Conner.

"I'm in that video, you know." Travis tugged at the bandage on his free hand. "It's being used in every GHA meeting in the U.S. I'm kind of famous."

Natalie wanted to ignore him. She knew exactly how he'd injured that hand, and even though she wasn't speaking to Dhiraj, there was nothing manly about three-on-one odds.

"Fame can be good." Natalie looked away from him and back toward the video, which was starting over from the beginning. "If you're famous for the right reasons."

Travis stood in front of her to block the view. "I've been told I'm supposed to show you around."

"They trust you with that much responsibility?" Natalie let out a chuckle. "You can't even throw a decent right cross."

Travis rubbed his bandage. "You know, I'm surprised you're even here." He placed his hands on Natalie's shoulders. "Using your real name, too. That's bold, seeing as you used to date the 'hero' himself."

Natalie placed Travis' hands back by his sides.

"Trying to be with the new Ted has gotten me stabbed in the back, literally, and double-crossed, figuratively," she said. "I think I'm in the right place."

Travis stuck his lips out a bit as he nodded. "Can I see it?" Travis gestured toward her back.

Natalie raised her eyebrows. "Seriously?"

Travis grinned. "Scars are cool."

Even though she tended to stay away from jocks, the smile helped Natalie understand why Travis rarely found himself without company. The way his face lit up compelled her to comply.

Natalie obliged, turning around and lifting up her shirt just enough to show the scar.

"Ted did that?" Travis asked.

Natalie pulled her shirt down quickly and glared at her peer.

"You know he didn't," Natalie said. "It was Nigel. The murderer who was working with your two friends, one of whom tried to kill Dhiraj with a rock."

Travis looked around in either direction and led Natalie away to a quiet corner. Natalie was surprised to see such concern on his face.

"Hey, you need to be quiet about that kind of stuff here, OK?" Travis looked convinced that someone would discover them at any moment. "I know about Jason and Phil. I realize Ted was only protecting you and your friends."

It didn't seem to add up for Natalie.

"Then why are you here?"

Travis looked at his watch. "We have a few minutes. Why don't I show you around?"

Natalie considered sticking with the crowd. After all, she didn't know what Travis was capable of. Then again, he didn't want to throw her out for speaking the truth about the Torellos. She figured that was a good sign.

Natalie nodded and Travis opened a door to an unpopulated part of the building.

He showed off the building's various renovations, including a state-of-the-art cafeteria, a conference room and several holding cells. The row of cells caught Natalie's attention. With the musty smell and the dim lighting, she wondered if the hall was one of the few parts of the building that had avoided renovation.

"Why would you need these?" she asked.

"If any of our members go out of bounds, we give them a little time to cool off." Travis tapped a metal door with his good hand. "The gentleman who threw the green paint balloons spent a couple of hours in this one."

When they reached the door they'd first entered, Natalie stopped her tour guide by the arm.

"I appreciate you showing me around, but you haven't told me why you're willing to lie about the Torellos."

The mild smile on Travis' face went away. He let a shallow breath out of his nose.

"Jason and Phil's parents needed something to latch onto." Travis paced away from Natalie and back. "I'd been over their house a hundred times. The movement gave them exactly what they wanted: someone to blame. It's a lot easier to blame Ted than something you can't see."

Natalie watched Travis as he moved back and forth. She wasn't sure what made the sympathy rise up inside, but her once-brash tone faded to sincere.

"I'm sorry they had to deal with that, but why are you here if you know the truth? You know that Ted isn't an alien."

Travis chuckled. When he did, Natalie could see his slightly crooked smile. She found herself kind of liking it.

"I was in kindergarten with Ted. I know he's not an alien. GHA isn't nefarious or evil. It's about pride and safety for people who are afraid of change."

They shared a moment of eye contact before a knock on the door startled the both of them. A scrawny classmate of theirs by the name of Nick poked his head around.

"It's time to meet about Operation Home Front." Nick turned his rat-like face toward Natalie. "What's she doing here?"

Travis walked up to Natalie with a knowing smirk. He took her hand. She felt a pang of nervousness in her stomach. Natalie knew Travis had hurt Dhiraj, but she didn't want him to go away. When he moved his face toward hers, she could have pushed, punched or kicked him so he never tried anything like that again. Instead, she let him. The chance to feel something like she'd felt with Ted was too good to pass up. His lips parted and they shared a deep kiss. Natalie closed her eyes and put her hand around the back of Travis' neck. The way his mouth moved made her feel alive. When he pulled away from her, Natalie kept her hand on his neck.

"She's a special guest." Travis gave her other hand a squeeze. "I've got to meet with some of the higher-ups about an outreach thing. Find you after the meeting?"

Natalie smiled and let a small sigh escape her lips. Travis seemed to enjoy her reaction a lot more than Nick did. The rat-lookalike gave Natalie one last wrinkle of his nose before the two GHA youth leaders exited. Natalie leaned against the wall and tried to dissect what just happened.

He's terrible. Why did I even let him near me?

Natalie wondered if Ted was right that being alone was getting to her. She ignored the thought and walked back into the main area. Chairs had been set up for some kind of presentation, and Natalie found an empty one toward the back. The seats were pointed toward a makeshift stage and a man who seemed to think he was important. When he spoke at the microphone, the tone in his voice was one of vanity and self-congratulation.

"Ladies and gentlemen, you have gone above and beyond the call of duty tonight," he said. "Your recent recruiting efforts have gained us more than 200 local members. Give yourselves a round of applause."

To describe the clapping as thunderous would be selling it short. Fanatical might be the better word, with a few hollers thrown in for good measure. The man at the front of the room held up his hand, and the crowd grew silent.

"Since Ted Finley has emerged with powers seemingly plucked straight from the devil, we've lost a local landmark and several jobs in the process." The man moved across the front, as if trying to connect with every row and column of the group before him. "We've also lost two teens who were very near and dear to our hearts."

Natalie wasn't sure if the man had seen much of the last few years at high school, but the closest the Torellos got to most people's hearts was when they were punching them in the chest.

He continued.

"Truth be told, we don't know what Ted can do. We've seen that he can move objects with his mind, turning anything into a weapon. But who knows what else he can do? Can he control people's minds? Turn a safe area into a radioactive wasteland? And if he can do more than meets the eye, how do we know that he's on our side?"

The man stopped his pacing. "Until we know more, Ted Finley needs to go."

The last bit got a rise out of the crowd. Natalie considered how her life in Treasure would change if Ted were gone. She had trouble convincing herself that it wouldn't be much, much simpler.

"I can tell you beyond a shadow of a doubt that with your help, we will get Ted out of Treasure and protect you and your families from the menace that he has wrought."

Natalie joined into this round of applause, which matched the fervor of the first. She wondered what Ted would think if he saw her clapping at a man who wanted to uproot and dispose of him.

She resolved to no longer think of Ted's feelings and sat on the edge of her chair to listen to the rest of the speech.

CHAPTER 11

Ted and Erica met up on the east edge of Treasure's Main Street, a strip of restaurants and shops that represented most activities in the quiet suburb. They'd already seen a dozen classmates coming in and out of the coffee shop, the movie theatre and the ice cream parlor. Thankfully, most of them had been willing to leave the resident superhero alone on his date.

After some polite catch-up conversation, it didn't take long for them to get into shop talk.

"You know, I've seen my fair share of mobs." Erica took a bite of the top scoop of her cookies n' cream cone. "A water balloon with paint is just the beginning."

Ted munched on some cookie dough. "So you're saying I should take up the DHS offer?"

Erica took Ted's hand and let their arms sway as they walked. "Since I'm not letting you do that, you need to think of another way."

Ted tried to think of a potential solution, but his mind was clogged with ideas for where on the street they should stop before he popped the prom question.

"Well, what would you do?"

"Me, personally?" Erica licked a bit of ice cream that had escaped her mouth. "I'd torture the leader, but it's probably not the best PR move."

Ted laughed until he started to wonder how many people Erica had tortured during her many lifetimes.

"I'll ask Dhiraj."

When they reached an empty gazebo, Ted let Erica inside. He heard the crickets chirping away at the nearby garden and smelled the clean spring air. It was a perfect location to do what he needed to do.

"Erica, I know that I've been putting this off, but will you–"

Just then, out of the corner of his eye, Ted spotted a fire in a building less than a block away. The flames raged through a couple of windows on the third floor of the brick structure. Erica's eyes took the same path as Ted's and noticed the fire as well.

"Holy crap." Erica crunched the remainder of her cone in her mouth. "We better get over there."

Erica leapt into Ted's arms. She felt almost weightless.

"Thanks for the ice cream," she said.

Ted breathed in deep. "You're welcome. We're going to come back to this."

"Sure thing." Erica smiled. "Enough talking. More flying."

I knew I should've asked before ice cream.

Ted planted his feet and concentrated on lifting the two of them off the ground. They took off into the night sky and flew toward the fiery brick building.

CHAPTER 12

Jennifer sat on the edge of her bed and leafed through one of her old yearbooks. She'd opened it to the page with 5th-grade Erica LaPlante so many times, the book couldn't help but open to the very same page. She looked at the book as if it were cursed, as if it were there to remind her of the death of her friend. Jennifer looked up at her walls, covered with photographs of the past. She grew angry at herself for going through the same routines over and over again and tossed the book to the other side of the bed.

Jennifer felt cold as her phone buzzed again.

The length of the text gave away the sender. Dhiraj was preparing to give an interview on national TV, his third since Ted had changed into something otherworldly.

"Tell everyone you know who has a Nielsen box to tune in," he said. "You also have to let me know how my hair looks. It was great seeing you the other day. I hope you're feeling better."

The text went on for another three paragraphs, telling Jennifer how prepared he was to debate the leader of the GHA. Jennifer breathed in deeply and shut the phone off. She reached back into the bottom drawer and pulled out a nondescript black binder. Unlike all her other scrapbooks, this one remained without a label.

She opened the book to the first page, which displayed an article from the local paper. The words "Local Teen Goes Missing" topped the story, followed by a picture of Erica smiling with her pompons. Jennifer wondered if she'd read the article over 100 times as she scanned for the part she hated the most.

"We're doing everything we can to find Erica," Deputy Daly had said. "If she's out there, we'll make sure she's back and in her parents' arms in no time."

The quote had always brought Jennifer hope before Erica had returned and the true nature of Deputy Daly had been revealed. Right up through the last time she saw Daly in the caves, she looked up to him and even thought he was sexy.

She pictured herself taking her stun gun and electrocuting her father's former co-worker right there on the rocky terrain.

Jennifer flipped the page past the other news clipping of Erica's disappearance until she got to articles from the past few months. The first one in the latest batch was called "Manhunt for Disgraced Deputy Begins." Jennifer had highlighted passages in pink and written notes in the margins. She flipped through several pages of printed phone interviews she'd conducted under the guise of being a CIA agent. Despite chatting with over a dozen friends and relatives, nobody seemed to have any idea where the murderous deputy had gone. Maybe if Erica's body was still underground, someone would have been more willing to talk.

When her doorknob began to turn, Jennifer felt a wave of panic come over her. She closed the book quickly and tossed it underneath her desk. By the time her father had fully opened the door, she'd already gone back to her pile of pictures in an effort to look completely innocent.

"Hey, honey. Sorry I'm late."

Jennifer hoped she'd wiped away all remnants of her tears. She couldn't handle her father asking what was wrong. Her emotions were held together with duct tape and dental floss as it was.

"That's OK, Dad." She put one picture on top of the other as if they went in some kind of order. "I'll be right down."

She could tell that her father detected something strange; after all, he'd become sheriff for a reason. He appeared to let it slide, nodding and closing the door. Jennifer tossed the pictures into the box and put her black binder back in order. She opened up to a grinning picture of Deputy Daly.

"You may have given up, Dad, but not me." She focused all her pain and rage on the deputy's eyes. "I'm gonna find you, Daly. And when I do, I plan on returning the favor."

CHAPTER 13

Erica couldn't help but feel somewhat aroused as she pressed herself against Ted and floated through the night sky. She was in a teenage body and she knew that a combination of hormones and emotional triggers made her want to kiss him deeply even though it would likely cause him to lose concentration, sending them both hurtling to the ground. Erica realized that the mixture of sexual attraction with the adrenaline of moving toward a burning building was making her even more attracted to Ted's hazel eyes, his increasingly muscular body and his winning personality. She didn't mind, either, because this part of the date sure as hell beat ice cream.

As they got closer to the building, she could feel the heat on her skin. The building was four floors high with six windows across. It was built to look like the businesses around it, and if it weren't for the orange flames, Erica wouldn't have given it a passing glance.

Erica looked into Ted's eyes as he attempted to lift one of the windows with his powers. "Having some trouble there?"

Ted glanced back. "This is harder than it looks."

Erica smirked. "Are you trying to say I'm heavy?"

Ted grumbled and dislodged a brick from the side of the building. He shot it forward like a bullet toward one of the windows. The glass shattered, leaving a hole large enough for them to fly in through. They zipped through the opening and landed on the carpeted floor.

"Good job." Erica squinted. "Though you have a bit of a chocolate stain around your lips."

She brought her lips toward his mouth and kissed off the sugar. The two them might have continued to help each other with the remnants of dessert if they hadn't heard a scream from the other room.

Ted turned toward the noise before spinning back. "More kissing later?"

"We'll see." Erica had her game face on.

Judging by the furniture, the building seemed to contain mostly condos. There would be multiple families at risk well before the fire department could arrive. They shared a glance and ran toward the screaming. Ted unlocked the door to one of the apartments from the inside and opened it with his powers. A mother was trying to pack something for her two children, one of whom was screaming in the middle of the room.

"You need to get out of here, miss," Ted said.

"Come with me." Erica gestured to the mother. "Show me the staircase."

The woman called her two children toward her and started to run down the hallway.

Erica looked back to Ted. "Check the other apartments."

Ted nodded and flew out the door, and she led the inhabitants through the door to the staircase. While doing so, Erica found herself thinking about Ted's powers.

We could have done this from a mile away, if I taught him everything.

Before Erica knew it, Ted had led a caravan of families toward the stairs. He flew through the hallway and back to Erica's side, where he coughed and kept low to the ground.

No. It's just too risky.

Erica put her arm on Ted's shoulder. "Check downstairs for any stragglers. I'll look on this floor."

"Are you sure?" Ted asked.

"Yes." Erica moved her hand to Ted's face. "Go. I'll be fine."

Ted took a deep breath and flew down the stairs above the escaping residents. Erica did a quick scan of the remaining apartments. All the rooms were abandoned; the fire continued to spread from one room to the next. When she returned to the stairs, the patriarch of one family said he recognized Erica from TV.

"You guys just saved all those people yesterday," he said. "You're all over the place."

"Right place–" Erica saw someone out of the corner of her eye. It looked like a girl around her age with curly, red hair. Erica had a sneaking suspicion she knew who the hair belonged to.

"Beth?" Erica turned to the man. "Is everybody accounted for?"

"I think so."

Erica saw the red hair zip around the corner and toward the fire. She ran in that direction.

"Wait!" The man could barely be heard over the sound of the arriving fire trucks. "Where are you going?"

Erica didn't have time to answer, as the person she was chasing moved too quickly for her. After going around two bends, Erica finally got a full glimpse of her. It was Beth. Her face was covered in black soot and she wore a vacant grin.

"What are you doing, Beth?"

Erica's friend wasn't the brightest egg in the dozen, but she knew well enough to stay away from fire. Unless she was the one who caused it.

Beth's grin grew wider.

"Homework." Beth dashed toward the smoke and Erica tried to catch up with her.

She doesn't even live in this part of town. Something isn't right.

Erica tossed off her shoes to move more quickly. She coughed as she grew closer to the source of the fire. Erica tried to bend lower as she ran, but it was no use. Erica thought of a past life in the desert as she got to a room that was completely engulfed in fire.

Beth stood right in the middle of it all. She didn't seem to be feeling any effects from the heat, the smoke or the fire.

"Beth, please."

"You know, I started this fire." Beth looked around from wall to wall. "And I knew you were going to be here. He told me you would."

Erica wondered if her friend was still alive. It was entirely possible she had been replaced with a dark soul, just like Sandra and the Torellos.

No, I would have felt it. She's still human.

The flames surrounded them and the smoke took over the room.

"Alright, Beth," she said. "The firefighters are going to be up here soon. Let's just get out of here together, OK?"

Erica felt a whoosh of air as Ted zipped around the corner and stopped right next to her.

"The fire marshal says this place is about to blow," Ted bent over and put his hands on his knees. "Why the heck is Beth here?"

"I'm here to help you reach your full potential." Beth walked up to one of the walls and started to lay her hand directly onto the fire.

"No!" Erica reached for her friend and felt the shudder of an explosion behind them.

Before she could react, Ted zipped ahead, grabbed Beth under one arm and gripped Erica underneath the ribs with the other. The three of them moved at an incredible speed through the air, smashed through a window and got far enough away from the building to avoid the burst of fire that followed them.

The three of them hovered in the night sky. Erica welcomed the cool air that brushed against her skin.

"Very impressive, Ted." Beth gave one last dreamy smile before digging her nails into Ted's arm.

Ted wrenched his grip from Beth's body and the girl plummeted toward the earth.

Ted's body tensed. "Hold on!"

Erica felt herself jerk downward as he attempted to hold onto her and fly at the same time.

He's getting good.

They punched through a cloud of smoke. Erica swore she saw a peaceful smile on Beth's face. Ted flew twice as fast as Beth's descent and snatched her up with his free arm about 10 feet before she hit the ground. The superhero slowed his flight and deposited his passengers safely on the lawn below.

Erica grabbed Beth's arms and wrenched them behind her before her friend could react. Meanwhile, Ted let himself collapse onto the grass.

"Let me go!" Beth squirmed as much as she could, but Erica's heightened strength was too much for her.

Erica watched Ted's chest heave up and down in rapid succession. "Is this nap time or something?"

Ted sounded like he'd just finished a marathon. "I... the flying... and... need a little break."

Erica couldn't help but laugh. Two firefighters came over to help restrain Beth – one of the apartment residents had seen Beth start the fire, and they had been looking for her. As much as Erica hated admitting it, she corroborated the story. When two deputies arrived shortly after, they placed Beth in handcuffs. Before they could take her away, Erica got her attention.

"Who did this to you, Beth?"

Beth whipped her long, red curls with a snarl. "Someone a lot more powerful than you."

As the deputies put Beth in their squad car, Erica sat down next to the still-recovering Ted.

She placed her hand on his chest, which had halved its previous rate of heaving. "You know, they say you're supposed to stand and stretch after strenuous activity."

Ted grumbled. "The guy who recommended that never flew through a burning building. Where's Beth?"

"They're taking her to the sheriff's office for questioning."

Ted took in a deep breath and sat up. "I don't think she did this alone. Was it the GHAers?"

Erica shook her head. "There's something else going on here. Something cosmic. Something from another world."

"Hashtag: Other world problems."

Erica rolled her eyes. "Date's over, funny man. It's time to get to work."

Chapter 14

Dhiraj's father had given him approval to take some of the money he'd earned from Ted-related speaking gigs to turn the basement into a television studio of sorts. It allowed him to make talking-head commentaries via satellite with ease. A freelance technician helped patch him into the feed while Dhiraj worked his earpiece into place. He spoke with the show's producer for a moment to get the rundown. Dhiraj and GHA founder Thomas Cobblestone would be introduced at the same time. He'd speak first, and from there, the two of them would alternate until fast-talking YNN superstar Rudy Bolger ended the segment.

The technician cued him in and Dhiraj could hear Bolger's used car salesman voice pipe in through the earpiece.

"Tonight, we have teenage entrepreneur and business manager for Ted Finley, Dhiraj Patel, on the program."

"Always a pleasure, Rudy." Dhiraj took a deep breath and let it out slowly.

"We also have the leader of the Go Home Alien movement, Thomas Cobblestone."

"I'd like to point something out, Rudy." Cobblestone's voice was clear and powerful. His voice was the kind people would listen to. It made Dhiraj feel self-conscious. "While I'm here representing my movement, Ted Finley is off using his powers to look up cheerleaders' skirts or something."

Dhiraj smiled and let out a chuckle, even though his instinct told him to come to Ted's defense. "Now we know what you'd do with telekinetic powers, Tom." Dhiraj thought he saw the technician laugh with him on that one.

"Gentlemen, please." Bolger put up his hands as if he didn't love every moment of conflict between his guests. The twinkle in his eye betrayed him. "Dhiraj, we'll start with you. Earlier this week, the GHA movement protested outside a robbery in which Ted Finley saved the lives of six hostages. Was this excessive?"

Dhiraj wondered if his face betrayed his belief that Bolger's question was one heck of an understatement. "Rudy, you know as well as I do that Ted Finley is a hero." Dhiraj let his eyes soften as he stared into the camera. "This week, he saved mothers, sons and daughters from armed men, doing what he could to keep families together. He was rewarded for his efforts by a couple of balloons filled with green paint to the side of his head. I wonder if Mr. Cobblestone would offer that kind of treatment if Ted had saved *his* children."

Dhiraj hoped he had Cobblestone backed into a corner. With a strong enough appearance, perhaps he'd be able to knock down enrollment numbers for new GHA members.

Rudy Bolger let out a "hmm" sound as he turned his attention toward Cobblestone. "Tom, do you think assaulting Ted after he saved six lives was out of line?"

Cobblestone laughed like everything he'd just heard was below his standards. "First of all, assault is one heck of a strong word for a little prank. We have disciplined the member who brought the tiny paint balloons to the protest." Cobblestone took in the air he needed for the long, prepared sentence he always spoke during his time on TV. "Ted Finley saved these families, but he'll never be able to atone for the murder of his two classmates, Jason and Phil Torello. The Torello family will never be whole again."

Dhiraj considered bringing up his stand-by defense: the fact that one of the Torellos tried to kill him with a giant rock. He decided to keep things lighter instead.

"Ted has mourned for the lives lost during the attacks of several months ago," Dhiraj said. "And now it's time for the GHA movement and Ted to work together: serving the public and using the power of many minds to solve problems."

Rudy Bolger turned his attention to Cobblestone. "Together everyone does achieve more, Tom." Rudy Bolger was amused at himself. "Could Ted and the GHA ever work together?"

From the breath Bolger took right before he spoke, Dhiraj could tell the GHA leader was in full attack mode.

"Work together?" Cobblestone let out an incredulous yelp. "We don't know how Ted gained these powers. We have no idea just how dangerous he could be. Ted is a nuclear explosion just waiting to happen — one that could kill everyone around him if we're not careful."

Dhiraj wanted to smack the rhetoric right off of Cobblestone's face. He knew exactly what to say to rile up his followers, and there was little Dhiraj could do to get him to change his tune.

"Could Ted be a threat, Dhiraj?" Bolger asked.

Dhiraj did his best to keep his cool. "Ted Finley is an honest-to-goodness hero, and that was the case even before he got his super abilities. He wants to keep everyone safe, including you, Mr. Cobblestone."

Cobblestone broke into the exchange immediately. "Keep me safe? Was that some kind of threat?"

Dhiraj rolled his eyes. "I'm just saying that Ted would protect you if you were in danger."

"Ted is the danger." Cobblestone was dead serious. "None of us are safe as long as he's allowed to roam freely. I'm nervous for Treasure and I'm nervous for the rest of the United States of America."

Dhiraj was unable to get a word in edgewise the rest of the interview until Bolger signed them off. As the show went to commercial, Dhiraj and Cobblestone remained on the line for around 30 seconds.

"What do you even want, Cobblestone?" Dhiraj asked. "A firing squad to gun Ted down?"

"It would be a start," Cobblestone said. "Take care, Dhiraj. Tell your friends I said hi."

Chapter 15

Ted missed the anonymity he used to experience when he walked into the main cafeteria. Before he'd gained the ability to move objects with his mind, it was rare for anybody to give him a second glance when he walked into the large hall filled with circular tables and semi-appealing smells. He'd had way too much attention when he sat down with Natalie the previous day in the Freshman cafeteria, and he had a fair amount of eyeballs on him as he maneuvered over to a table where Erica and Dhiraj sat waiting for him.

On most days before his powers, Ted would sit in a quiet corner with Natalie and Dhiraj. Natalie would discuss her latest game or sports in general. Dhiraj would talk about the newest money-making scheme he'd heard on a podcast or webinar. Ted would simply listen and enjoy the company. Nowadays, he was expected to contribute much more to the conversation than a smile and a nod.

"I checked her body for the symbol," Erica said. "As far as I can tell, Beth is still alive."

Ted smirked at his friends. "For once, can't we talk about who's hooking up or the latest cat video or something?"

Dhiraj raised his chin. "Personally, I like the one with the cat on the tiny sailboat."

Erica sighed and looked away as Ted stared in her direction with a smile.

Dhiraj did the same.

"Fine," she said. "I saw the sailboat one, too. It was cute. Can we talk business now?"

Ted nodded.

"If Beth wasn't a dark soul, why was she burning down a building?" Dhiraj asked.

Ted couldn't help himself from glancing at Erica's hands, tracing up her arms and looking at the body of a girl he'd wanted to hold his entire life. He could've done without them having to talk burning buildings and dead people, but he figured he'd take what he could get.

Erica tapped her fingernails on the tabletop. "Dark souls may not be in play here, but there are many other worlds beside the Realm of Souls and yours."

Erica had mentioned other worlds before, but she'd remained tight-lipped about them during their training. Ted didn't know if there was some kind of pain there or if the living soul was on a need-to-know basis.

"Are the people on the other worlds like the dark souls?" Ted took out his chicken salad and started to devour it.

"No. Like yours, they're impacted by the war, but most of them don't support one side or the other."

Ted got the feeling Erica was holding something back, but he wasn't sure if he should pry. His girlfriend would tell him everything he needed to know to protect the town and his friends, wouldn't she?

"Beth didn't seem like herself, right?" Dhiraj asked. "Maybe something was controlling her. Like the same kind of thing you did with the sheriff."

Erica stared at the stir-fry stand to their left for a second.

"Erica?" Ted put down his fork. "Are there creatures from another world who can do what you can?"

"Usually they aren't powerful enough to take over a person's mind for any extended period of time." Erica munched on a celery stick slathered in peanut butter. "Sometimes, when the living soul crosses over, the power used in the process can be harnessed."

Ted narrowed his eyes at Erica. He wondered why this was the first he'd heard of this.

Dhiraj broke the silence. "Like a turbo button in a video game."

Erica laughed. "Sure."

Ted smirked at Erica. "Hey, you guys were the ones who picked a couple of nerds to keep the world safe. Would this turbo charger thing be in Page's?"

As Ted watched Erica, he couldn't help but wonder if she was trying to determine what to tell him and what to hold back.

"There's a chance the power could have been trapped on paper. Leaving some kind of magic book."

"The books on the walls." Ted began to nod. "Of course. I think they're at the library now."

Dhiraj looked as happy as a kid in a candy store. "Turbo buttons, magic books. I love how this is all turning into some kind of video game."

"Please." Ted grimaced. "Please do not try to adapt this investigation into some kind of playable app or something."

Dhiraj grinned. "You know, I hadn't had that idea until now, but I appreciate you contributing to the think tank."

Ted shook his head.

"As long as you don't try to sell it on YNN." Erica sighed. "Good interview yesterday, by the way."

As Dhiraj thanked Erica and began to speak about his experience, Ted noticed something from across the room. Bringing up the GHA chat made Ted glance at the designated GHA clique table. It seemed to have gathered a few extra people since the previous day.

When he saw the unmistakable black hair of his ex-girlfriend at the table, he couldn't help but feel sick to his stomach.

Ted turned back toward Dhiraj and Erica, but he couldn't hear any of the words they were saying. The room spun as he thought back to the previous day in the freshman cafeteria.

Was I the one who pushed her to hate me?

This time, Erica was the one who noticed something was off with him. "You don't look so good, Ted."

"Then why are you going out with him?" Dhiraj asked.

"I meant right this second. In general, Ted is very cute."

Ted looked down at his hands. They were shaking.

Dhiraj leaned in toward him. "You need some water, man?"

Ted shook his head and stood up. He left his lunch bag on the table and walked toward the exit. He felt like the room was closing in and the only way he could get any oxygen was by getting out of there. The collection of orange lunch trays rattled as he walked by, and several students shrieked when their backpacks started to shudder. Ted tried to pick up the pace of his stumbling walk. As he neared the exit, he heard a voice calling to him.

"Hey, Finley." Travis looked over his shoulder at Ted from the seat next to Natalie. "You look a little pale."

Natalie turned in his direction as well.

Travis put his arm around Ted's ex. "Feel better soon, OK?"

Ted tried to read Natalie's face, but it was completely void of emotion. He continued to exit the room and used his powers to open one of the hallway windows. At least, he tried to just open one window, accidentally opening an entire row of windows. The outdoor air felt good in his lungs.

Dhiraj and Erica reached his side just a few moments later.

"What is it, buddy?" Dhiraj asked.

Ted continued to breathe in the air through the window. "Natalie."

It was the only word Ted could get out. That was all it took for both Erica and Dhiraj to understand.

"I'm sure it's just a one-time thing, Ted," Erica said. "She's not a part of the group. There's no way she could ever hate you."

Dhiraj scrunched his nose and looked back toward the lunchroom. "I'm going to give her a stern talking-to later today about this."

Ted lifted his hands and accidentally backed both of his friends up a few steps. It took him a second to even realize that he'd used his powers. "Sorry, guys." He shook his head. "What did I do wrong?"

Dhiraj and Erica couldn't give him a straight answer, so they hugged him instead. Ted swore that of the many eyes watching the three of them embrace, Natalie's were among them.

CHAPTER 16

Erica felt the role reversal as she took her turn staring at Ted during Mr. Redican's English class. Ted looked straight ahead and hadn't even glanced back at Erica once for the entire 40 minutes. She missed having his eyes on her.

She wondered how Ted would react when she told him the truth.

"Here's the big question." Mr. Redican scribbled something on the blackboard. "Is he ready to become the most important person in the realm?"

Erica's ears perked up. Redican seemed to glance at her as soon as the question ended, but Erica admitted that could have just as well been in her head. She'd been paranoid about the safety of her mind since the incident with Beth. Her friend's empty desk loomed beside her.

"Is Prince Hal ready to become the king?"

Erica watched as Ted's hand sprung up. A few of the students around him flinched. Ted's participation in class wasn't exactly a regular occurrence.

"Mr. Finley."

Ted's face remained stoic. "It's not like he has much choice."

Redican nodded. "That's a good point." He paced to the other side of the room. "When his father dies, he's going to be the man."

Several students chuckled. Erica didn't notice even a hint of a smile on Ted's face.

"The question is: is our bar-hopping, sword-fighting prince ready to become the leader of the people?"

In an instant, she thought about the possible future for Ted. If they all survived high school, which was no certainty, Ted would continue to find out about his other abilities. As his power grew, her control over the situation would diminish. There was a chance that Ted was the once-in-an-era hero who wouldn't let the burden and beauty of power turn him against the forces of good. If he wasn't, she knew exactly how Gan and Reena would alter her mission from the other side. Erica tried to suppress the tightness in her stomach.

Redican's question went unanswered as the bell rang. Ted came right up to Erica's desk at the end of class, and she felt some of the tension release from her stomach.

"I'm sorry." Ted's face contorted into an almost smile.

"You don't have to apologize." Erica pretended she wasn't judging his every movement as she put away her books.

"Yes, I do. Just because my ex-girlfriend has joined some kind of cult doesn't mean I should ignore you and it doesn't do me any good to lose control."

Erica tucked away her assignment book and zipped her backpack. "Apology accepted. How did it feel to be stared at all class long?"

Ted tightened the straps of his bag. "Kind of creepy actually. Does it feel creepy when I—"

"Yes." Erica grinned and the two of them walked stride-for-stride out of class. "Up for a trip to find some magic books?"

After last period, they hopped into Ted's car and took a trip to the Treasure Public Library. As they walked inside, the scent of books took her back to several of her past lifetimes.

They reached the librarian in charge of the special stacks. The woman wore a low-cut blouse and a lot more makeup than most librarians she'd known. Her bright orange scarf also helped her to stand out against the beige library walls.

"Hello," Ted said. "I'm—"

"Resident superhero Ted Finley?" The woman's perkiness hurt Erica's brain. "I know who you are. It's an honor."

Ted smirked back at Erica. She gestured for him to move it along.

"That's true, but I was going to say we're looking for the books that were donated from Page's."

The librarian let out a mini-squeal and pulled something up on her computer. "Of course." Her fingers clacked against her keyboard at a rapid clip. "It must be like a little trip down memory lane for you."

Her grin was disarming. The librarian couldn't have been much older than college age.

"I'm a sentimental soul."

"I can tell that about you." The librarian adjusted her glasses. "It'll just take a sec. The woman who used to run the stacks took off to Cancun with her dog all of a sudden."

Erica caught Ted looking dreamily at the librarian. She nudged him in the back.

"What?" Ted phrased the question as if he knew exactly why she'd bumped him.

"Focus."

The librarian got to her feet.

"Right this way, kids." She gestured behind them as two security guards walked over. "They're here to make sure you two aren't disturbed. Celebrity status and all."

Ted followed close behind the busty librarian as Erica eyed the guards. She wasn't so sure they were there to prevent autographs. The five of them went down one floor on the escalator.

Erica tapped Ted on the shoulder, but before she could say anything he took a defensive pose.

"It's just my thirst for knowledge," he whispered. "Librarians are like sexy nurses for me."

"Sexy nurses?" Erica recoiled. "This isn't about her."

"Oh," Ted said. "Forget I mentioned it."

She couldn't.

"I was going to tell you to be careful. Something seems—"

The librarian cut off her whisper. "They're just down this hall. Start getting excited."

The quickening of Erica's pulse had little to do with excitement. When the librarian took out her keycard to open the door, she gestured for Ted and Erica to go in first. Ted bolted in before Erica could get his attention. She'd been around long enough to detect the odor of a trap, but she followed him in anyway.

The room contained three bookcases filled with older works. Erica considered whether or not they could be used as weapons.

As soon as the door closed, the librarian turned primal and ran across the room shrieking. She jumped on Ted's back and attempted to choke him. Meanwhile, the two security guards closed in around Erica.

"Oh great, the superhero gets his version of a 'sexy nurse.'" Erica crouched down in a fighting stance. "And I get you two lugs."

"Them's the breaks." The first guard threw a punch at Erica.

She moved to the side to let the fist go by and wrenched the guard's wrist into an arm bar. When the second guard ran in for a kick, she pulled her first attacker into a human shield position. After the guard kicked his own partner in the gut, Erica pushed them into each other, resulting in a head-on-head collision.

She looked back over to Ted. Her boyfriend was now on the ground with the librarian on top of him. The woman swung wildly at Ted's face.

"Use your powers." Erica kept her eyes on Ted while easily deflecting a blow from one of the now-concussed guards.

"I don't want to hurt her." Ted's voice was nearly drowned out by the woman's shrieking.

Erica blocked another punch and sent one right back into the guard's arm. She swept his legs out from under him, and the guard stayed down.

"I'm sure that's the reason she's still on top of you."

When the second guard dove for her legs, Erica leapt up onto his shoulders and locked her knees around his throat. It didn't take long for her to choke him to unconsciousness. Before he could fall, Erica rolled backward and caught him. When she laid him gently on the floor, she saw Ted float the screaming woman off his body and into a chair across the room. He took the scarf from around her neck and used it to tie up her arms with his mind.

"Took you long enough." Erica rolled up the sleeves of one of the unconscious guards.

"I had the situation under control."

When the librarian began to shriek again, Ted used his powers to keep her mouth shut.

Erica pulled up the sleeves of the other guard. "They aren't dark souls. I think they were controlled, just like Beth."

Ted took a glance around the room. "I don't see the books from Page's here. I think they led us down here to keep us away from them."

Erica nodded as she picked up the librarian's key card from the ground. "Let her talk."

Ted waved his hand and the librarian let out another shriek. Erica dashed in front of her and the woman stopped.

"Tell us where we can find the books."

The librarian laughed. "Why would I ever tell you?"

"Because you're a librarian?" Ted shook his head.

The woman's face darkened. "You're never going to find them. There are hundreds of rooms here and millions of books."

Erica held her hands a few inches apart. A burst of blue lightning went between them.

"Mind control," Erica said. "It's a two-way street."

After the librarian gave Erica the exact directions to the books from Page's, along with her phone number, they attempted to sneak their way in there.

"Whoever messed with their brains might have done the same thing to anybody who works here," Erica said. "Tread carefully."

Ted proceeded to knock over a potted plant, though he caught it before it could completely tip over.

"Sorry."

Erica rolled her eyes and directed him into the elevator. When the door closed, Ted went back to his standard volume.

"Is this mind control guy like you? Is he a light soul?"

Erica shook her head. "I should be the only one on your world right now. But I have a theory."

Before Erica could share it, the elevator doors opened. There were five librarians and a security guard waiting for them.

Erica glanced over at Ted. "Looks like your fantasy come to life."

"One librarian gets you a little excited and people think you have a fetish or something."

Ted and Erica clenched their fists and sprung into action.

Chapter 17

Jennifer opened the Daly file to a half-filled page titled "Leads." She dialed a number from the text.

"Hey, can I speak to Cheryl?" Jennifer affected a southern accent, though she wasn't sure why she chose southern. "Thank you, dear."

Cheryl picked up on the other end.

"Hey there, Cheryl." Jennifer had her pencil ready to take notes. "I just got a text that said you spotted my deadbeat ex-husband shopping at your store?"

Her father's office hadn't gotten far on the Daly case. She blamed the Nigel situation and the precinct attack for the lack of devoted resources. Jennifer had made much better progress on her own once she'd learned that Daly had a prescription medication for his thyroid that he couldn't live without. Working state by state, she'd been calling every pharmacy she could find. Several thousand calls later, she had her first lead, in upstate New York.

"I saw him, alright," Cheryl said. "We aren't really supposed to give out this kind of information, but you said it's been two years since he's given you a dime?"

Jennifer affirmed the lie. She couldn't very well tell people that she was looking for someone who murdered her friend when her friend was alive and kicking. The child support story seemed to elicit a lot of sympathy among female employees.

"Give me your number one last time, honey." Cheryl seemed to share Jennifer's pain over the phone. "He's using a fake name, but I'm sure it's him. I'll send you over his address right now. I hope you catch the bastard."

Jennifer hoped she would to. After she got off the phone with Cheryl, Jennifer plotted out the directions on her computer. As she did, she spied the last picture of Erica she had that wasn't sitting in a box on the top shelf of her closet. The framed photo was from just last year. Erica, Beth, Winny and herself were pretending to hold weapons as they tried to look cute.

Jennifer opened the same drawer the Daly file came from and reached all the way in the back. She took out a gun.

"I can get there tomorrow morning. Scope him out all Saturday. This could be all over by the end of the weekend."

Jennifer checked the magazine and put it back into place.

"Let's go for a little drive."

CHAPTER 18

Natalie felt a little more comfortable at the next GHA meeting than she had at the first. After all, this one had a different vibe, with many of the participants preparing to join in some field games. When sports were around, she couldn't help but feel like she was in her element. The parking lot had been transformed into a carnival atmosphere with bright colors, games and life replacing the rows of cars she'd spotted last week.

Natalie tried to suppress the image of Ted shaking every tray in the cafeteria when he saw her with Travis. He hadn't so much as blinked when he saw over a hundred protestors earlier that week. She was the one who made him upset. Natalie knew it was proof that Ted cared about her, but she wasn't the kind of person to back down from her commitment. As soon as Natalie was about to join in on a game of horseshoes, Travis grabbed her by the arm and pulled her behind a booth set up for a softball toss game.

Travis smelled like a man to Natalie. There was no hint of detergent or fruity shampoo, as there had often been with Ted. It was like the difference between white and dark meat. His scent was richer, somehow. More dangerous. She started to become self-conscious of how she smelled when Travis had them sit down on the concrete base of a tall lamppost.

"Can we play a game?" Travis had a crooked smile with a reputation. Natalie could see why.

"You mean like softball toss?"

Travis stood up and faced her. "This one is more mental than physical. I'm going to examine you and tell you exactly what you're looking for in a relationship, and then you'll do the same for me."

Natalie scrunched her face. "Okay."

Travis waived his hands. "No, I swear, it's going to be great. I'll start."

Natalie leaned back against the metal post and folded her arms. She gave Travis a look that said she was ready for his impending subpar performance. "While we're young."

Travis cleared his throat. "You want someone who can keep up with you, both physically and emotionally. You want a guy who listens to what you say and what you aren't saying. A person who is sweet, sensitive and strong all at the same time." Travis focused on Natalie's eyes. "And you deserve all of that and more."

Natalie tried not to betray how she felt, but her shallow sigh gave it away. Travis knew exactly what she felt like she needed in a man.

Words are easy. I'm not.

"Are you trying to say that you have all these qualities?" Natalie pursed her lips to suppress the laugh.

Travis opened his mouth wide. "I would never talk of myself so highly."

Natalie couldn't help the giggle from slipping. "Uh huh. I've only been here since 7th grade, Travis, but I'm not blind or deaf."

Travis blushed. Natalie didn't even know he was capable of such a thing. She hoped she hadn't gone too far.

"Fair enough." Travis shifted and straightened his shoulders. "But I'll tell you this much: I'm working on it. I want to be better, and I want to be this ideal guy. Both for myself and for you."

Now Natalie was blushing. She tried to look away and hide it, but it was pretty obvious that Travis spotted it. The smile on his face declared victory.

"That was smooth, Travis." Natalie stood up and circled around her suitor. She gestured for him to sit down. "Now it's my turn."

Travis sat and took the pose of a cherubic angel.

"Alright. You want someone who will believe all your horsecrap and sleep with you on the first date."

Travis opened his eyes wide and Natalie sat back down next to him. After a few moments of silence, they burst out into laughter.

"That was good." Travis laughed so hard that tears came to his eyes. "I deserved that. Man, you're amazing."

Natalie wiped away the tears from Travis' face. "I'm not going to disagree with you."

Travis took Natalie's hand and leaned into her. He bent his head to plot a collision course with her mouth. Natalie felt her stomach flutter as she closed her eyes and waited for contact. It never had the chance to come.

"Hey!" The voice of Nick, the classmate from the other day, rang out. "You're wanted in the command center."

Natalie had given some dirty looks in her day, but none as angry and intense as the one Travis gave to Nick. Natalie touched his shoulder to try to lessen the ire.

"It's alright." Natalie looked at Travis' lips. "I'll still be here when you get back."

"No, they want both of you to come."

Natalie had been as relaxed as she'd felt in weeks before Nick told her what was coming. She held her breath.

"That's great." Travis gave Natalie's shoulder a squeeze. "You're in the inner circle."

Natalie scrunched up her face. "Just when I was getting used to the outer circle."

"Come with me." Nick waved them inside.

Natalie suppressed her nervousness and followed.

Going from the color and noise of the outdoor activities to the cold, lifeless interior of the command center felt like going from day to night. Something about it made her feel unwelcome, as if she should turn around and try to escape.

This is a bad idea. A really bad idea.

She continued forward anyway. When they reached the door, a pencil of a man held out a tray and collected Travis and Nick's cell phones.

"And who are you exactly?" The man's eyes zipped from left to right with alarming speed.

Natalie gulped before sharing her name.

The man's countenance brightened. "Ah, Ms. Dormer. We've been expecting you. Phone, please."

When she hesitated, Travis put his hand on her back. "Don't worry, it's just while you're in the room."

Like most teens, she felt strange parting from her phone for any time period other than sleep. The reassuring look in Travis' eyes gave her the strength to pass it over. When she let the device go from her hands, she had a strange feeling that she might never see it again. The stick of a man placed the phone in the container beside the others. Travis smiled as he led Natalie forward.

The room was filled with giant TV screens, most of which were turned off. The one that wasn't looked like it was displaying the first slide in a presentation. It read "Operation Home Front." She watched a few other people file into the room, most of them older than Travis and herself. She recognized Thomas Cobblestone right away. It took her a moment to place the man he was speaking with, but then she realized it was none other than David Torello, the father of Jason and Phil.

Cobblestone took out a long, rolled-up sheet of paper and placed it down on the room-length table. As the paper unfurled, Natalie could see that it was a blueprint for a house. She spied the downstairs area, the bedrooms and the backyard all very clearly. Alarm bells started to go off throughout her brain.

I've been in that house.

A few other people filed into the room and gathered around the blueprint. Travis followed and Natalie stayed by his side. She could feel herself beginning to sweat.

You've made it this far. Keep it together.

Travis glanced over at her, and Natalie did her best to relax her face and smile. She felt confident she'd kept up appearances well enough when he grinned back.

"As you all know, we're only a few hours away from Operation Home Front." Cobblestone cleared his throat. "The equipment is in place nearby, as are our operatives."

Nick's long-fingered hand rose into the air. Cobblestone nodded in his direction.

"If we're gonna wait till Ted's asleep and everything, why don't we hit him with something harder? We could just kill him."

Natalie couldn't help the sharp inhale. She looked back over at the tray of phones. There were at least three people between her and contact with the outside world. When she glanced back to the table, Cobblestone caught her eye for a split second before he answered the question.

"I appreciate your dedication, Nick, but we're trying not to bring too much suspicion back on us." Cobblestone smiled with easy confidence. "It should be a simple act of vandalism gone wrong. Not a full-out hit."

Mr. Torello coughed. "Plus, we're not going to stoop to his level."

Natalie felt for Mr. Torello, a person who was an innocent bystander in all of this. Even though his son had tried to kill her friend, she knew his sense of loss was genuine. Cobblestone wrapped up the meeting and told the attendees to get to their positions. Natalie waited until everybody's attention was elsewhere before she tried to walk over to the box of phones. Travis caught her hand before she could get halfway.

"Don't you want to meet him?" Travis interlocked his fingers with hers.

"Of course," Natalie said. "I just got nervous that somebody texted me."

"You're just so damn popular." Travis led Natalie toward Cobblestone.

Natalie could tell how the man would be trusted with leading an entire movement. Even his body commanded attention. Layers of bulky muscle lined his frame. Natalie figured it'd be difficult to guard him in the low post. She hoped this encounter wouldn't come to anything physical.

"Tom." Travis sounded proud when he dropped the leader's first name. "I'd like you to meet Natalie Dormer."

There were layers to Cobblestone's reaction. She could see the surface smile all right, but there were a few things underneath that were impossible to assess.

"Ms. Dormer, how good of you to come." Cobblestone put his arm around Natalie. "It's so important that we have you as an ally. I'd actually appreciate if we could talk in private for a moment."

Natalie wasn't sure if she could pull off the same number of emotional layers as the GHA boss, but she tried her best to hide the fear.

"I'd like that. I'm free almost all weekend—"

"Now, actually." Cobblestone shooed everybody out of the room. "Let's talk right now."

Travis was the only one left until Cobblestone gave another wave of his hand. Natalie watched as Travis attempted to give one last crooked smile before exiting.

"You've had an interesting few months, Ms. Dormer." Cobblestone paced around the room as Natalie stood still. "You broke Ted Finley's heart, took a knife in the back, won a state championship and then joined our humble movement."

"You do your homework." Natalie fought the urge to fidget.

"We do a little more than homework, Ms. Dormer."

Cobblestone took to a step to his left and pushed a touchscreen button. A sound clip featuring her voice played from the speaker.

"Hey, this is Natalie Dormer. I know you might not be expecting this, but I want to know how I can help."

The other voice on the recording was Erica LaPlante's.

"Natalie," Erica said. "This is surprising. But you couldn't have called at a better time."

Cobblestone fast-forwarded the recording.

"Once you're inside," Erica continued, "You need to figure out what they're planning to do. Do not let Ted know about this. You need to act like a true convert. Alright?"

Natalie's mouth hung open in dread.

"You want me to spy?" Natalie heard her voice ring throughout the room. "Sounds like fun."

Natalie grabbed the closest chair and tossed it in Cobblestone's direction. She sped toward the box of phones and tried to find hers in record time.

"Guards!" Cobblestone lumbered toward Natalie.

The door opened to reveal three or four men who'd been standing right by the door. It was as if they expected this to happen.

When she couldn't find her own device, Natalie picked up another phone and attempted to dial 9-1-1, but the guards had her by the arms before she could do any such thing.

"Looking for this?" Cobblestone pulled a cell phone out of his pocket.

Natalie recognized the solid black case around her phone.

"We've got plans for this, sweet girl," Cobblestone said. "We've got plans for you, too."

CHAPTER 19

When the librarians and guards charged forward, Ted didn't hesitate. He used his powers to lift all their opponents up into the air, over their heads and into the elevator they'd just exited. This time, it did feel like they were at the lair, doing their normal training routine together. Ted felt comfortable using his powers around Erica. It was almost like he was a student trying to impress his teacher.

He swore he saw Erica smirk as he shut the doors manually and used his powers to keep them that way.

"What?" Ted couldn't help but smile, himself. "I just needed to get warmed up, OK?"

Erica stuck out her tongue. "Eyes on the prize. The books should be right this way."

Erica used the librarian's keycard to get into a room that was only a few feet behind the desk where they'd first inquired about the books. When Ted crossed into the room, he could feel something different inside. It was the same kind of energy he felt when he got his abilities and when he wielded the dark soul-smiting sword. The old power in there began to give him a buzz.

"Do you feel this, too?"

Erica nodded as she shut the door behind them. There were five pedestals in the center of the room. While four of them sported books from Page's, one of the spaces was empty. Ted heard a low humming sound coming from the book closest to him and reached out.

"Ted, wait!"

Before Ted could process Erica's warning, he touched the front cover of a first-edition *The Sound and the Fury*. All of a sudden, he wasn't in the library in Treasure anymore. He was everywhere at once. Ted could see his bedroom, the school and Erica's house from multiple angles at the exact same time. He also saw different worlds that he didn't recognize. There was a kingdom and an army before him as well. The last image he could make out was his face on the body of a man who was leading a force of thousands of men, when his consciousness came back to him.

He came to on the ground approximately 10 feet away from the book. His fingers burned.

"That's OK." Erica helped him back to his feet. "Don't listen to me or anything. I'm just trying to keep you from short-circuiting."

"What happened?" Ted sucked on his burned fingers. "I felt like Google Earth for a second there."

"You were almost Google Death. We need to get these somewhere safe." Erica wheeled over a cart and slid one of the books off of its pedestal without touching it.

"What are these?" Ted moved his hand around to get the oxygen flowing. "Why is one of them missing?"

When Erica got the last book onto the cart, she had a disappointed look on her face. Ted couldn't tell if that was meant for him or for herself.

"There are certain things you're not supposed to know, Ted. For your own protection."

Ted glared at Erica. "I don't understand why you wouldn't tell me everything."

Erica pushed the cart out of the room and they walked toward checkout. Two librarians who'd been brainwashed came running toward them. Ted floated the librarians into a private room with his powers and wedged a chair under the doorknob to keep it locked.

"Have you heard the story about Pandora's Box?" When a security guard came running at Erica, she took his weight and rolled backward to flip the man behind her. She got up like nothing had happened and continued pushing the cart.

"Does it have something to do with online radio stations?" Ted saw another librarian approach and used his powers to set her up on the top shelf of the stacks.

"It has to do with no turning back." Erica reached the checkout area, grabbed a tote bag and tilted the cart until the books fell inside. "I'm trying to keep you from hurting yourself. And others."

When two security guards tried to stop them at the exit, Ted spun them around with his powers until they dizzily collapsed.

"I don't know what you're talking about. But you need to trust me."

Erica sighed. "You're right." Erica glared at the stolen book detector when it beeped at them. "It's just complicated."

When they reached the parking lot, the sound of a revving motor approached. Ted's car screeched to a halt right in front of them. The driver's seat was empty and the trunk popped up seemingly on its own.

"Pretty cool, huh?"

Erica tossed the books in the trunk and shut it. "Mildly impressive." She put her hand on Ted's shoulder. "I'm going to need you to fly home again."

Ted squinted at Erica. "You're gonna hide these books, aren't you?"

A noise from the library's front door grabbed their attention. Several librarians weren't ready to part with their dear books quite yet. Ted used his powers to push the pursuers back into the building before breaking the lock off inside the door. The brainwashed librarians pounded on the glass.

"I bet I'll have to pay a fine for that."

He looked back at Erica. "I think I deserve an explanation here."

"And you'll get one." Erica hopped into the front seat and rolled down the windows with the flick of a switch. "Tonight. Dinner. My treat. I'll pick you up at seven."

The crash of glass falling to the ground made Ted turn away from the car. When he turned back, Erica had already sped away.

Ted could have caught up to the car if he'd wanted to. When they started doing some speed training together, Dhiraj purchased a radar gun to see how fast he could go. Ted topped out at around 90 miles per hour. But instead of flying after the car, he simply took to the skies to be alone with his thoughts.

Erica is treating me like I'm dangerous. Am I?

Ted found himself remembering his encounter with Nigel several months earlier. The dark soul had told him that Erica had no interest in saving Earth. He said it was a lie and that Ted shouldn't trust anyone. While Ted had his doubts about Erica at first, she'd saved his life and had dedicated the last few months to training him. Why would Erica hide other powers from him if she wanted to train him to be stronger? Something didn't add up.

They had been out on several dates, but this was the most formal of all of them. Ted wished he didn't have to bring up business.

"I need to ask you about my pow–"

"This place is really something." Erica took a quick sip of her water. "I'm really impressed."

Ted could see right through her, and as much as he wanted it to be a normal date, there was no way that was possible.

"Thanks, but I need to know more about what I can–"

"Good evening, Mr. Finley." The waiter had a mild French accent and wore attire that matched the upscale establishment. "The owner is a big fan. She'd like to offer you anything you'd like tonight, on the house."

Ted couldn't help but let out a sigh of relief. Erica gave him a glare.

"That's very generous of your owner." Ted looked over at his date's beautiful, judging face. "Please tell her thank you. We'll be ready in just a couple more minutes."

The waiter bowed and left them.

"Erica, I need to–"

"Alright." Erica straightened her posture and looked deeply into Ted's eyes. "I realize that I lied to you about who I was before and now I'm lying about what it is you can do. In both cases, I was trying to protect you."

"If I know more about what I'm up against and how my powers work, won't I be safer?"

The answer was delayed a moment while the waiter came back to take their orders. When he left, Ted stared at Erica until she answered.

"It's complicated." Erica looked away before glancing back at Ted. "Becoming what you are is no picnic. Trying to learn it all at once is like tearing off a Band-Aid that's covering your entire body."

Ted took a gulp of water as he played that image in his head. "One of your best friends tried to kill a bunch of people in a fire. A dozen librarians tried to murder us for a book that wasn't even there. I appreciate you trying to take it easy on me, but maybe we need the Band-Aid approach this time."

When the salads arrived, Erica put her silverware onto her plate and placed the napkin on her lap.

"You have immense power, Ted. Few living souls have ever been able to tap into all of it."

"Why?" Ted munched on a leaf of lettuce before he put his fork down as well.

"Because most don't live long enough to try."

Ted wasn't sure if a piece of crouton went down the wrong pipe or if his throat closed up on its own. "And the ones who have?"

He could see the pain in Erica's eyes.

"They've gone crazy in the process."

Ted was starting to understand why Erica might want to hold some things back.

"But if I keep training with you, I'll be fine, right?"

As Erica's eyes started to water, Ted wished mind reading were one of his powers.

She dabbed a bit of makeup onto the corner of her napkin. "Hasn't gone so well in the past."

Ted could see deep pain in Erica's eyes. It reminded him that despite her teenage appearance, Erica had seen war and death and countless other things Ted didn't even have a concept of. After the waiter brought them their main course, the conversation wandered off the topic of powers until Erica asked if they could head back home.

She didn't say much in the car except for a request to go back to Ted's house, and he complied.

When they reached the front door of the pitch-black house, Erica took him by the hand. "I want to show you something."

Ted was surprised when she spoke up. He couldn't tell if she was deeply sad or angry, but her lighter tone made him question his previous assumptions. Erica kicked off her heels and he followed his barefoot date down the back of his yard and into the pond area. A full moon spilled some light onto the sparsely wooded spot of nature. Several crickets sang their song as a twig snapped beneath Erica's feet. In an area typically undisturbed and natural, the small table with a bakery box on top looked out of place.

"What's this?" Ted peeked through the plastic top of the mostly brown paper box. It was a small, white frosted cake.

"Dessert." Erica gestured for Ted to sit at one of the two chairs.

As he did, Erica opened the box and cut off a piece for him, revealing the strip of raspberry jam on the inside. She placed a fork from inside the box beside a small plate and served him the treat.

"I'm actually pretty lucky that some woodland creature didn't try to take it." Erica cut off a piece for herself.

When Ted began to dig in, Erica went to one knee and started to take something out of her purse. Ted gave her a sideways glance.

"Erica, what—"

"Shhh," she said. "Ted, you've indulged me on all this superhero stuff, training hard and protecting your world. But you're more than I ever imagined you could be." Erica took out two tickets from her purse. "Ted Finley, will you go to prom with me?"

Ted covered his face and laughed. He and the old Erica had shared hundreds of hours by the pond. He'd loved her during all of them. Ted couldn't see his own face, but he imagined it was bright red and smiling wide.

"Yes." Ted felt a massive weight fall from his shoulders. "Oh man, yes." He imagined a limousine and Erica walking down the stairs in a beautiful dress. "It's going to be awe—"

Before Erica could get off her knee, the sound of an explosion blasted through the air. The smell of burnt carbon quickly wafted over from the Finley residence. The scent reminded Ted of the model rockets he and his father used to launch in the backyard.

Dad. Mom.

He dropped his fork and looked at Erica before running back up to his house.

"Ted, wait!"

The backyard light came on when Ted entered the automatic detection zone. The shining spotlight couldn't block out the flames engulfing his bedroom.

Erica caught up to him and took his hand. "I'll call 9-1-1."

They shared a moment before Ted leapt off the ground and smashed through his bedroom window.

CHAPTER 20

When Ted crashed through the window, he could tell that most of flames were coming from the upstairs hallway. That's when he heard the cries of his mother. She was saying his name over and over again, though her voice was much weaker than usual. Ted flung his door open wide with his mind and saw her lying in the middle of the fire, which had engulfed the doorframe to Ted's bedroom.

"Mom!"

Ted attempted to control the fire that was surrounding his mother and climbing up the hanging quilt in the hallway. Seeing her in pain sent his emotions off the chart. His efforts to move the fire only made it worse.

"Damn it!" He took off through the air and grabbed his mother out of the fire with the flames lapping at his clothes.

He ignored the heat and pain as he landed on the ground floor. She screamed as she dropped to the ground, rolling out the patches of fire on her pajamas. A hiss of air and foam zipped through the air and Ted turned to see his father using the extinguisher to get the last of the flames that were lapping at his wife.

"Dad." It was all Ted could get out when he looked at them.

"I was downstairs for a snack when I heard it." Ted's mother yelped as his dad tried to cradle her.

Ted used his powers to open the front door. "Take her. I'll—"

Mr. Finley put his hand on Ted's shoulder and handed him the extinguisher. He picked up Ted's mom and walked out the front door. While Ted had flown too fast for his clothes to catch fire, he noticed a deep, stinging sensation on the back of his hand. Ted shook off the burn and flew back upstairs. The fire had spread from the hallway to both his room and his parents' room. Ted released the contents of the extinguisher, which emitted a hissing sound and took out the fire with ease.

When all the flames were gone, Ted saw several pieces of metal lying just outside his room, indicating where a bomb had detonated. He kicked a hole through the wall before he noticed Erica standing at the top of the stairs.

"The ambulance is here for your mom."

Ted was about to fly down and out the front door when he saw Erica's outstretched arms. He stopped and let himself melt into them for a few seconds. He knew he'd be in front of television cameras soon, but this was a place where he could show his true emotions.

Erica ran her hand down Ted's back. "It's gonna be OK."

Ted nodded against Erica's shoulder. "You'll tell Dhiraj?"

Erica put on her best possible smile given the situation and nodded. Ted gave her one last look and bolted for the ambulance.

Ted and his father rode to the hospital. The EMTs had given Ted's mother something for the pain, and she was breathing calmly. The medics said the burns weren't life-threatening, but the wounds Ted could see on his mother's arms and torso looked ghastly.

"They were trying to get me." Ted looked at his father. "They saw my car in the driveway and tried to kill me in my sleep."

His father grimaced. "We don't know that for sure."

"Dad. This wouldn't have happened if I—"

Ted's father took his hand. "We love you, Ted."

He gripped his dad's hand and let his eyes well up with tears.

The EMTs were right about his mother's burns, and it didn't take long for the doctors to tell Ted and his father that she'd heal with very little scarring. As Ted had the small burn on his hand examined, Sheriff Norris came walking up with a grim look on his face. Erica had seen him enter from the waiting area and followed close behind.

"You alright, Ted?"

Ted did his best to look strong. He'd been practicing the face during the many photographs and videos the media had taken of him in the last half hour.

"I'll survive. My mom will survive. It could've been worse."

The sheriff crinkled a document in his hands. "There's... We've got a lead on the bomb."

Erica asked the nurse to excuse them. Ted shifted on the hospital bed and the paper beneath him noisily moved to accommodate.

"You don't look happy about it." Erica put her hands on her hips.

Erica was right: the sheriff looked downright uncomfortable.

"Natalie Dormer's phone was found at your house. Prints on the phone match the ones on the bomb."

Ted pounded his fist on the bed and the curtains that surrounded them fluttered upward as if a gust of wind had gone by.

"I knew it. There's no way she would've hung out with those GHA dicks unless she was brainwashed like Beth."

Ted expected to see the same look of realization on Erica's face. Instead, she looked embarrassed.

"Actually...."

"Actually what?" Ted asked.

"I kinda, sorta... sent Natalie undercover to infiltrate the GHA."

Ted laid his head back onto the bed and groaned. "We just had a whole conversation about you being more honest with me!" Ted sat up and scowled at Erica. "You give me a cake, you ask me to go to prom—"

"Did he say yes?" Sheriff Norris asked.

Erica nodded.

"Oh, congratulations."

"Thanks." Erica let a momentary smile escape before turning back to Ted.

"Ugh. Where's Natalie now?" Ted was hoping for a more positive look from the sheriff.

"She didn't come home after school. There was a GHA meeting to-night, but they're denying that she was there."

"Ted, I'm sorry about Natalie." Erica touched the side of the bed. "We're going to find her."

Ted caught the sheriff's eye. "I want to see him."

The sheriff folded the document and put it in his pocket. "I don't think that's such a good idea."

Ted scooted himself to the edge of the bed. "I want to see Cobblestone and I want to see him now."

CHAPTER 21

Dhiraj was halfway to the first part of "early to bed, early to rise" when he received word about the bombing via a text message from Erica. He took the neatly folded clothes sitting on the top of the dresser and changed into them without a second thought. Dhiraj switched off the loudest alarm clock in the country and remade his bed, dollar-bill comforter and all. He had a nervous feeling in his stomach.

There'll be no sleep tonight.

By the time he turned on the TV, they were already pegging Natalie as a potential suspect. He tried to get in touch with her via phone and social media, but there was complete radio silence.

After his text conversation with Erica, the first person Dhiraj called was Jennifer. She told him she could give him a lift to the hospital, and he was happy to take the ride, given his current level of sleepiness.

Dhiraj told his father where he was going and lugged his stuff downstairs. He opened the front door just as Jennifer was about to come in. The two of them hugged for a full minute.

"I'm sorry, Dhiraj." She was breathing heavier than he expected. "She's going to be OK."

Dhiraj hated the fact that the comforting from Jennifer made him feel aroused. He decided to blame it on teenage hormones instead of a sick mind.

"Thanks. I know she will."

They packed Dhiraj's stuff into the car. He noticed a large cooler in the back. "What's with the cooler?"

Jennifer fidgeted with the car keys and almost dropped them before she responded. "In case the hospital food is terrible, I brought a few meals."

Dhiraj could tell Jennifer was uneasy.

Did the bombing really make her that nervous?

The first thing Dhiraj noticed about Jennifer's car was the clutter. A few folders and school assignments, as well as a field hockey stick, littered the back. The vehicle smelled like a concentrated burst of the Norris household, which made Dhiraj's heart race.

As Jennifer pulled out of Dhiraj's neighborhood, she put on a classical station and drove on the empty road.

"Are you alright, Jen? Between the other day and now, you seem a little on edge."

Jennifer let out a quiet laugh. "I've been out of it lately. Still trying to get my head on straight after Erica... and Ted...."

Dhiraj put his hand on Jennifer's shoulder. "I totally understand."

Jennifer let out a deep breath. "I think I'm moving toward a solution, though."

Dhiraj yawned. His typical sleeping plan tended to take a hit during these late night encounters.

"Excuse me." Dhiraj rubbed his eyes. "That's good. You know, you can always talk to me."

"Thanks, Dhiraj."

Dhiraj yawned again. "Except for right now. Do you mind if I take a little catnap?"

Jennifer chuckled. "Not at all. I'll let you know when we're there."

Dhiraj leaned back against the comfortable seat and let sleep wash over him.

When he woke up, the faint hint of light left in the sky was gone. Dhiraj could swear he saw a sign for a town in New Jersey. When he glanced over at Jennifer, she stared straight ahead with a slight lean forward. It was as if everything in her mind and body had focused on what was coming.

"I think you missed the turn."

Jennifer didn't even look over at him. "I know exactly where we're going."

Dhiraj felt himself go from sleepy to alert in the course of a few seconds. The same Jennifer who wanted to skip school and make out with him on a whim was driving them to an unknown destination.

"We need to see Ted's mom and how everybody's doing."

Jennifer gave a quick glance over to Dhiraj and then back to the road. "We've got something more important to do."

Jennifer's tone had more bite to it than Dhiraj had ever heard escape her mouth.

"And what's that?"

Jennifer moved her neck to the side. Dhiraj could hear the joint crack to relieve some tension.

"Retribution," she said.

CHAPTER 22

Natalie woke up the next morning on the cold, hard bed she'd curled up on the previous night. There was a wool sheet on top of her that made her body warm enough to sleep. It also caused her to itch like crazy, but contracting something from a communal blanket was the least of her worries.

After a short stretching routine and a few dozen pushups, she walked over to the tiny view through the locked door into the room. There were two new guards stationed outside, each of them brandishing batons and pistols. Last night, she'd done everything she could to plead with them. She said she didn't even want to get out. She just wanted to know if Ted was OK. Aside from the plate of food they'd tossed in when she'd dozed off, they'd completely stonewalled her.

"Good morning, sheep." Natalie made the tiniest of waves when one of the guards looked through the window.

She stalked around the room for what felt like the millionth time as she looked for potential ways to escape her prison cell. The room was bare except for one hopeless escape route: the door to the hallway.

Natalie had been given the grand tour during the previous GHA meeting, and since her captivity she'd deconstructed exactly how she'd escape. If she could just get into the hallway.

As she stood at the opposite end of the room, a guard unlatched the lock and slid in a tray of food. Before Natalie could even plant her feet for a mad dash, the door was already closed and locked. The apple and buttered toast didn't interest her nearly as much as the newspaper on the other side of the tray. She took the items back to her bed and chomped on the apple as she scanned the front page. It didn't take long for her to lose her appetite. The Treasure Tribune, a paper that had listed her accolades since middle school, now cited her as the primary suspect in the bombing. The article sported a picture of Ted's house on fire and described the injuries of his mother. Natalie's muscles tensed and her brain told her it was time to punch somebody.

That's exactly what they want. No more getting jerked around.

Natalie thought about her call to Erica, asking to be of some assistance to the cause.

"You've been distant." Erica sounded mad over the line. "I bet the kids at school think you hate him right about now."

Hearing Erica's voice say "kids" made Natalie think about just how many lifetimes the girl had led.

"I'm sorry." Natalie had known it was a bad idea to call.

"No." Erica's tone brightened. "It's perfect actually. Would you mind having people hate you for a little while?"

Natalie smiled. "I always play better in away games. I love it when they boo."

The girlish laugh on the other end made Natalie hopeful.

The prisoner didn't expect she'd be this hated, though. She could picture the town dividing into two. On one side, there would be the teammates, coaches and friends who knew the real Natalie. On the other would be the GHAers and people who believed everything they read or heard online. She hoped the one side would be louder than the other, but just in case it wasn't....

Natalie took out the paper's advertising section. She tested the hard, sharp edge of the paper before she used it to slice open her palms. It took a few tries, but before long, she had a faint trickle of blood running down to her wrists. Natalie had learned not to let pain get to her during years of knee-to-knee collisions and semi-intentional eye gouges. As she squeezed her hands, she watched the blood rush through the small lacerations.

"This oughta get their attention."

Natalie crept up to the door, staying low enough to avoid the guards' gaze. When she'd pushed enough blood out of her cuts, she rubbed it all over the window. Natalie wiped the rest on her shirt and screamed the highest pitch sound she could muster.

One of the guards spied the blood and opened the door. As soon as his leg crossed the entrance, Natalie kicked with all her might. His leg made a cracking sound as the heavy door smashed into his knee. He shrieked with pain.

"Your scream is way better than mine." Natalie kicked the door again in rapid succession until the guard had collapsed and wedged the door open.

With a running leap, Natalie sprung out of the room and into the other guard before he could draw his weapon. Both of them toppled to the ground and Natalie could hear an alarm sound. She looked up at a flashing red light.

"No time for finesse."

Before the guard could fully recover, Natalie kicked him squarely in the crotch and ran for the exit. She didn't even look back to see him crumple to the ground as she pushed her way through a door and out of the hallway. She ignored a cramp in her side as she used memory and instinct to move her from one room to the next.

"Almost there."

When Natalie reached the foyer of the building, she saw the door that would bring her freedom. She'd never run as fast as she ran right then, until she felt the bullet hit her in the back. She'd been moving so quickly that when she fell forward, her body skidded several feet on the painted cement.

The pain from the projectile was excruciating. When she reached back to feel for blood, she was surprised not to find any.

"Rubber bullet," Travis said. "Cobblestone says he's not quite ready to kill you yet."

As much as it hurt to move, Natalie turned over to a sitting position and attempted to melt Travis' face with her eyes. She wondered if someday that trick would work. Natalie expected that Travis' face would be villainous and cruel. He actually looked more hurt than angry.

"Shooting someone in the back is kind of a dick move." Natalie tried to inch her way closer to the exit door.

Travis kept pace-for-pace with her, gun drawn and pointed directly at her head. "So is pretending to be someone you're not."

Natalie growled. "I think bombing a classmate and injuring his mother wins the psycho contest." Natalie stopped a few inches short of the door. "So congratulations to you and your hateful organization."

Travis fired another shot. This one whizzed by Natalie's ear and ricocheted off the door.

"I'm not afraid to shoot you again."

Natalie pushed past all the pain in her back and stood up. "You may not be afraid to shoot me from point blank range, but you are afraid. Afraid of telling the truth."

Travis cringed. "The truth doesn't matter."

Natalie stood as tall as she could manage. "You've got a room full of people who are going to cheer for Ted's mom getting injured. If they knew the truth–"

"It's too late." Travis' face began to twitch. "You're going back in the cell."

"You know what happened to the Torellos. You know that Ted is a hero." Natalie noticed the two other guards enter the room. "You're a good guy, Travis. I know you'll do the right thing."

Natalie watched Travis' gun hand shake while the other guards used a plastic tie to bind her wrists. Even when they kicked her in the back of the knees to send her to the ground, Natalie never took her eyes off Travis. When the guards pulled her back to the cell, she saw her classmate over her shoulder, continuing to stand in the very same position. She wondered if getting to him was her only hope of making it out alive.

CHAPTER 23

Erica took careful steps into Beth's hospital room, which happened to be only a floor up from where Ted's mother was recovering. The room was sterile and smelled of rubbing alcohol. Beth looked directly at her when she walked through the door.

"Oh my God, Erica!" Beth squealed. She emphasized almost every other syllable she spoke. "What is going on? You have to help me."

The hospital staff had bound Beth's wrists to the bed to keep her from trying to escape. Erica knew she'd have a hard time convincing the nurses to let her loose after 24 hours of raising hell.

"Hey, hun." Erica gave her friend a hug. "I'll see what I can do. How you feeling?"

"How am I feeling?" Beth did her best to gesticulate without the use of her hands. "I have doctors coming in every two hours treating me like a crazy person. I'm tied to the bed like some wild boar." She jerked her head to one side of the room and the other. "And I haven't even touched Facebook for two straight days. My life is the worst."

Erica sat down at the chair beside her bed. "I'm sorry." Erica forced a smile. "At least you'll probably drop five pounds from the terrible hospital food."

Beth started to cry. Erica did her best not to hate all teenage girls at that

113

moment.

"You know, before your boyfriend got superpowers, everything was fine." Beth wiped a few tears on her hospital gown. "You were there to hang out with me and play 'Who Wore It Best' in the hallways. We were all everybody cared about. Now, everybody just wants to see Ted hover off the ground."

Erica considered telling Beth that she was worm food before Ted changed, but she caught herself. Erica took Beth's hand.

"We don't always have a choice of what happens around us. It's all about what we do with those circumstances that makes us who we are."

Beth looked at Erica for a moment before closing her eyes. "Ugh, I fell asleep. You were too boring."

Erica knew that her previous inhabitant was just as terrible as Beth before the crossover, but that didn't make her any less angry. She did her best to cover it up.

"Do you remember anything about the person who told you to start the fire?"

Beth opened her eyes and leaned back into the pillows. "The doctors seem to think it's some kind of voice in my head. I don't remember anything that happened after Redican's class on Thursday. Maybe someone told me in there."

Erica exchanged some cheek kisses with Beth. "You're wonderful. Feel better soon." Erica walked to the door. When she turned back, Erica felt the room grow dark.

While Beth was still sitting on the bed, Erica could tell that another person had taken control. A look of hatred washed over Beth's face.

"You can't keep him from the truth, protector." Beth's voice had changed from bubbly to devilish. "Or is there too much blood on your hands for you to even care?"

Erica glanced into the hallway. She waited to step back into the room until a nurse moved out of earshot. "Who are you?"

Beth smiled like she knew all the secrets in the world. "Someone with nothing to lose." The redhead leapt toward Erica, but her restraints snapped her right back down into the bed. Beth growled and pulled at her shackles with all her might.

"It doesn't have to be like this." Erica moved closer to the bed. "You've lost people. So have I. That's what happens during a war."

The rage on Beth's face changed into pain. "It wasn't our war. The dark souls wouldn't have even bothered us if you'd given them Earth."

Erica pursed her lips. "Give someone an inch and they'll take a mile."

Whoever was in control of Beth's facilities ignored Erica's response. "Consider this your last warning. Give the boy access to all his powers. Let him end this war and bring peace to all the conquered realms."

Erica stood her ground. "And if I don't?"

Beth's confident smile sent a chill down Erica's spine. "Then I'll make everyone you know and love suffer. Including your boyfriend."

As the message ended, Beth collapsed back down to the bed. Erica ran back over and attempted to rouse her. Beth opened her eyes and looked through Erica as if she wasn't there.

Erica shook her head and felt tears come to her eyes. "Damn it."

She wanted to run to Ted right away to tell him what happened, but she remembered that he was still waiting for his mother to wake up.

It's not the right time.

Erica sighed.

Not that there's ever a right time.

Erica decided on the next-best person to talk to.

She found Sheriff Norris typing away on a laptop in the cafeteria. The room was so white, the light reflecting in through the window threatened to blind her. While the rubbing alcohol scent was absent from the room, the aroma of food that replaced it certainly didn't make her want to order an early breakfast. The sheriff had stayed in the hospital all night with the Finleys. Erica sat down next to him with two cups of coffee.

"Catching up on fan mail?" Erica handed him one of the cups.

"Thanks." The sheriff took a large gulp and continued typing. "I wish. What do you want, Erica?"

She feigned surprise. "I'm just trying to be of assistance to the hardest-working lawman in all of the U.S.A."

The sheriff closed his laptop and leaned his chin onto one of his hands. "Uh huh." He took another sip of his coffee. "Just don't put another whammy on me, OK?"

Erica had promised Jennifer she wouldn't use her powers on Sheriff Norris again. It was mighty tempting to get everything she wanted without much asking, though.

Erica handed over a list of names to the sheriff. "Long story short, someone on this list may have put a spell on Beth to make her start that fire."

The sheriff took the paper and glanced it over. "Fifth period English?" He gulped his coffee.

"One of these people may have a book that lets them control a person's mind."

The sheriff shook his head. She imagined he liked it better when he was dealing with jaywalking and parking tickets instead of the strange and mystical.

"Should this really get priority over whoever bombed the Finley house?" the sheriff asked.

Erica sipped her own coffee. "What scares you more: a cult or the possibility of 1,000 brainwashed students walking around starting fires?"

Sheriff Norris let out a long sigh. "I can start making some phone calls about a magical brain book."

"Thanks, Sheriff."

As she left the cafeteria, Erica walked past a wall of photos that showed the hospital under construction. The image of girders and a cement foundation brought her back to memories of screaming, the crunching sound of a tumbling building, and an overwhelming sense of loss. She shook off the past and kept walking.

CHAPTER 24

Jennifer had hoped to make the entire drive on her own. She knew she could trust Dhiraj to protect her, but she worried that his form of protection might involve calling her father and taking them back to Treasure. There were still two hours left of driving when she felt herself start to tire.

"How are you feeling?" Dhiraj caught Jennifer's eyes as she glanced over.

She could feel the genuine concern radiating out of him. "I'm more awake than I've ever been."

Dhiraj chuckled. "Is this opposite day or something?"

Jennifer giggled, despite her determination to stay grumpy. "You're ridiculous."

Dhiraj let the words sit for a few moments. "You know, people who care about you are going to start wondering where you are pretty soon."

Jennifer had already steeled herself against any such arguments. She knew her father would be worried when he got home from the hospital, but she figured there are just some things you can't involve your parents in. The new Erica hadn't paid her much attention since she'd returned, which wasn't so different from the old Erica who'd shunned her for her stick-in-the-mud attitude. Aside from the two of them, Dhiraj was the only one who seemed to want her to be happy and healthy, and he was right along for the ride.

Jennifer smirked. "You can tell them we eloped."

In a three-second space, Dhiraj's face went from joy to melancholy. "Seeing as I'm on a need to know basis, that's as likely to be the truth as anything else."

"I'll tell you more when we get there." Jennifer suppressed a yawn.

Dhiraj shifted his weight toward the driver's side. "So I can't talk you out of it?"

Jennifer made a sharp exit off the highway and into the parking lot for a rest stop. She watched the flickering neon lights of the convenience store as she parked beside an empty fuel pump.

"If you don't want to be here, you can leave right now." Jennifer took the keys out of the ignition. "If not, you can get me an iced coffee."

Dhiraj opened the door. "I need to pee anyway."

As she watched Dhiraj enter the store, Jennifer felt herself wishing he would come back to the car. As the hours crept into the middle of the night, she'd gotten more and more unsure of herself. Having someone there to keep her from a mental breakdown might be the only thing that would give her the revenge she sought.

Jennifer filled the tank and watched the door of the convenience store. She didn't notice the man standing behind her until he'd tapped her on the shoulder. As she turned around, the first thing she saw was the beige deputy uniform. A gun rested in Daly's holster and he appeared to reach for it as he spoke.

"Excuse me, miss?"

Jennifer's shriek was so loud, it caused Dhiraj to come running out of the mini-mart, iced coffee in hand. "Jennifer?!"

She backpedaled until she was pressed up against the trunk of her car. Jennifer felt her hands shaking as they tried to grab anything they could to escape.

The Daly-lookalike put up his hands, backing away as quickly as he could from the sound. "I was just going to ask you to move your car up a little. I didn't mean to—"

"Long drive." Dhiraj put his hand on the Daly-apparition's shoulder. "She's on edge. We'll be out of here in a sec."

Jennifer watched as the man changed to his actual form. His skinny frame and glasses made him look like Daly's opposite rather than his twin.

The man glanced at the coffee. "I hope that's decaf." He looked at Jennifer like she belonged in an asylum and went back to his car.

Dhiraj put his free hand on Jennifer's arm. "Are you okay?"

She let out a deep breath and nodded. "Yeah. But maybe you should drive."

Jennifer figured Dhiraj must have sensed that she didn't want to talk about her crazy screaming at the station, because he changed the subject to anything but her outburst and the reason for the drive.

The cool beverage and polite conversation was just what she needed to settle down.

"We're just about there." Jennifer eyed the odometer and kept her eye out for a certain motel sign.

"I'm surprised you even know where there is." Dhiraj smiled to himself. "No GPS. No printed directions. You're sure we've reached this magical spot you've kidnapped me to?"

Jennifer felt herself relax even further as she stuck her tongue out toward Dhiraj. The motel sign came into view.

"Not everything needs to be digital. You memorize a few numbers, check the mileage and before you know it...." Jennifer changed her tone to the GPS voice. "You have arrived at your destination."

Dhiraj gave Jennifer a goofy grin. "More like, you and your captive have arrived at your destination."

Jennifer opened her mouth as if she were offended. "That's it, we're not eloping anymore. I had a great ceremony planned and everything."

Dhiraj rolled his eyes. "I'll get the cooler."

Jennifer had been in the company of a lot of different guys in the past couple of months. This was the first time, however, she could say she truly felt comfortable around one of them.

When they checked in, there was only one room left and it sported one queen-sized bed.

They assessed their belongings. Jennifer's cooler would keep them well fed, while the extra toothbrushes and supplies in Dhiraj's overnight bag for

Ted would make sure they were hygienic.

Jennifer changed into the outfit meant for Ted – a generic t-shirt and a pair of pajama pants covered in cartoon meatloaf drawings. "Why meatloaf?"

"Never a bad time for meatloaf." Dhiraj looked straight down at the carpet and sat. "Would you mind lending me a blanket for the floor?"

Jennifer held out her hand. "Unh-uh." She lifted him up off the ground. "You're getting half the bed. Besides, it'll make it easier for me to hear you sneak out."

When Dhiraj stood straight up, they were eye to eye. She wanted to kiss him, but she didn't know if it was her instinct from months of kissing every boy in sight, the fact that she was a teenager alone in a hotel room with a boy or that she actually cared about her friend in that way. When she moved close to him, she could feel his body shudder.

"I'll take half of the bed." Dhiraj's breath quickened. "Thanks."

Jennifer put her arms around the back of Dhiraj's neck. She breathed in his scent and drew her body closer.

"We don't have to sleep yet." She brought her lips close to his to see if he would close the distance himself.

Jennifer felt him inch forward a tiny bit before he pulled back. She moved ahead and kissed him anyway. She wanted Dhiraj to take her by the waist and toss her onto the bed. She wanted all her emotions thrown out the window for several minutes of pure instinct. Before she could lose herself in the moment, Dhiraj jerked his lips away.

"This isn't right." Dhiraj tried to touch Jennifer's waist to push her away, but his hands were too shaky to do much of anything. "It's what I want, but not the way I want it."

Jennifer sidestepped Dhiraj and sat down on the bedspread. He joined her.

"You don't like me?" Jennifer sniffled.

Dhiraj steadied his hand and took a hold of hers. "It's the opposite. I love you. And you're my friend. I don't understand what you're going through, but I want to."

With that, Jennifer let her emotions fly out in the form of tears. She lowered her head into Dhiraj's lap and wept. He cradled her head with one hand and put the other around her waist. She laced her fingers with his and cried until she fell asleep.

CHAPTER 25

When Ted woke up the following morning, he was surprised he and his dad had been able to pass out on the blue upholstered chairs given the consistent beeping of the machines hooked up to his mother. When Mrs. Finley's eyes opened to see Ted and his dad sitting by her side, she smiled so wide that even Ted was almost convinced that nothing bad had happened.

"My boys." She reached for them, and they obliged her with a gentle hug. "I'm so glad you're OK."

When the embrace ended, Ted let out a tear and a laugh. "You almost die in a fire and you're glad we're OK?"

Even with heavy pain medication, Ted's mother gave him a quick smirk. "I was afraid you two wouldn't last four hours without me, let alone an entire night." She grew serious. "How's the house?"

Ted's dad shook his head and smiled. "Aside from that terrible quilt and a few burned patches of carpet, we made out OK."

"The quilt?" She somehow smiled wider than when she'd first spied them. "The bomb was truly a gift from God, then."

His mother's smile soon gave way to a quivering lip. When she started to sob, Ted's heart completely broke. He and his father began to cry as well.

Ted sniffled. "Mom, why'd you try to find me?" He took her hand. "You could've gotten yourself killed."

She tightened her grip and let out a shallow exhale. "You can't take the mother out of the mom."

Ted couldn't help but think what would've happen if the weapon had been more powerful. What if it would've taken his mother from him? Ted felt his face grow hot.

"What am I supposed to do, guys?" Ted pulled back and turned away from his parents. "These people could do this again. And they might have Natalie stashed somewhere. If I could just get my hands on Cobblestone."

"Theodore Finley!" Ted's mother could be just as stern from a hospital bed as she could from a standing position. "You're old enough to make your own decisions, but you're smart enough to make sure they aren't made in anger."

Mr. Finley took his wife's other hand. "I don't know, Deb." He glanced over at Ted. "I'd kind of like to strangle Cobblestone right now myself."

Ted appreciated the support, but he could see his father's comment start to pierce his mother's calm.

"Vigilantes? Are those the people I've married and raised?"

"But Mom—"

"But nothing, Ted." His mother looked stronger as she sat up in her bed. Past all the bandages and the beeping machines, she was still a mom through and through. "If you make this emotional, you've let the bad guys win. They want you to hurt somebody else or hurt yourself. You want justice, but they want to turn you into one of them. I'm going to be fine, but I won't be if you let them win."

Ted attempted to let himself relax. He wasn't sure how well it was working. "Alright."

Ted caught Erica talking to two men out of the corner of his eye. He recognized them as Agents Vott and Harding. "I'll try my best. Be back in a sec."

Ted kissed his mom on the cheek and hugged his dad before heading back into the hallway.

Ted joined Erica's side. She covertly took his hand and gave it a squeeze before going back into business mode. Ted wondered how many people Erica had lost in her many lifetimes.

Would seeing that many people die make you care more or less?

Vott and Harding barely even noticed Ted's entrance into the chat. Ted assumed they had figured out that Erica was the one who needed more convincing than he did.

"Natalie Dormer is still missing," Agent Vott said. "She remains our #1 person of interest until we find some more evidence."

"But I already told you, she was set up." Erica had come a long way from pretending she was too stupid to function around the DHS. Now she was talking to the two agents as though *they* were too stupid to function. "You need to search the GHA headquarters. They probably have her in a bunker. If she's still alive." Erica looked over at Ted. "Sorry."

He nodded. "It's okay. I know she's alive. I can feel it."

"The GHA is protected by some major players in Washington," Agent Harding said. "The chances of us getting clearance to search their building are unlikely."

Ted wondered who in the government disliked him enough to protect the same people who'd just bombed his house. Whoever it was, he certainly wouldn't be voting for them when he was old enough to hit the polls.

Agent Vott cleared his throat. "Now, if you join up with us, we can make this problem go away and keep your family safe."

Erica scowled at the agents. "Ted's mom is in the hospital. It could've been Ted himself who was maimed or killed. Then you wouldn't even have a chance to sign him up for your little club."

Ted took Erica by the shoulder. "Hey, let's talk about this in private for a sec. Guys, can you excuse us?"

The agents nodded and Ted took Erica to the other side of the waiting area. She pushed Ted's arm off and started to pace away from him.

"I don't trust them and you shouldn't, either." Erica folded her arms and continued to walk.

"Of course I don't trust them. But just because I don't trust them doesn't mean I might not need them."

Erica gave Ted a death glare. "It's part of the job that people you love will be in danger."

Ted considered telling Erica that he didn't exactly apply for the position.

He had a feeling that line of reasoning would be met with a swift kick in the gut.

"I know." He took her shoulders and did his best to look calm. "But most of the time these living souls have a secret identity. I don't, and I need to keep my family safe."

Ted's attempts to bring Erica down to a simmer were having the opposite effect. She was as tense as he'd ever seen her.

"When I was a living soul, I nearly died trying to live a normal life." She pounded her fist into her other hand. "If I'd just listened to my protector, I might have died knowing the people I loved lived happy, fulfilled lives. I didn't listen."

Ted scrunched his forehead and tried to understand exactly what Erica had just said.

"You were a living soul? You were like me?" Ted pictured Erica flying through the air at top speed.

She let out a groan. "Yes. I was like you. I wouldn't listen and I got the people around me into trouble by being an idiot."

Ted didn't know why Erica was so on edge, but it was starting to damage his calm. "So, you're saying the bomb was my fault?"

Erica smacked the nearest wall, leaving a several-inch crack in the wake of her outburst. The noise from the structural assault caused more than a little attention from nearby patients, visitors and nurses.

"I'm saying there will always be human problems to worry about. You need to care about bigger things now, Ted. What's the point of protecting a few people when the whole world could go down in flames?"

Ted didn't care if people were looking at them, and they certainly were. He couldn't believe Erica was treating him like this.

"I already saved the world. The world isn't in 'peril' anymore."

"Your world is always in danger." Erica pulled the collar of Ted's shirt toward her. "If you join up with the DHS, maybe you'll save a few people from a hurricane or something, but right now we need to focus on whoever stole that book."

Ted heard his mother's calming voice in his head and ignored it. He felt the anger bubbling over. "How do I even know I can trust you?"

Ted had never seen Erica's eyebrows go so high. "Excuse me?"

Ted seethed. Erica had been the one who let Natalie walk right into a trap. She'd held back on telling him about powers that for all he knew could have thwarted the bombing. And when a solution presented itself to deal with the GHA, she was the only thing that stood in the way. As much as he wanted look at her and see his girlfriend and protector before him, all he could see was a liar with ulterior motives.

"There's always one more secret." He paced away from her. "You say you're here to protect me, but it seems like you're just putting everyone I know and love in danger."

Erica grabbed his shoulder and turned him around. "The danger was coming already. If it wasn't for me—"

"Natalie and my mom might be safe."

Erica let out a roar of anger as she pushed Ted back into the wall. "You want to blame me for what happened? Fine. But this is bigger than Natalie and your parents. It's even bigger than the two of us. We have a responsibility to every world and every person in it." Erica backed away from Ted. "Call me when you're ready to handle being the man you were meant to be."

With that, Erica stomped off down the hallway and out to the parking lot. Ted knew his mother had said not to make decisions in anger, but how could he avoid it when he felt like his body was about to explode? As he thought about Erica and the way she was talking to him, three pictures fell off the wall and crashed to the ground.

Ted turned his attention back toward the DHS agents. He didn't care about his so-called responsibility to people on worlds he'd never even seen. Ted knew he had to protect his family and find his friend.

"I need a gesture of good faith."

Agent Harding was still looking at the broken picture frames on the ground. His partner smacked him and concentrated his attention on Ted. "And then you'll join us?"

"You do what I ask, and I'll consider it much more strongly."

Agent Vott folded his arms. "Name it."

"I want to meet with him." Ted stood up straight. "I want to meet with Cobblestone."

Chapter 26

Ted sounded angry on the phone when Dhiraj got a hold of him. Despite staying up way past his bedtime, Dhiraj couldn't help but get up at the crack of dawn. He wasn't sure when Jennifer would wake up, so he went out to get them some breakfast at the nearest bagel shop and called Ted along the way from his Bluetooth.

"Why the hell are you in upstate New York?" Ted sounded snippier than usual.

Dhiraj wished he could tell him, but even he didn't know why Jennifer had whisked him away in the middle of the night. He wasn't sure why she tried to make out with him, either, but he was more interested in conquering Ted's problems that particular moment.

"I'll let you know when I find out." Dhiraj tossed a few napkins into a bag of bagels and rolled the opening. "You sound like you want to punch somebody."

Ted paused like he'd just been caught with a handful of cookies. "I am perfectly calm."

"I don't think I've ever heard you perfectly calm." Dhiraj hoped his friend could survive a couple of days without him. Having superpowers could get you out of most jams, but emotional conflicts were a different story. "Why am I hearing this buzz about you meeting with Cobblestone?"

Ted grumbled. Dhiraj swore he could hear Ted put his head underneath a pillow, even over the phone.

"How do you always find these things out before me?"

Dhiraj grinned. "It's called the internet. I hear it's going to put the pencil sharpener out of business."

Ted mumbled something indecipherable.

"Look, Ted, just don't do anything stupid." Dhiraj reached the motel parking lot. "I want to be there when you do stupid things. It's more fun that way."

Ted's sigh nearly shorted out Dhiraj's Bluetooth. "No promises. You be careful, too."

Dhiraj nodded through the phone. "You've got it, buddy."

He opened the motel room door with care and saw that Jennifer was still asleep. When he'd woken up naturally before the sun rose, her arm was draped over him as if he were in his favorite dream. He'd imagined being married to his landmark crush a million times over, picturing himself expertly removing her arm every morning before heading off to his study to make them the money they deserved. He'd never imagined the same scene in a shady motel room with no idea why he was there.

When Dhiraj fished the bagels out of the bag, Jennifer began to stir. He caught himself wondering why she'd been acting so strangely. Could it still be the attacks messing with her brain? Dhiraj had almost been killed by an undead bully, but she'd been strangled half to death and learned about her best friend biting the dust. There was hardly a comparison.

"Where'd you go?" Jennifer spoke with the covers still on her face.

"There's this great place around the corner for people who've been kidnapped." Dhiraj cut his bagel in half, cream cheese oozing onto a branded napkin. "It's called Stockholm Syrup. Real fresh bagels!"

Jennifer pushed herself out of bed. She hiked up the meatloaf pajama pants that were several sizes too big for her and stood next to Dhiraj.

"You're too chipper." She took one half of the bagel and sat back on the bedspread. "This is the time of day for crazy people."

Dhiraj could feel his face betray him by reacting to the word "crazy." He thought back to the morning he brought her to school and yesterday's loud shriek in the gas station parking lot. He'd been spooked for sure, but he had no intention of pressing Jennifer on her behavior. She noticed his concern before he could return his demeanor to a neutral state.

"And these days, I'm the expert on what's crazy." She munched on the half-bagel.

Dhiraj forced a smile. "What do you mean?" He attempted to nonchalantly pick up his breakfast.

"You don't have to pretend, Dhiraj."

"Alright. You've been skipping classes. You freaked out when some nerdy stranger got your attention. Plus, you kidnapped me and took me across state lines for what seems like no—"

"I found Daly."

Dhiraj's mind snapped back to the moment in the cave when the twisted deputy pointed his gun at Erica's head. If it weren't for Natalie, he might have been dead as well.

"As in deposed murderer Deputy Daly?"

Jennifer nodded.

"Where is he?" Dhiraj felt the fear double in his stomach.

"Nearby." Jennifer spoke through a half-full mouth. "He works the graveyard shift at a convenience store close by. He's going under a fake name. I have his work address."

Dhiraj felt his mouth gape open. He knew Sheriff Norris didn't like to let go of cases, but Jennifer wasn't the bounty hunter type. Then again, she hadn't been the girl he'd known since telekinesis, resurrection and mind control became part of their day-to-day lives.

"What are you going to do?"

"We're going to catch the man who killed my friend." Jennifer hopped off the bed and reached for another piece of bagel.

Dhiraj wanted nothing more than to protect Jennifer, but she was making it pretty hard.

"We should call your dad. And the local cops."

Jennifer stared into Dhiraj's eyes. "We need to make sure it's him. Besides, he's a former cop. He'll know when people are after him and we may never find him again."

"But what if something happens? Nobody even knows where—"

"I've been seeing him." Jennifer put the bagel down on the counter. "The man at the gas station. Friends. Even my dad once or twice. I freaked out because I thought it was Daly."

Dhiraj stood up and took Jennifer's cold hand in his. He felt an internal buzz of electricity as he did it.

Jennifer gripped his hand tightly. "I need to be the one to find him. I need to end this so I can sleep at night. So I can be me again."

Dhiraj attempted to relax his fear away. "What's your – our plan?"

Jennifer looked happier than he'd seen her the entire trip.

As they got dressed and ready for the day, Jennifer explained that Daly's shift would end in the next half-hour. They would stake out the street until he headed home. Once they identified him, then they'd call the cops and nail him. Within the next 10 minutes, Jennifer and Dhiraj had pulled up their car across from the convenience store. The middle-of-nowhere shop was as beat up as their middle-of-nowhere hotel room. Dhiraj figured it wasn't as much a town for living as it was a town for hiding. Sure enough, the man behind the counter had the same build and height as Daly, though the advertisements stuck to the windows prevented the confirmation of his identity. As the man stood behind the counter, Dhiraj tapped Jennifer on the shoulder.

"Before... all of this goes down, I need to ask you about last night."

"I told you. In the parking lot—"

"No." Dhiraj started to squirm. "I mean, you trying to kiss me."

The look on Jennifer's face didn't inspire Dhiraj with much confidence. "I'm sorry. You've always been so nice to me and I tried to take advantage of you."

Dhiraj tried to start a reply several times, but he wasn't quite sure how to process Jennifer's words. "You... I... trust me, Jen, I'd be lucky to have you take advantage of me. If I'd done nothing, it would've fulfilled about 45 of my top 50 fantasies."

Jennifer's grin helped Dhiraj to relax. "That's creepy. But also sweet."

"You don't have to make up for her being gone." Dhiraj hoped he wasn't crossing a line. "You're amazing and you don't need to compensate for Erica.

It sucks that she's not who she was anymore, but the world would really lose out if you became someone you're not."

Jennifer's eyes blinked several times as some tears built up inside. Before she could respond, however, they both saw the man leave the convenience store. As he entered the daylight, it became clear that it was Daly.

"Should I call the—"

Jennifer stopped Dhiraj with her hand. "We're going to follow him home first."

When Daly pulled his car out of the parking lot, Jennifer allowed another car to pull behind the mark before she tailed him. They kept silent, as if Daly might hear them if they spoke. A few minutes had passed when Daly turned into a row of apartments that were as worn as everything else in town. Jennifer parked on the other side of the lot and watched as Daly entered his unit on the third floor.

After Ted got his powers, Dhiraj had seen his own adrenaline capability tested, but this was as fast as he could remember his heart beating. "Now we call the cops?"

"Open the glove compartment." Any sentiment Dhiraj had built up in Jennifer was gone. She sounded all business.

Dhiraj complied. On top of the insurance cards and the owner's manual sat a gun. He heard a large breath to his left.

"It's for protection."

Dhiraj considered grabbing the gun and fleeing to the nearest pay phone. Instead, he stayed in his place as Jennifer reached across him and took the weapon. Dhiraj wasn't sure what Jennifer needed more: protection against Daly or protection from herself.

CHAPTER 27

Ted felt like he was moving into enemy territory when he passed through the front door of GHA headquarters. Even though the dark exterior of the building had given way to a bright, posh core, Ted couldn't help but continue to feel darkness all around him. The people who met within these walls wanted his head on a platter, which made it hard to enjoy the interior design. Agents Vott and Harding were on Ted's left and right, respectively, and half a dozen DHS guards walked in behind them. He'd been told that more than a hundred people would take part in meetings that discussed his family and his future. There were only about a dozen people in the building now, but all of them looked like they considered him sub-human.

It wouldn't take much. Just a flick of the wrist and you'd be on the ceiling.

Ted tried to keep his mother's words in mind to take anger out of the equation. Between the looks the GHAers were giving him and his fight the previous day with Erica, anger felt like the only emotion within his grasp. And the more he attempted to suppress it, the more the feeling seemed to grow.

Ted thought about where these men and women might have been within the mob outside of the jewelry store. He figured it was much easier to people to taunt him when a hundred people had their back. Could one of these people have been responsible for sending his mother to the hospital?

The idea made the legs of an antique table in the corner of the room start to rattle.

Agent Vott put his hand on Ted's shoulder. "Not the best idea, Ted. Keeping your powers in check is a way better plan."

Ted concentrated on the table and the rattling stopped. He took a deep breath. "If it'd been your mom?"

Before Agent Vott could chime in, Agent Harding piped up. "I'd crush 'em."

While Vott's sensibility was important for a time like this, Ted would take Harding for a night on the town any day. The two agents went into a room ahead of Ted, giving him the opportunity to scope out his surroundings.

The interior of the building had sprung up so recently, Ted could still smell the fresh paint on the walls. Given how long construction work typically took, Ted imagined that whoever backed the GHA had deep pockets.

What would some rich guy or company have against me?

Before he could brainstorm further, the door ahead of him opened and Agent Harding waved him forward. Cobblestone was sitting at the head of some kind of command center table with a half-dozen armed men of his own. It reminded Ted of the underground White House bunker he'd seen in movies when the President had come under attack. He looked at the head of the GHA and pictured him as a movie villain stroking a purring, white cat.

Cobblestone opened his arms wide in Ted's direction. "We're honored to have you here today, Ted. It's amazing that a small advocacy organization like ours could command a sit-down with an important person like yourself."

While Ted couldn't smell the bullcrap, he certainly knew what it sounded like. "Mr. Cobblestone."

"Please, call me Tom." The man's boisterous tone changed to solemn in a hurry. "I'm so sorry to hear about your mother. We are working around the clock to find Ms. Dormer and put her behind bars."

Agent Vott put his hand on Ted's neck.

"Thank you." Ted considered pointing all the GHA weapons directly at Cobblestone and seeing if he'd give up Natalie's location. "Tom."

A few beats of silence passed.

"I'm sure your time is as valuable as mine." Cobblestone leaned back in his chair. "How can I be of service?"

Ted had never tried it, but he wondered if it would be fun to try to yank out one of Cobblestone's teeth from the root. He suppressed the urge. "Do you mind if the two of us talk one-on-one for a moment?"

Tom waved his hands and the men around him stood up. "Of course, Ted. I figured you might want that. Agents Vott and Harding?"

Ted could hear Vott's low grumble behind him. The DHS agents shuffled out just as Cobblestone's men had.

"Be smart." Vott gave him one last pat on the shoulder before he and his partner exited.

Cobblestone's posture changed when the two of them were alone. He leaned forward as if he were trying to stab Ted with his words. "It's nice to be able to talk candidly with someone. Even if it is with a murderer."

The insult made Ted feel more at ease than when he'd had to play nice. "You put on a good face for the crowd, Tom."

Cobblestone coughed. "Don't address me, you abomination. You should be in jail for what you did to the Torellos."

Now Ted leaned back in his chair. He knew now it wasn't Cobblestone's choice for him to be there. "The Torellos were already dead. They were the ones possessed by… aliens. I stopped them in self-defense." Ted cleared his throat. "Trying to kill my mother and frame my friend for it is a lot worse than what I've done."

Cobblestone laughed. "Nobody was going to die. It was a warning shot. If you do what we say, nobody else will get hurt."

Ted seriously considered sending one of the room's flatscreen TVs through Cobblestone's skull. "My mother is not a bargaining chip."

Cobblestone acted like he didn't hear him. "If you and your girlfriend leave Treasure forever, we'll give you back your friend and protect your family from future… harm."

Ted stood up. "She's here, isn't she?"

Cobblestone got out of his chair and looked Ted in the eyes. "Catch her if you can."

Agent Vott opened the door to see them staring at one another. "Everything going okay in here?"

Cobblestone changed his demeanor from evil leader back to friendly used car salesman. "Thank goodness you're back, Agent Vott. Mr. Finley here was getting a little heated."

Ted could tell Vott didn't trust Cobblestone's tone of voice, but he played along just the same.

"Ted, I think it's time to go. You got what you came for."

Ted took a deep breath. He was about to go against Dhiraj's advice from earlier that day.

"No, Agent Vott." Ted glanced at the room's exit. "At least, not yet."

Vott attempted to close the door behind him, but Ted was too quick. He went completely horizontal and shot through the opening and back into the lobby. Ted continued to push himself to full speed to zip past the DHS guards and back to the front of the building. When he landed back on his two feet, an alarm sounded throughout the building.

This could be bad.

Ted saw a spinning red light shine down from the ceiling. Several of the men who'd been milling around the lobby earlier surrounded Ted. They drew weapons and pointed them right at the hero's chest. He felt his stomach churn in double time, but he refused to let the fear get in the way of his finding Natalie.

"Nice place you've got here." Ted's voice shook. "Can you set me up with your decorator?"

One of the men held his hand up when the others reached the desired position. "Down on the ground, alien, before we take you out."

Ted smirked. "I'll just look her up online, then."

Before any of them could pull the trigger, Ted rocketed to the other side of the building and headed straight for a locked door into the other part of the complex. He lowered his shoulder and shut his eyes. The door gave way and smashed open, sending the deadbolt out of the wall and clanging to the ground. Ted didn't turn back to admire his show of strength.

Nat, if you're here, I'll find you. Or die trying.

CHAPTER 28

Erica spent a few extra minutes primping in front of the mirror. The ancient part of her had spoken with people of all ages, including Presidents, foreign dignitaries and murderers. The part of her that was still a teenager had never met with a teacher outside of class before. Sheriff Norris had set up a meeting with Mr. Redican at a local coffee shop, which would give Erica the chance to ask him questions about the case.

The sheriff had planned to accompany her, but as soon as word got out that Jennifer was missing, that proposal went out the window. The way Jennifer had been acting lately, like Erica's former inhabitant in training, she wasn't surprised her friend had run off. Any worry she had about the situation evaporated when she heard Dhiraj was with her.

They can handle themselves. And so can I.

Erica finally approved her outfit and makeup in the mirror and looked down at her phone. She and Ted hadn't spoken since they'd blown up at each other in the hospital.

They planned the meeting for noon, and by the time Erica reached the coffee shop, the place was packed with students, families and other caffeine connoisseurs. The smell of espresso beans mixed with caramel and filled the room.

If there's one thing this world has improved on, it's coffee.

Thinking back to some of the black sludge she'd downed in previous lifetimes made her gag. It was right at that gagging moment that Mr. Redican flagged Erica down from the corner of the room. She almost didn't recognize him at first, given he'd shed his typical button down shirts for a casual polo. It felt strange to walk up to this man, who now seemed much closer to her age, and interact with him outside of school. Teachers were people, too, she supposed.

"Just when I thought I could get away from you blasted kids." Redican grinned when he shook Erica's hand. "I'm surprised Ted isn't here. The two of you seem inseparable."

Erica blushed a bit and took the empty chair across from her teacher.

"I'm here on his behalf." She scooted her seat closer to the table. "He can't be in two places at once, right?"

Redican nodded in silence. It was as if he were gesturing more to himself than Erica.

"How can I help Team Ted?" Redican sipped from a long blue straw, letting the end of the drink make a slurping sound at the bottom of the cup.

"This won't take long." Erica took out a small notepad and scribbled a header at the top. "I need to know if you saw anybody chat with Beth before... the incident."

Redican leaned back in thought. Or was he pretending to think? Erica couldn't shake the feeling that Redican was hiding something from her.

"I don't remember her chatting with anyone in particular." Redican looked right into Erica's eyes. "She always acted odd in my class. I think your friend had a schoolgirl crush on me." He laughed and nearly knocked over his cup with a giddy gesture.

"Oh, that crush remains active," Erica said. "No past tense about it. You're a cool teacher, Mr. Red."

As Redican beamed, Erica remembered something Beth had said to her. During the building fire, Erica's friend had said something about homework.

"Likewise. Except the student version, of course. Sometimes, it seems like you're in another league than your classmates entirely."

Erica shared a glance with her instructor. "A month on the streets gives a person perspective."

There was something in the way Redican was smiling that made Erica uneasy.

"Ah yes, I heard about that. You disappeared and came back without a scratch on you."

Beth was doing an assignment. It was a teacher. It was—

Erica stopped her train of thought, realizing that the man before her was more than he appeared. In fact, it was very likely that Redican could hear everything she was thinking.

Erica did her best to keep a poker face. "You've been helpful, Mr. Red, but I really should see how this interview with Cobblestone is going—"

Erica tried to stand up out of her chair, but her legs refused to move. It was as if the commands from her brain weren't reaching their intended destination. Redican's face changed from his smiling teacher persona to something much more sinister.

"It's so hard to get help at these places." Redican raised his hand in the air and three baristas came to their table at once.

"How can we help you?" The three of them spoke the question in unison.

Erica stopped trying to use her legs and began thinking of the best possible plan of action.

"Could you lock the door, my dears?" Redican half-grinned, half-scowled at the baristas as they walked in a single file toward the front door.

Erica noticed that everyone had frozen in place. One gentleman with a sandwich had it clutched an inch away from his mouth. A little girl with a smoothie had a straw chomped between her teeth. Only the hum of the espresso machine remained.

"Neat trick, Mr. Redican." Erica glanced toward the emergency exit. "Seems like you're using an awful lot of power on little old me."

Redican snapped his fingers and all the patrons in the room put down their food. They stood straight up and looked toward their corner table.

"You had such promise, Erica." He paced around the outside of the table. "Even though you aren't really a student."

Erica wondered how many of her memories Redican had gone through without her knowledge. "What do you want?"

"See, I like it when we can be more direct. Enough of this pussyfooting around like we belong here." Redican put both hands on the table and looked at Erica. "I want the living soul to reach his true potential. I want him to take back my world and turn the dark soul army into a pile of dust."

Erica felt the hint of a plan and made sure to stow it deep within her mind to keep Redican from sniffing it out. "You know that's not how this works."

Redican sneered. "Ted is your lapdog. It was smart getting into bed with him. Making sure he'd protect your home world without question." Redican stood up and began speaking as if the words were meant for his ears only. "But there are other worlds in danger. And with a little change in programming, I think you'll make sure he saves them as well."

Erica felt Redican enter her mind and she put her plan into action. With dozens of lives worth of memories, Erica had access to more storage than most. She jumped from memory to memory and life to life as fast as her brain could handle. Erica watched Redican begin to shake as he tried to process all of Erica's thoughts at once. Redican let out a gasp of pain as he went down to one knee. Erica could feel her legs again and used them to run out the back door.

Erica had gotten about a block down Main Street when she turned back. Redican didn't appear to be in pursuit. She passed by the empty gazebo when a girl a couple of years her junior grabbed Erica from behind.

"You think you can escape?" The girl's eyes looked enraged. "You think you can have the living soul all to yourself?"

Erica looked back toward the coffee shop and saw Redican walking slowly toward her. She pushed the girl away from her and continued to run.

When she checked on her pursuer, a running stroller crashed into her side and sent her into the pavement. The mother and her child screamed at Erica in unison as they went for another pass. This time, Erica leapt over the stroller and kept going without turning around. She heard a short, repetitive honking noise and tried to outrun it. Two cyclists zipped down the street and closed in on her from either side.

The biker with the longest reach grabbed for Erica. "There's no use."

The other one made like he was preparing to ram her. "You'll suffer.

He'll suffer."

Erica jumped and did a split kick in midair. Both bikers hit the pavement hard and Erica grabbed one of their bicycles. She'd made it about a block and a half before she felt her legs fall under Redican's command. She did a U-turn and headed back toward her teacher. Erica attempted to reach into her purse and alert Ted through her phone, but she felt like her hands were glued to the handlebars. As she got closer to her teacher, Erica hopped off the bike and let it careen down the street until it turned sideways and skidded along the blacktop.

As Erica reached the ground, she tried her last ditch effort. With all her effort, she dove toward Redican and sent a bolt of blue electricity between her hands. If she could reach him, perhaps she'd be able to put him under her thrall. Her legs got within two feet, but they never came close enough to his body to do any damage. She was stuck in place, and Redican easily shut her power off like he might fix a leaky faucet.

"All these lifetimes, all these powers." Redican walked up to her frozen body. "Wouldn't it just be easier if you were a regular teenager?"

Erica gasped. "No, please!"

As Redican touched her forehead, Erica could feel the world slip away from her as she collapsed to the ground.

CHAPTER 29

As Ted crashed through the door to an unknown area of the building, he felt the sting of at least three rubber bullets colliding with his body. The pain was immense, and he was certain his alarming speed toward the shooters had made the impact even worse. Distracted from his flight path, Ted caromed into a wall and crashed to the ground. His shoulder got the worst of the landing, sending even more pain through his body. He felt woozy when he looked up at the guards as they readied their weapons to fire a second volley. He reached back toward them and used his mind to smash the guns into the wall.

His vision wasn't at 100%, but he could still see the three figures coming toward him ready to kill him the old-fashioned way. Ted would have gladly obliged some hand-to-hand combat if he'd had more time. Instead, he pointed at the largest of the three, lifted his body into the air with his powers and swung it around by the legs like a rag doll. The man-turned-weapon screamed as his body smacked into the other two guards. The crack of skull on skull knocked all three of them unconscious. Ted laid them on top of each other and shook off the mental cobwebs. Instead of flying, he went running at super speed down the corridor, willing his legs to move faster than ever before.

Natalie would kill for these legs.

Ted went through another door, which led to a hallway that resembled a prison. Two guards stood in front of a room that Ted rightly assumed led to his captured friend.

The nervousness he'd previously felt had vanished. Between the pain and the slight dizziness, Ted was running on pure instinct. He put his hands on his hips and puffed up his chest at the guards. "Hey, guys. My friend is in there and the two of us need some private time."

One of the guards took one look at Ted and ran in the opposite direction. Ted couldn't help but laugh, which seemed to demoralize the remaining guard.

"I don't want any trouble." The guard's declaration came out more like a question. "Just stay away, OK?"

Ted continued to walk toward the guard. The man fired a shot. Ted used a flick of his hand to guide the bullet around his body and into the door behind him. Another shot fired out of the guard's gun, and once again Ted moved the projectile around him. His confidence started to grow.

I am such a beast right now.

When the guard fired a third time, Ted stopped the rubber bullet in midair, turned it back around and placed it against the guard's forehead. He dropped his gun.

"You say you don't want trouble." Ted floated the man up in the air. "Then you shoot at me. With a gun. It's kind of a mixed message."

The man whimpered. "I'm realizing that now."

Ted shook his head. "Stay up there for a while, will ya? Shout if any more guards come in."

"No promises." The man's legs flailed as Ted opened the door to Natalie's cell.

The room was dim, but once Ted's eyes adjusted, he could see Natalie right away. She was chained to the wall and had red-stained gauze wrapped around her hands. Ted used his mind to rip the chain off the wall and unlatch Natalie's wrists and ankles.

Natalie looked up at him with a sly smile. "I thought I heard some idiot running in here."

"Are you alright?" Ted ran over to Natalie and put his arm over her shoulder. They hugged.

"Not anything a little choking won't solve." Natalie flexed her free arms and legs. "I'm sorry about your mom."

Ted felt the anger tie in with his adrenaline. The GHAers had injured him mom and chained his ex-girlfriend to a wall. Somebody would have to pay for this.

"Thanks. She'll be okay." Ted gripped Natalie's waist with his arms. "But we're gonna need to move fast to do the same."

Natalie nodded. As Ted was about to take back off, he heard the floating guard's shout echoing through the hallway.

"He's in here with the girl!"

Ted grinned.

"What are you so happy about?" Natalie asked.

Ted pulled away from Natalie and used his powers to shut the door to the room before twisting the handle and lock all out of shape. "The guy actually did what I asked him to do."

Several of the guards attempted to enter the room, but Ted had broken the handle and fixed the lock in place. They pounded on the door with no chance of getting in.

Ted felt a sense of pride. "And now the guards are trapped."

"So are we." Natalie let out her trademark growl. "Was this all part of your plan?"

Ted's excitement sunk. "Um." He looked around. "It was part one?"

Natalie shook her head. "Come over here. I've got an idea."

Ted followed Natalie to a part of the wall that sported a six-inch crack. She gestured to it. "Well? Do your thing."

Ted cocked his head sideways. "What's my thing?"

"Ugh!" Natalie put her hand over her face. "It's so hard to find good heroes these days." She moved Ted's shoulders until he directly faced the crack. "Use your powers to grow the crack until it busts a hole through the wall. Do you think you can do that?" Natalie looked back at the door as one of the four hinges holding it snapped off and fell to the ground. "And quickly?"

"Alright, alright. I'm not a mind reader." Ted did as he was told. As soon as he started to concentrate on the crack, it doubled in size. The crack spread throughout the wall and Ted could hear the sounds of breaking wood and ripping insulation. When the crack had gotten large enough, he made a pushing motion and a hole the size of a garage door smashed through the side of the building.

Light streamed into the room and Natalie shook her head. "See, now was that so hard?"

Ted felt like he'd just bench-pressed a Buick, but he didn't want to share that with the strongest girl in town. "Easy-peasy. Let's fly."

Ted put his arms around Natalie's waist. She tightly gripped him back, and they flew out of the building.

"Where are we going? The lair?" Natalie had to speak loudly to get over the sound of the air whipping past them.

Ted did the same. "No. We're going to turn ourselves in."

"Seems counterproductive."

Ted laughed. "I've got the first half of another plan."

They circled the building and landed in the parking lot. As they did, Ted and Natalie came face to face with the DHS agents, Cobblestone's security detail and the GHA leader himself. Ted didn't enjoy having a dozen guns trained on him, but he figured it was better to face the music now than to attempt to be a celebrity fugitive.

"I want this criminal arrested for assault and causing massive damage to my property." Cobblestone stomped around, but Ted imagined this was exactly how he wanted things to shake out. It amazed him how some of the most terrible people in the world were killer actors.

"Do what you want with me." Ted looked toward Agents Vott and Harding, who had joined the rest of the agents in the gun-pointing party. "Natalie was here all night, chained to a wall. The evidence is pretty compelling that the GHA framed her for trying to kill my family."

"I will admit to kicking one guy in the junk, though." Natalie's frown turned upward for a moment. "As long as we're being honest."

Ted looked for a reaction from Vott. He put down his weapon and walked over to Ted.

"You shouldn't have done that." He looked over at Natalie and back at Cobblestone. "Now it's your word against his. There's no way any of his guards will back up your story."

"I have proof!" The voice that echoed through the parking lot surprised Ted more than the rubber bullets had. It was none other than GHA bully Travis Conner. "We had a security feed on Natalie all night. She couldn't have done it."

Ted looked at Natalie. "But why would he...?"

Natalie touched his arm. "And the truth shall set you free."

Travis held a flash drive in his hand, which Ted snatched using his mind and guided to Vott's hands. "There's your evidence."

As Travis passed by Cobblestone's security detail, the GHA leader lunged forward and slapped the boy in the face. Travis fell to the ground, and the DHS agents pointed their guns at Cobblestone.

"Tell your men to holster their weapons, Cobblestone." Agent Harding's voice seemed to go down an octave when he made the command. "You're coming with us."

After the DHS had gathered up Cobblestone and his guards, an EMT tended to Natalie's wounds at the back of an ambulance.

"I thought you'd really turned to the dark side." Ted examined one of the welts from his rubber bullet wounds. "It was scary."

Natalie grimaced as the EMT put some iodine on her cuts. "It had to be convincing or else they weren't going to buy it. Some good it did."

Ted put his hand on Natalie's face. "My mom is going to be fine. Besides, Vott said that Cobblestone is bound to get some jail time for this. You did good, Nat."

Ted wanted to kiss Natalie right then. He had a feeling she felt the same way. Ted reached up and kissed her on the forehead instead.

After Natalie was all patched up, Ted turned down a ride from the agents and hitched one with her instead.

When the car pulled into Ted's driveway, someone on Ted's front porch came into sight. At first, neither of them could make out who the figure was. Natalie turned off the engine and walked by Ted's side of the car as he flipped on the porch light with his mind.

"Hey, baby." The familiar voice was slurred. "I was wondering if you'd ever get home."

Erica took a swig from a clear bottle until she'd sucked out the last drop. She let the bottle fall down the stairs and land in the grass of the front yard.

Ted moved with alarming speed to the base of the porch. "Erica?"

Erica stumbled when she tried to get up. When she found her footing, she put her arms around Ted, paying no mind to Natalie standing to their right.

"I know you missed me so much." Erica blew her vodka-laden breath onto Ted's face. "But don't you worry. I'm back."

CHAPTER 30

Jennifer inspected the gun to ensure it could be used if needed. Being a sheriff's only child came with weapon-related perks. She'd grown up on firing ranges and even spent one of her birthday parties shooting targets and plastic milk jugs with her best friends. She knew her way around a handgun better than most suburban teens, but Jennifer could tell that Dhiraj didn't care about any of that. His skin had grown several shades paler since the reveal of the weapon.

"If we're going up there, I don't think you should bring that with you." Beads of sweat rolled down Dhiraj's forehead.

Jennifer reached over her friend to pull a holster out of the compartment as well. "It's for self-defense. This guy is a murderer."

Dhiraj took Jennifer's wrist in a tight grip. "I understand that. There's just a lot of emotion tied up in this. It's better to let people who aren't involved handle things."

Jennifer mulled over Dhiraj's argument. It was sound, but she needed to see Daly squirm. She had to be the one to make him pay.

Dhiraj could tell his words weren't hitting home. "You've tried to kiss me twice this week, and the only reason I didn't reciprocate is because I love you."

Jennifer's train of thought halted. She looked straight into Dhiraj's eyes as if he were some kind of curiosity.

She stammered as she spoke. "I... I think I knew that. Somewhere in my messed-up brain."

Dhiraj took Jennifer's hand. "That's why I can't let you do this. We need to call the police right now."

Jennifer sighed. "No. That's why I have to do this."

She took out a pair of handcuffs from underneath the driver's side seat. Before Dhiraj could react, she'd slapped the cuffs on the steering wheel and his wrist.

"Jen!" Dhiraj struggled to yank his arm free of the cuffs.

Jennifer opened her door and stepped out. A light spring breeze played with her hair as she turned back to her captive.

"I wouldn't have done this if I didn't love you, too."

Dhiraj lurched after her with his free hand. Jennifer shut the door.

She walked away from the car to the sounds of Dhiraj pleading with her through the inch-open car window.

"Please come back!" Dhiraj pounded his fist against the door. "Jennifer, don't do it! It's something you'll never be able to take back." He screamed at the top of his lungs. "Can't we just talk this out?! Jen!"

By the time Jennifer reached the second floor of the apartment building, she could no longer hear Dhiraj's voice.

"He's going to understand." She took in a deep breath and let it out slowly. "They'll all understand eventually."

Jennifer continued to walk up the stairs, beset by peeling white paint on all sides.

When she reached for the door handle, Jennifer could feel her hand shake. She knew that if she opened the door, nothing would ever be the same. Jennifer made herself think of the way Daly had tricked them all. His aw-shucks demeanor and work with her father had made them all think highly of him. She then thought of Erica, her body made stiff and rotten by the man who resided beyond that threshold. She thought of him stabbing her to death and covering her up with the earth. The fear turned to a simmering anger.

Jennifer opened the unlocked door.

The stench of mildew was the first thing to hit her as she walked into the room. She guessed there wasn't much time for cleaning when you were hiding from the law. She recognized several plastic bags and half-eaten containers of food from Daly's workplace. Toward her right were stacked up dirty dishes in the kitchen. When she turned to the left, she saw the light from a television and heard a creaky, old ceiling fan.

As she took a few steps toward the TV, the man she sought came into view. Daly was still wearing his uniform from work as he sat in a recliner that appeared to be straight out of a dumpster. The man's eyes were shut, his head turned to the side as he dozed. After weeks of visions of Daly populating her nightmares and bleeding into her life, she was finally seeing him for real. Every warning signal her body possessed started to go off at once. Instinct told her to run, but she refused to listen.

Jennifer thought about how easy it would be to punish him right here and now for his crimes. All she'd need to do was take out her gun and unload a few shots into some key areas. Unless Dhiraj had called the cops, he'd be the only one who knew she was there. It would be clean and it would be quick. But Jennifer knew she wasn't just there to put an end to Daly's life. He needed to know what he'd done and why he was going to pay for it.

Jennifer slammed the front door behind her and Daly sprang to life on the chair. His first look was bewilderment until the recognition sunk in.

"Sheriff's daughter." Daly wiped his mouth and relaxed as he faced her straight on. "I thought it'd be the superhero."

Daly had put on a few pounds since she'd last seen him in the caves several months ago. His five o'clock shadow had been replaced by the start of a beard.

Erica wouldn't have been caught dead with a guy like that.

Jennifer hoped Daly would cry or scream, but he only let out the same grin she'd admired dozens of times. She wanted to shoot the smug look right off his face. Jennifer took her weapon out of the holster and pointed it directly at him.

"I think you'll find that I'm full of surprises."

CHAPTER 31

Natalie could tell what happened to Erica almost immediately, even if she didn't understand it. She'd never examined her as intently as Ted had, but all the old personality quirks were there. Erica's voice was different, as if she was trying to get someone to go to bed with her through every syllable and phrase. Erica was also more physical than she'd been the last few months, seeing as she grabbed at Ted's crotch when he got close enough to her. On top of everything else, she was completely plastered.

Natalie watched as Ted fell over himself to avoid being groped in front of his ex-girlfriend. She appreciated the effort, but Natalie could tell that Ted had no idea what or who he was dealing with.

"I bet it would feel good to do it on the lawn." Erica got her hand close enough to take Ted's zipper half way down before he slapped away her advances.

Erica only giggled and tried harder. Natalie couldn't help but feel her anger build. She'd done enough picturing of Ted and Erica being intimate together, and she certainly didn't need to see such images live and in surround sound.

Natalie watched as the confidence of Ted's triumph against the GHA faded away.

Ted stammered as he fended off another one of Erica's approaches.

"What are you– Erica, this isn't like– Natalie's right here."

Natalie crossed her arms and waited for the show to be over. The stench of liquor from Erica's breath reached her, even as she kept her distance. It reminded her of a girl she'd needed to tend to at a sleepover basketball camp. Their room smelled like vomit the entire week.

"Nadre the Giant can watch if she wants." Erica stutter-stepped and went down to one knee in the grass. "Ooh, we could do a video."

Natalie gave it another few seconds before Ted finally seemed to realize what had happened.

"Erica?" He looked over at Natalie before bending down next to their drunken friend. "What do you remember?"

Natalie caught a glimpse of Erica's eyes when she looked toward Ted. It didn't seem like anybody was home.

"I remember thinking that you're hot." Erica pulled at Ted's shirt.

When he tried to back away, one of the buttons ripped loose.

Natalie growled so loud, she nearly scared herself. "That's it! Enough of this freak show. Get her inside. Float her if you have to."

It took a few tries to get Erica through the front door, but once they did, they each sat beside Erica on the Finleys' downstairs couch.

Natalie and Ted forced Erica to drink an entire glass of water before she had permission to speak again. Whenever Erica made a motion off of the couch, Natalie commanded Ted to use his powers to keep her there. When she finally settled down, the interrogation began.

"Where do you last remember being before you – fell off the wagon?" Natalie wished she had a lamp to shine right into Erica's eyes.

"I remember going on dates with Ted." She gave a brain-free smile in her boyfriend's direction. "I remember him touching my body and putting his lips against–"

"I'd rather not hear the details." Natalie snorted at Ted before she turned her attention back to the drunk girl on the couch. "Do you remember Nigel and the dark souls?"

Erica gave a puzzled look. "Is that a band? Are we in a band?"

Natalie gestured to Ted. He appeared stunned by Erica's response and needed a second before he shook out of it.

Ted's voice was tentative, as if he wasn't sure whom he was truly addressing. "You remember our dates, but what about Beth and the burning building?"

Erica gave the same confused look, but this one came with a smile. "Sorry, I don't remember a building. You're looking really sexy. Are we almost done?"

When Ted smiled back, Natalie considered taking a ceramic figurine from the end table and throwing it through the TV screen. She could feel the anger seeping out of her like fiery sweat.

Ted must have sensed Natalie's mood, and his smile faded. "It's like someone selectively changed parts of her brain."

Natalie stared at Erica. "Changed? Or erased?"

"Changed. The other memories have to still be in there." Ted tugged at his shirt. "They just have to."

"I could've blacked out the memories. It happens." Erica lurched forward. "I think I'm going to be sick."

Ted and Natalie guided Erica to the downstairs bathroom. As the door opened, she ran toward the toilet and started to puke. Natalie gave Ted a dirty look as she put her hands around Erica's hair to pull it back.

"So, this is your golden girl?" Natalie spoke loud enough to be heard over the noise of Erica's vomiting. "The one you were still in love with when you dated me?"

Ted frowned and leaned back against the wall. "I never had to hold her hair back."

Natalie gripped Erica's hair more tightly. "Lucky you."

"I'm never drinking again." Erica's voice echoed from inside the toilet bowl.

Natalie patted her on the back. "I'm sure you've never said that before."

After Erica was through, Natalie and Ted carried her the old-fashioned way back to the couch. She curled up and fell asleep within the next minute. The other two sat on the floor with their backs against the base of the loveseat.

"I'm sorry, Ted." Natalie put her arm around his shoulder. "I shouldn't have tried to make you feel bad. This isn't under your control."

Ted stared straight ahead.

"When we were kids, Erica was never satisfied with doing what everybody told her. She wanted to make life bigger, better and more exciting." He sighed. "When she took me along for the ride, I felt more interesting. More fun. When she left me behind, all I wanted was to get back to how she made me feel."

Natalie didn't know what to say at first. This was the first time she'd heard Ted open up about the girl who had his heart. "It sounds like you were more in love with the idea of a person than the actual person."

Ted broke his stare at the wall and looked over at Natalie. He let out a labored breath. "You might be right." Ted pulled his knees toward his chest and rested on his arms. "But none of this matters. Without the new Erica, we're pretty much screwed." Ted buried his face.

Natalie pulled him toward her. "We're gonna figure this out."

"No, we're not." He lifted his head. "This is something from another world, Nat. It messed up Erica's head and it could do the same to all of us."

Natalie saw the tears start to form in Ted's eyes. She couldn't tell if he was more scared that the new Erica might be gone for good or that they were in way over their heads.

Natalie tried to push down her own feelings of fear. "Look. You wanted me to be a part of this team. Well, here I am. Let's go stop this guy, fix Erica and save the freakin' world."

"So…." Ted wiped his eyes and his lips almost formed a smile. "You're in?"

Natalie rolled her eyes. "Sign me up. But no tights."

Ted sniffled and hugged Natalie. She felt herself grow nervous and warm at the same time.

"Thanks, Nat."

As good as it felt, Natalie shrugged out of the hug. She stood up and pulled Ted with her. They took a long look at the sleeping, brainwashed Erica.

"Thank me when we win," she said. "If we win."

CHAPTER 32

Dhiraj yanked at the handcuffs until his wrists were as raw as his throat. His cries for help hadn't even gotten a glance out of an apartment window from the complex. Even when he unlocked and opened the doors, nobody seemed to hear him at all. If they did, Dhiraj guessed they didn't care.

It'd been several minutes since Jennifer walked through Daly's door. He was relieved that he hadn't heard a gunshot, but there was no way to know what was going on up there. He pictured the worst-case scenario of Daly lying in wait for her, tossing Jennifer to the ground and stabbing her to death just like he had the old Erica. He pictured another scenario in which Jennifer shot Daly to death and ended up going to prison for murder. He watched her try to explain how the man had killed her friend, even though Erica was still alive. Dhiraj had to believe that neither situation had occurred. It was the optimistic escape he had to believe.

"Escape." Dhiraj looked at his phone as the idea formed in his head. "Of course."

He flipped through the phone's touchscreen to find the video app. He searched for ways to escape handcuffs. After a few low-rated videos, he found exactly what he needed. He hunted around the car to find an object to pick the lock, eventually settling on the metal ring from his house keys. Dhiraj nearly took off his fingernails in an effort to straighten the metal, but it was all worth it when the video's tactics actually worked. As he wrenched his arm free, the handcuffs made a clacking sound against the dashboard.

His first instinct was to call the police as he ran to the stairs to help Jennifer, but he pushed the plan to the side. If they found out that Jennifer had broken into Daly's home and pointed a gun at him, she'd go to juvenile hall at the least, and he'd be the accomplice. Dhiraj likewise ditched the idea of running in and trying to save her. If he dashed into the middle of some kind of standoff, he'd potentially get himself or Jennifer shot. Instead, he opted to take it slow.

He walked up the stairs, attempting to make as little noise as possible. When he reached the door handle, he turned it in slow motion and let it open inch by inch. When he wasn't blown to bits, Dhiraj figured it was safe enough for him to go all the way in. The smell of mold washed over him as he saw Jen pointing the weapon at Daly. He thought he'd get it aimed in his direction as well. Instead, Jennifer was so focused on the former deputy that she barely acknowledged her friend's entrance.

"Hey, Dhiraj." Jennifer's tone had reached an alarming level of intensity. "I was telling our comrade here about some of his transgressions."

Dhiraj produced a guttural noise in response, but he wasn't sure how much more to say. He was worried he'd take her attention off the man sitting in the recliner and Daly would charge the two of them. Then again, the man looked quite calm for a guy who might be shot within the next few minutes.

"What is this, a teen beach party?" Daly fidgeted in the chair.

Jennifer scoffed and aimed the gun at Daly's crotch. "As a person who slept with a 16-year-old girl because he was too immature to handle anything else, this is probably playing right into your fetishes."

Daly looked like he wanted to snarl at Jennifer, but he kept his facial expressions as neutral as possible given the insult.

Jennifer continued. "You were just so scared someone would find out you were such a pervert. So you killed my friend. My best friend."

Dhiraj reconsidered his idea of calling the cops. Under the age of 18, he figured Jennifer couldn't get too much time for breaking and entering. As long as he could keep her from firing that weapon.

"Two points." Daly changed his expression to a grin. "Erica never mentioned her bony, squeaky hag of a friend, so it seems like it was a one-way relationship. Second, your friend is still al–"

Jennifer moved closer to Daly, and Dhiraj followed suit. The man flinched when Jennifer made a motion with the gun. Dhiraj could feel his heart beating through his chest.

"You and I both know the person in Erica's body isn't her." Jennifer cranked her neck to the side and focused back on Daly. "You killed the friend I knew and there's no reason I shouldn't go eye for eye on your a–"

"Jen!" Dhiraj didn't even realize he spoke until Daly looked over at him. "You can't do this. If we get the cops in here, Daly is going to go to jail. It won't be for murder, but–"

Jennifer roared. The primal sound shocked both Daly and Dhiraj.

"That's not good enough, Dhiraj." Jennifer shifted the gun and fired a bullet through the glass porch window.

Dhiraj covered his ears as shattered glass crashed to the ground. Daly kicked off his heels, nearly causing the chair to topple over backwards before it balanced itself back into place.

Jennifer moved the gun back to its original position: trained right on Daly's body. "He killed her and he should be dead, too."

Dhiraj couldn't let this go on any further. He did the stupidest thing he could think of: he wedged himself in the space between Jennifer's gun and the man who had murdered Erica LaPlante.

"If you kill him–"

"Move, Dhiraj!"

"Your life'll be ruined."

"It already is!"

Dhiraj felt something he didn't expect. Amidst all the fear and uncertainty, he stood up straight and looked right into Jennifer's eyes. "If that's what you really believe, then I don't know how to help you." Dhiraj stepped out of the line of fire but kept his eyes fixed on Jennifer's. "If your entire existence revolves around the lives of other people, then you never had a life to begin with."

Daly started to laugh. "Look at Indian Tony Robbins here." Daly stood up from his chair and took a step toward Jennifer. "The truth is, Sheriff's daughter, it was fun. Stabbing a girl who wanted me oh-so-badly and watching the blood drain out of her."

Dhiraj refused to let Daly get to him. "Screw other people, Jen. Who needs Ted or me or Nat or Erica? Don't throw everything away because of any of us."

Daly took another step toward Jennifer, and she took one back.

"I did it all under your father's nose, too. When I put the last pile of dirt on your friend's cold body, I knew I was going to get away with it. I have gotten away with it."

"Don't you dare come any closer!"

Dhiraj pulled out his phone. "If you think your life isn't worth it, Jen, you can kill him right now. But if there's some chance that you want to become something other than a friend and a killer, I will get the police here right now."

Daly took another step toward her and when Jennifer inched away her back reached the front door. Dhiraj knew he had to buy more time. He ran toward Daly. The man took a wild swing and Dhiraj felt a painful slap against his cheek as he tumbled to the ground. Dhiraj ignored the stinging sensation and turned toward the standoff.

"It's just you and me, Jen." Daly closed the distance between them once again. "You want to go out just like your BFF did?"

Dhiraj dialed 9-1-1 as he watched Jennifer's trigger finger twitch. He was surprised to see a smile spread across her face.

"Nope." She aimed the gun exactly where she wanted the shot to go. "I'm gonna go my own way."

The gun went off, sending a bullet in Daly's direction. Dhiraj closed his eyes and prayed.

CHAPTER 33

Ted ran the gamut of emotions as he floated Erica into the back of Natalie's car. She'd passed out after throwing up two more times in the toilet. Ted wondered if the girl he'd grown up with was actually back for good. If that was the case, he couldn't help but be happy that a dead childhood friend had come back to life. Then again, the new Erica was his protector, a girl who had led many lives and a person he was beginning to fall in love with.

"We should go through her pockets." Natalie stared straight ahead as they drove across town. Despite her ordeal from the last day and a half, she seemed focused on dealing with the issue at hand. "Maybe we can find a clue."

Ted shook his head and grinned. "That's brilliant. Teammate."

Natalie snorted. "It was in a movie. Now, which one's her place again?"

They parked about a block away from Erica's house and Ted waited until the coast was clear before floating his unconscious friend around the back of the house. Ted used his powers to fly all three of them into Erica's room.

"So, this is where the magic happens?" Natalie looked like she'd rather be next to an active volcano than in the peach-colored room.

"Hardy har." Ted began rifling through Erica's pockets. "You wanna check her purse?"

Ted hoped to find Erica's phone, but they came up empty. They spread out everything they found on the bedspread. Aside from a few coins and her car keys, the only thing of value was a receipt to the coffee shop on Main Street.

"Seems like as good a place to start as any." Natalie squinted and walked over to the air conditioning vent. "Hey, there's something in here."

Ted used his powers in lieu of a screwdriver to reveal the hidden item. It was a short bottle filled with clear liquid. He uncapped it. The burning aroma confirmed its contents.

Ted sighed. "We should see if there's any other booze hidden in here."

They found three other secret liquor hiding locations throughout the room: underneath a miniature dollhouse table, in the back of an end table bottom cabinet and in a storage container beneath her bed. They poured all the alcohol they could find down the drain.

As Ted poured the final bottle down the bathroom sink, Natalie stood in the doorway with her arms folded.

"I think you should be prepared."

Ted rinsed the bottle out with cold water. "Prepared for what?"

"We don't know what happened, but for all we know, the old Erica could be back to stay."

Ted feared that Natalie could be right, but he refused to believe it. He squeezed past her and back into the bedroom. He looked at Erica, as if he was trying to pull additional information out of her mind.

"She remembered going on dates with me. When she sobers up I'm sure she'll...."

For a moment, he thought he saw the image of a man sitting across from Erica. He almost had a clear picture before the memory zipped away from him. When he tried to do the same thing again, the image was gone. Ted leaned back against the wall. He felt tired for some reason.

"Are you OK?" Natalie asked.

Ted wondered if the location of the image he'd seemingly pulled from Erica's head had been a meeting at the coffee shop.

"When I looked at her, I almost... I think I saw a memory."

Natalie gave him a sideways glance. "What do you mean you 'saw a memory'?"

Ted shook his head. "I'm not sure, but we have to go there. See if there are any clues." He looked back at Erica and felt his stomach start to work overtime. "Leaving her here like this... it doesn't feel right."

Ted pulled the covers over Erica, who instinctively wrapped them around herself. He sat down beside her.

Natalie cleared her throat. "If we don't find out who did this to her, it could be a lot more than one brainwashed girlfriend we're dealing with."

Ted nodded. He pushed some hair away from Erica's face and kissed her on the cheek. She murmured a whispered response and went silent again.

"You're right. Let's get a smoothie."

When they arrived at the shop, a crowd of patrons surrounded Ted. He thought it was funny that people who would've passed him by just three months earlier were now hounding him for a selfie or an autograph. He figured it was a good thing he didn't like coffee, or getting his morning fix would be a major pain.

Natalie squirmed as the patrons gathered around them. She spoke loudly enough to be heard over the masses. "I should tell them how pale you look with your shirt off. Maybe they'd be less impressed."

Ted pinched Natalie in the side. "I would float you off a cliff." He gestured to a barista who stood by an open table. "Potential witness #1."

Ted recognized the girl as a Treasure High alum from the previous year. Despite the fact that she was at least two years older, the barista was in a losing battle with her attempt to suppress several girlish squeals. "Oh my gosh." She almost knocked over one of the chairs as she tried to pull it out. "Ted, here's a table for... can I get you something... I just can't."

The girl started to turn away in embarrassment when Natalie took her arm. "Would you be interested in sitting at a table with the one and only Ted Finley?"

The sound that came out of the barista's mouth scared Ted. He could best describe it as the midpoint between a tire screeching and a dog's squeaky toy.

"I... I would love that."

It took a minute for the girl to stop hyperventilating, allowing the crowd to settle as the espresso smell wafted over. When the barista calmed down, Ted cut to the chase.

"This girl." Ted presented a picture of Erica on his phone. "She was here yesterday. Can you remember if she was with anyone?"

The barista's eyes showed that she recognized Erica, but she wasn't very interested in answering the question. "You know, it's great to date someone your own age, but you can learn a lot more from an older girl."

Ted felt the barista's leg touch his underneath the table, rubbing up against him and causing his cheeks to go from peach to bright red. It took a fair bit of willpower for him to push it away.

"Erica's an old soul." Ted put the phone back in his pocket.

"Really old." Natalie leaned back in her chair, aware of the physical flirting going on. "Like, nursing home old."

Ted kicked his shoe into Natalie's. "Can you please answer the question?"

The barista told them that Erica was in there with an older guy the previous day. "I was in the back when a whole bunch of weird stuff started to happen."

"What kind of weird—"

"People were saying stuff at the same time. They didn't have control of their own bodies. It was...."

"Weird." Natalie looked at Ted. "Sounds like what happened to Beth." She put her attention back on the girl. "Do you guys have a security tape or something?"

The barista contorted her face and looked like she was about to cry. "We – we looked for it yesterday. We were going to try to post the weirdness online. But then we erased it. It wasn't by accident – it was like we didn't remember doing it."

After the barista made a last-ditch pitch for him to go on an "extra-long date" with her, Ted and Natalie exited the coffee shop, smoothies in hand. They walked a block or so until they found a secluded-enough bench for them to talk in private.

"She was nice." Natalie took an extended sip of her drink and smiled.

"Can we focus here?" Ted put his hand on the bench, accidentally grazing Natalie's. He pulled it away and felt himself starting to blush again. "I... so... Erica was here with some guy."

"Erica and older guys don't mix." Natalie didn't blink.

Ted attempted to ignore her. "We need to figure out what Beth and Erica have in common."

Natalie took another sip. "They're both sluts. Or at least they were."

Ted let out an exasperated groan and stood up, kicking the concrete base of the side of a building.

"Come on, Natalie!" He turned to face her. "My girlfriend – and my partner in all of this inter-dimensional insanity – is gone, maybe for good. There's something going on that I can't explain. Plus, I just saved you from a creepy cult's headquarters. Can't you stop cracking jokes for one second?"

Natalie's smile turned back to neutral. She stood up to meet Ted's gaze. "I'm sorry."

Ted didn't know what he expected from his ex, but he knew from experience that sincere apologies like this one were rare.

"I'm lost with this stuff. What do we do now?"

Natalie paced in the opposite direction. "We should call the sheriff. Maybe he knows something we don't."

Ted agreed, though he dreaded the call. Dhiraj had sworn Ted to secrecy about Jennifer's whereabouts. Before the GHA meeting, Ted had ignored Sheriff Norris' call in an attempt to avoid lying. He took a deep breath and dialed the number.

"Ted." The sheriff seemed frantic over the phone. "Jennifer is missing, I need to—"

"She's safe." Ted hoped Dhiraj wouldn't disown him as a friend for sharing part of the secret. "I know she's with Dhiraj and he's trying to help her, but I don't know all the details."

The sheriff was silent on the other line. All Ted could hear was his shallow breaths.

"That's all I know about that, Sheriff, but we're in a crisis here too. Did Erica tell you about any kind of—"

"She met with your teacher." The sheriff's tone of worry had completely gone. It was replaced by pure rage. "Redican. Good luck." Sheriff

Norris hung up.

"What'd he say?" Natalie asked.

"Two things. I think Dhiraj is a dead man. And the bad guy might be Mr. Redican."

"The sub?"

Ted looked around the alley. "Beth and Erica are both in his class. So am I."

He didn't understand. Redican seemed to be one of the only teachers who cared that they learned anything.

Ted felt a deep pit in his stomach. "We need to get somewhere safe before he does the same thing to us."

They tossed their empty smoothie cups in the garbage and ran back to the parking lot. Natalie hit the unlock button on her key ring. Instead of hearing the clicking sound of the locks, something different happened completely. Natalie's car vanished, leaving an empty parking space.

Natalie looked around in every direction. "What the hell?"

"Language," a voice said from across the lot.

Ted and Natalie looked back to see Mr. Redican walking toward them. "Hello, children."

CHAPTER 34

When Jennifer let the shot ring out, nearly every part of her cried out to end Daly's life. Only, she didn't kill him. The bullet blazed through the air beside Daly's face and clipped his ear.

The murderer dropped to the ground and clutched the side of his head. He cursed her out with every dirty word she'd ever heard and some that she hadn't.

Jennifer felt numb as she watched the man squirm on the ground. Dhiraj came up to her side and touched her arm. She hadn't realized that she was still pointing the gun where Daly had been standing.

Dhiraj's voice wavered as he spoke. "Are you OK?"

Jennifer nodded, though she wasn't as sure as her head indicated. "Call the cops. Call my dad."

The local police arrived within the next few minutes. When they got there, Jennifer showed them the multiple warrants out for Daly's arrest. They said they'd need to question her about her tactics, but she was free to go for now. Jennifer sat in a daze on the trunk of her car. Everything that had consumed her the last few months was gone in an instant.

She didn't get nearly as much relief as she'd hoped for.

Jennifer had forgotten about her second request to Dhiraj, until he came up to her about as pale as she'd ever seen him.

"It's your dad." Dhiraj shook as he handed her the phone. "He's not quiet."

Jennifer prepared herself for the worst. She watched Dhiraj walk away to the far side of the lot before she spoke. "Hey, Dad. I got him."

Sheriff Norris paused for a moment on the other line. Then she heard the sound of tears flowing and a hearty sniffle.

"You had me so worried, honey." The sheriff blew his nose into a tissue. "I thought about Erica and search parties. And autopsies. You shouldn't have done that to me."

Jennifer hopped off the car and sat down on a curb as she watched Dhiraj pace from afar. "I know. He's a murderer, Dad. He killed her."

"And he could've killed you. How do you think that would've made us feel? You have people who love you, Jen."

Jennifer caught Dhiraj staring at her. He quickly turned away when their eyes met. "I know, Dad. I'm sorry." She took in a deep breath. "It's over now."

Her dad sighed. "I wish that were true. You two should get back to town."

As Jennifer finished the call, she thought back on all her previous relationships with boys. She wondered if any of them would've gone to the lengths that Dhiraj had to keep her alive and safe. Her partner in crime was checking his phone when she walked up to him.

"Why didn't you call the cops when you got loose from the car?"

Dhiraj put his phone into his pocket. "You needed this." He stood up and walked to within a foot of her. "It was stupid and you could've gotten yourself killed, but it was obviously something you felt you had to do. Who am I to deprive you of that?"

Jennifer closed the distance between them. "That's a good question, Dhiraj. Who are you?"

Dhiraj squinted. "I'm... I'm your friend. Friends help friends heal."

Jennifer put her arms around Dhiraj's neck. She could feel him twitch from the contact, but she had no desire to pull away. "I've never really dated a friend."

Dhiraj gently put one hand on Jennifer's midsection. "I've heard good things. There was this whole piece in GQ about—"

Jennifer stopped his sentence with her lips. She'd spent the last few months kissing whomever was interested in helping her cope with the pain, as long as they could get something in return. This was different. Dhiraj didn't want anything other than her happiness. She could feel the difference when he began to kiss her back. She let herself enjoy the moment and felt a peace wash over her. When she pulled away to catch her breath, she didn't see a hallucination of the man she'd been hunting. All she saw was the pure bliss on Dhiraj's face. His joy made her feel light and bouncy.

She pulled him in tight for a hug. "I've got an important question for you."

Dhiraj gave Jennifer a short kiss on her neck. "If you're going to ask if I'd like to do that again, the answer is yes."

She giggled. "Actually, I wanted to see if you'd go with me to prom tomorrow."

Dhiraj moved back to look into her eyes. She swore she saw a firework go off in his brain. "Prom? I'd need to get my tux refitted." Dhiraj started speaking faster and faster with every passing word. "And get a matching tie. I think I know someone who can get us a limo at a good deal. Can we reserve corsages 24 hours ahead of time?"

Jennifer put a finger up to his lips. "Dhiraj. You need to answer first. Will you go with me?"

Dhiraj started to laugh. "I thought the answer was so obvious, I didn't even need to say it." He took both of her hands in his. "It would be an honor."

They kissed one more time before they walked toward the car. Dhiraj started to chuckle.

"What is it?" Jennifer asked.

"I was just thinking, I should've taken you on a vigilante shooting spree years ago. It would've saved a lot of trouble."

Jennifer shook her head. "And give up years of you pining after me? Never."

They got in Jennifer's car and began the long trek home.

CHAPTER 35

Natalie woke up beside the car, which had seemingly coming back into view when she'd been knocked out.

What the heck happened?

The second thing she spied after the car was Ted's lifeless body. Natalie watched him for a few moments to see if the air was inflating his lungs or not. After a few motionless seconds, she threw patience to the wind and shook her friend. She held her breath until Ted made a low grumbling noise.

"My head." Ted opened his eyes and smiled when he saw Natalie. "I'm alive. No more shaky."

Natalie obliged. "Good."

Natalie remembered their attacker. She looked back to see if Redican was still approaching. There was no sign of him, and everyone else on the street was moving around as if nothing had happened at all.

"It doesn't make any sense." When Natalie stood up, the blood rushed to her head, causing a wave of dizziness. "If he wiped Erica's brain, why didn't he do anything to us?"

"Performance problems?" Ted stood up and almost collapsed.

If it weren't for Natalie's quick move to the side, he might have gone back to the ground.

He looked into her eyes with a sheepish grin. "Thanks."

Natalie hoisted Ted up by his arms and leaned him on the car. "Don't mention it."

She wasn't sure why, but Ted's scent started to wash over her. The aroma led to memories of them together that she'd rather push back to the recesses of her brain.

"What's wrong?" Ted rubbed Natalie's arm as if it were the most natural thing. As if they were still together.

Natalie pulled away. "It's nothing." She unlocked the car. "Can we go home now?"

They headed back to Ted's house.

"Redican knew that we were there." She glanced at Ted. "He couldn't have gotten there so quickly otherwise."

Ted caught Natalie's eye and smiled. "Do you remember when we broke into that practice facility?"

Natalie had the day burned into her brain. It was an encounter she looked on as one of the highlights of their relationship. "Of course. It was fun."

Ted looked almost goofy as he turned toward her. "We make a good team. I'm really glad we get to do this together."

Natalie rolled her eyes. "I'm sure it would be exactly the same if your girlfriend didn't have selective amnesia."

Ted put his hand on Natalie's leg and moved it down to the knee. "I'm not thinking about her right now. I'm thinking about us."

Natalie felt her cheek twitch. "Oh, yeah? And what is it you're thinking exactly?"

Ted leaned over from the passenger seat, as if to deliver his message as a whisper. "I think I'm ready to tell you that 'I love you' back."

Natalie's heart began to pound and it took an unintentional jerk or two of the wheel before she steadied the car. Ted removed his seatbelt and moved his lips to Natalie's neck. She took in a deep breath and inhaled the familiar scent. She wished the words had come several months earlier. Everything could have been different. As Ted moved his lips up to her ear, Natalie could only think of one problem with her current scenario. None of this was real.

As she was about to pull onto Ted's street, Natalie yanked the wheel all the way to the left, sending Ted bouncing away from her and back into his chair. She slammed into a mailbox and gunned the accelerator up the lawn of one of Ted's neighbors.

"What are you doing?!" Ted's voice cracked as he attempted to gain control of the wheel.

"Just a little reality check." Natalie gunned the accelerator.

They bore down on the front windows of a two-story home. Ted screamed and covered his eyes.

And then, nothing happened at all.

The car didn't have a scratch on it as Natalie sat alone in the vehicle. Ted had disappeared and the neighborhood had been replaced by a dry waste-land.

Natalie was more shaken by the fake declaration of love than she'd been by the fake crash into the house. She closed her eyes to shake it off before stepping out of the car. Her feet landed on a crack in the dusty earth. Everything around the vehicle was desolate and hopeless. Though she had a distinct feeling that she was being watched.

"I know you're here, Redican."

The teacher appeared without hesitation on the other side of the car. He looked different than he had when the man had approached them in the parking lot: he appeared stronger, and an inch or two taller. Natalie figured it was some kind of projection of his ideal self. Maybe he felt like a real man when he was invading people's minds.

"I'm impressed, Natalie." Redican walked around the front of the car before he leaned against one of the headlights. "Maybe the light souls picked the wrong champion."

Natalie crossed her arms and glared at this supposed authority figure. "You're in my brain. I guess you can do anything you want while you're in here, huh?"

Redican smiled. "That's correct. Some people put up more fight than others, but that's generally the case."

"Then why even talk to me?" Natalie asked. "Why not just have me go blow up a bridge or whatever the heck you're controlling me for?"

Redican pouted. "It's easy to control someone. I'd rather convince you that what I'm doing is right."

Natalie took a few steps away from the car. She could feel the heat from the fantasy world beat against her exposed neck. "I guess you have a captive audience. What do you want to convince me of?"

Redican walked up to Natalie and looked off into the endless view of cracked, vacant ground.

"This is what your world will look like if Ted continues down this path. Erica and the light souls are using him as a weapon, but he's meant to end the war and bring peace to all the worlds it's affecting."

Natalie looked at Redican. He seemed sincere, but it was impossible to tell what was fact and what was fiction in this place. "You realize that goes contrary to everything Erica's been telling us."

Redican sighed. "You say that I'm the one with the mind control, but Erica is the one brainwashing all of you." He paced, each step kicking up more dust than the last. "It's not her fault. She's a pawn for the light soul regime. Just like Ted, she never chose this. But she's here to keep the living soul on their side, preventing him from his true destiny."

Natalie thought for a moment. "You're saying he's powerful enough to be king of all the worlds, not just a hero of our world."

Redican eyes seemed to glow with her response. "He's not just strong enough to rule over all the realms. It's his true destiny."

Natalie couldn't even think of Ted as the student body president, let alone some Grand Poobah of worlds they'd never even heard of. Then again, that was the old Ted. The new one had stopped an apocalypse and saved her from the clutches of a semi-evil cult.

"And what am I supposed to do about all of this?" Natalie kicked at the dirt.

Redican lifted Natalie's chin up, allowing them to look eye-to-eye. "You're his friend. You can help him to see reason."

Natalie growled. "And if I don't, you'll warp my brain back to kindergarten, right?"

Redican stepped back and smiled. "No. You'll die. But not by my hand – by somebody stronger than me."

Natalie put her hands to her face and ran them through her hair. She looked away from her mental captor.

Redican continued to back away. "You can think it over, Ms. Dormer. But time's a wastin'. I think it's time to wake up."

Before she could say a word to the man walking away from her in the wasteland, Natalie's real eyes fluttered open.

Chapter 36

Ted and Natalie woke up at the exact same moment, and they looked at each other for several seconds before speaking.

"We need to get out of here," they said in unison.

They picked themselves up off the pavement and drove for several minutes of silence before Natalie broke it.

"So. What'd you dream about?"

"Nothing. Why?"

Natalie sighed. "Redican got in my head and tried to recruit me. He thinks you could bring peace to all the worlds."

Ted raised his eyebrows. "How 'Nightmare on Elm Street' of him. We need to get the real Erica back and make sense of this stuff."

When they reached a stop sign, Natalie changed her turn signal from left to right. "Just what I wanted to do today. Go to Little Miss Perfect's house twice. I hope she left you an instruction manual."

Mrs. LaPlante's cheeks turned red with happiness when she saw Ted at the door to Erica's house. "I'm so glad you're here." She gestured for the two of them to enter. "Erica was talking about graves and death and who knows what. I could barely stand to listen to it."

Ted and Natalie shared a look and inhaled the aroma of potpourri.

"Where is she?" Ted asked.

"In her room." Mrs. LaPlante flattened out her dress. "She hasn't made a peep for hours."

Ted left Natalie downstairs for some small talk as he bounded his way up. He walked into Erica's room and immediately felt the draft from the open window. Ted noticed something out of place. He moved the dollhouse to its usual location, but he put it back when he saw the giant hole in the wall.

"She's gone." Ted touched Mrs. LaPlante's shoulder. "I'm sure she's just waiting at my house."

Mrs. LaPlante sniffled briefly before the waterworks started. She fumbled around for a tissue until Natalie found the box and handed her one.

Within a few minutes, Mrs. LaPlante had stopped crying and the two friends were back on the road. Ted explained what he'd seen in the room.

Natalie let out a short laugh. "Great. So our little alcoholic realizes that she used to be dead and that she has super-strength. I wish we had a police blotter right about now."

Ted leaned back in his seat. "I think I know where she is, but I should probably go alone." He put his hand on Natalie's arm. "Besides, you haven't even seen a bed in two days."

Natalie shook her head. "You mean a shower, Ted. I haven't seen a shower in two days. That's what's bothering you."

Ted ignored her. "You're coming to prom tomorrow, right?"

Natalie pulled into Ted's driveway. "We have a supervillain who can mess with our brains, your date is probably off on a rampage somewhere and nobody even asked me." She looked over at Ted with a smirk. "So, no, I think I'm gonna sit this one out."

Ted took in a deep breath. "Alright, suit yourself, but it's okay to go with friends. I bet Dhiraj'll rent a limo if he gets back in time."

Natalie unlocked the doors. "I'll consider it. Now, go find your girlfriend before she knocks over a 7-Eleven."

Ted patted Natalie on the shoulder. He couldn't quite read her face, but there seemed to be something she was holding back. Ted opted to let it go, and when she pulled away he took to the skies.

It felt peaceful to fly through the wind as the cold air pressed against his cheeks. The whooshing sound that filled his ears helped him forget everything that ran through his mind. His trust remained with Erica, but it felt strange that both Nigel and Redican had said the same thing. They both thought that he was being used. Whether or not they were right, how was he supposed to know? After all, he was taking Erica's word for it.

Ted recalled his ordeal in the caves a few months ago as he flew over the fence to the woods. Sure enough, when he reached the overturned tree and the clearing where Daly had done the deed, Erica was sitting there alone on a tree stump. When he got closer, he saw that her hands were covered in dirt and that she was gripping a bloody knife. Ted's eyes grew wide as he landed.

"Oh my God, are you—"

"Don't worry, it's old blood." Erica didn't sound like either person Ted had known in that body. She let out a dark laugh. "It's my murder weapon. I guess I should put it in a shadowbox or something."

Ted froze in place. "I – I'm glad you're OK."

"I'm not OK. I'm dead." She cackled again. "And even worse than that. I'm sober."

While Ted was mildly concerned Erica might stab him, he sat beside her on the tree trunk anyway. "You remember everything?"

She nodded. "I remember getting stabbed and buried alive. After that, it gets blurry until I saw you yesterday."

Ted put his hand on Erica's thigh. "I wish I could've saved you."

She gave Ted a sideways glance. "Oh, come on. I was terrible. To you. To my parents. If not then, I probably would've ODed in college or gotten mugged and left for dead outside some skeezy club."

Ted started to put the pieces together. Erica didn't just drink because she was addicted. She drank to rid herself of these depressing, morbid thoughts.

"I never cared that you had issues." Ted scooted closer to Erica. "I just wanted to be there for you."

Erica's lip quivered. "I knew." She put her free arm around Ted's neck. "And I loved you for it."

Erica drew Ted close and kissed him. It wasn't like the deep, sloppy kiss they'd shared on his front porch. This one was real. He wanted to keep pressing his lips against hers for the rest of time. Unfortunately, that wasn't what Erica had in mind.

She pulled away from him and stepped off the stump. "Thank you for that. But I've already used up my time here."

Erica took the knife and moved it toward her abdomen. She was about to stick it in the same exact spot that had ended her life when Ted used his powers to fling it away. The knife stuck into the side of the turned-over tree, and Erica began to sob. As she slinked to the ground, Ted put his arms around her.

"I'm sorry." He tightened his hold. "I wish I could make you feel less pain. I want to bring you peace."

A strange sensation came over Ted. He felt himself looking into Erica's brain. For a second, it was as if he could find the part of her that was broken. He saw memories as if they were thousands of images on a digital screen. For a moment, he saw Erica's death at the hands of Deputy Daly. Another picture displayed the battle with Nigel and the dark souls. The last one he could see clearly seemed to be him standing with Erica at the altar of an outdoor wedding. At least, it was someone who looked like him.

The memories swirled around before him and seemed to re-order themselves when a burst of blue light shot out through his hands and enveloped Erica. Frightened, he stepped away and the light dissipated. Erica started to convulse. A dizziness came over Ted, and he leaned against the tree for support. As he did, Erica coughed herself back to consciousness. The tears were gone from her eyes. She looked around as if there was danger close by.

"What the... why are we in the forest?" Erica got up to her knees. "Where's Redican?"

Ted lowered himself to the ground and put his arms around Erica's waist.

"You've... you're—"

Erica glanced around and back at Ted. Her face relaxed, which softened her features.

"You did it. You fixed me."

CHAPTER 37

Erica was too weak to let herself free from Ted's grasp. It wasn't that sensing his grip around her body didn't feel good. A part of her wanted to relax and take the necessary time to recover, perhaps while nuzzling up to Ted under a nearby sycamore. The part of her that won out, however, was the one that stood up way too fast and grabbed onto the overturned tree for balance. She couldn't help but be reminded her of her most recent crossover into this world.

One of the key differences was that this time Ted was the one who brought her back.

"You don't remember anything from the past couple of days?" Ted offered a hand to help Erica steady herself.

She took it. "No. The last thing I remember is Redican chasing me down."

Ted appeared to chew on the last thought like taffy, both methodically and carefully. "You'd forgotten everything about your other lives. You were pure Erica."

Erica was tempted to take a tour through Ted's brain. It would be a shortcut to figuring out what the combination of a furrowed brow and a smile really meant.

She rubbed his arm. "I - I'm sorry. Was it terrible? Did I do anything—"

Ted took her hand and kissed it. "No. It was good, actually. I got to say goodbye."

Erica nodded. She felt some of the strength return to her body like a battery recharging. Erica stepped away from the tree and stretched her arms to the sky.

She looked back at Ted. "Why didn't you leave her – me – the way I was? You could've had the Erica of your dreams."

Ted spun her around so he could face her. "I needed you." He moved a few strands of hair away from her face. "We'd probably all get brainwashed if you weren't here to help."

She'd been hoping for more, and the sigh betrayed her thoughts. "Okay."

Ted pulled her close. His sweet smell surrounded her.

"I wanted *you*." He smiled. "Also, I kind of didn't know what I was doing when I messed around with your head, so it all worked out for the best." Ted's smile didn't last. He bit his bottom lip. "Which reminds me. How did I fix your brain? Can I do what Redican can do? Is that one of my other powers?"

Erica didn't need all of this. Her consciousness had just come back from who knows where and Ted was teetering very close to the edge of her authority.

"Yes." Erica wiped the dirt off her clothing and started to walk toward the fence. "Now, let's get back to—"

Ted flew through the air and landed ahead of her. "I have the ability to control people's minds and you're just gonna gloss over it?"

She took in a deep breath and forced a smile. "Um... yes?"

Ted's voice grew faster and higher in pitch. "Oh, no. You're not getting out of it this easy, protector-girl. Redican stole one of these books. Between that and the other ones, there's a ton of power that's supposed to be a part of what I am, right? Maybe I can use them to stop him."

Erica let out all her pent up emotion. "No! You can't!"

Erica thought she had been back to full strength, but the shouting made her dizzy. She stumbled back over to the tree stump and sat down.

Ted seemed to consider comforting her before keeping a few feet of distance. "You think I'm not good enough or something?"

Erica tried to look up into his eyes, but they were pointed straight at her feet. "It's just too much power for one person to handle."

"Shouldn't I be the one to make that decision?"

Erica met Ted's sincere gaze. She knew he was hurt by her omissions, but there were some things more important than hurt feelings.

"The last time I let a living soul choose to take on all the power at once...."

Erica didn't want to continue.

Ted knelt down so he could look right at her. "Tell me."

She took a deep breath. "Forty years ago I was sent here to train another living soul. His name was Adam." The memory of crunching steel came back to her like it was yesterday. "He was strong before he got his powers. Always wanted to be stronger. All I wanted to do was help, so I taught him how to use his mind to change the minds of others."

"He pulled a Redican on you, didn't he?"

"While I was under his control, he made me teach him everything. Every power, whether or not he was ready for it." She chewed her cheek. "It overwhelmed him. He went a little crazy and started plotting the end of the world." She looked into Ted's eyes. "So me and his friends brought an entire building down on him."

A few beats of silence followed as Ted considered the implications. "Do you really think I'd be capable of all that?"

She pursed her lips. "I don't want to think that, but every time I picture you studying those books and gaining a new ability, I see that building coming down around someone I used to call a friend."

Ted squinted at Erica before his eyes grew wide. "It's part of your orders isn't it? If I go crazy or turn to the dark side, you're supposed to kill me, aren't you?"

Hearing the truth laid out gave Erica a headache.

There's nothing like telling your boyfriend you might have to kill him if he goes nuts.

"And that's why we're taking things slow... powers-wise."

Ted stood up and paced. "If I can't use the power and Redican can, how are we going to stop him?"

Erica tapped her nails on the side of the stump. "I'm not sure yet. But if

I put a bet on when he'd strike next, it would be tomorrow. At prom."

Erica loved seeing Ted's face light up at the p-word. Even though they might encounter certain death at the dance, at least they'd look good while they did it.

Ted helped Erica up to her feet. "It's a good thing I already rented my tux."

CHAPTER 39

After Natalie arrived home and told the short version of events to her parents, she conked out for the next 12 hours. When she woke up in the wee hours of the morning, she couldn't tell at first if she was in a cell or a bed.

Or if she was in fantasy or reality, for that matter.

Upon checking her texts from the previous night, she learned that Erica was back to normal. Natalie was glad that they had another weapon back in their fight against Redican, but she wondered if Ted, Erica and the rest of them stood a chance against a person who could invade their minds. After all, she was half-convinced that Ted had given up on Erica and wanted to get back with her. The image of Ted saying he loved her felt as real to her as their first date or their breakup. Unlike a dream that feels sort of real, there was no blurring at the edges. Natalie hated that some part of her brain believed that Ted Finley was in love with her.

Five minutes after she posted a comment on a picture of Dhiraj's tux, he arrived at her doorstep. For a guy who almost witnessed a revenge killing, he appeared excessively upbeat.

"I've already got it all planned out." Dhiraj didn't seem to care that Natalie was silent. "Dinner at Grazie beforehand, a limo ride to the dance and a private after-party. And because I worked out some sweet sponsorship deals, it's all gonna be free!"

Natalie gave a nod of acknowledgment.

Dhiraj raised his eyebrows. "You know, it'll be better with you there."

Natalie wasn't sure if there was enough room for her eyes to roll as much as they needed to. "Uh huh."

"You're my co-best friend. I need a wing-woman."

"You don't need a wing-woman. You've already got the girl. Everybody's got someone but me." Natalie lay back down on her bed and stared at the ceiling. "I don't want it to be awkward."

Dhiraj lay down next to her. "Do you really think that you could possibly be more awkward than Ted? You've seen him dance."

Natalie pictured her ex-boyfriend attempting to bust a move. The image brought a smile to her face. "You can't even call it dancing. They need a new word to describe it."

Dhiraj rolled to his side and rested his ear on his hand. "We could come up with the right word together."

"I don't know, Dhiraj." She looked toward her closet as if she could see through to her homecoming dress. "I need to clear my head. I'll let you know."

Dhiraj popped off the bed and grinned. "Alright. There's definitely a spot in the limo for you." He glanced at his phone. "I better get to steppin'. I've got a mani-pedi at nine."

Natalie pushed onto her stomach and chuckled. "You're one of a kind, Dhiraj."

"That makes two of us." He moved toward the exit before turning back. "You know, both of us got kidnapped this weekend."

Natalie nodded. "That's true. And we both got out alive. Must be pretty resourceful, you and I."

Dhiraj flashed a smile. "Must be. I'll see you tonight."

Try as she might, Natalie couldn't go back to sleep. At the first sign of daylight, she changed into shorts and went for a run. She took her normal path around the neighborhood before jogging onto the trail along a canal that ran behind her development. Natalie thought about what Redican had said when he was inside her mind.

She wondered if Erica truly was holding Ted back from becoming the most powerful person in the universe. Even if she would consider convincing Ted that he should explore his powers, Natalie had no idea what she would say. As she attempted to clear her mind of the issue, something caught her eye on the trail ahead. There was a small flame in the middle of the dirt path about fifty feet away. Natalie slowed her pace.

That's weird.

When she got closer to the small fire, it began to grow. The flames reached up until they were almost as tall as her. Natalie's heart beat faster. She started to run back in the direction she came, but the flames followed her. Natalie looked over her shoulder and watched as the fire seemed like it was trying to catch up with her. The nervousness grew inside of her as she tried to double her pace. The red and orange flames sped up as well, and Natalie could feel the heat on her calves and ankles.

Not good. This is not good.

Natalie put all she could into her legs and leapt off the trail into a patch of grass. The flames whipped past her and continued down the trail. She could feel the heat pressing against her as the flames grew even higher. Before she knew it, the fire moved off the path and surrounded her in a circular wall. She looked in every direction, but there was no escape. Natalie considered making a break for it through the fiery barrier when a thought crossed her mind.

She ignored the parts of her brain that triggered pain and fear, and she reached out and touched the flames.

"It doesn't burn." She touched the fire with her other hand. "Redican."

A voice came from the fiery wall around her. "You have the power to convince him, Natalie."

"You're still in my head, aren't you?" She growled. "Why don't you just pretend you're me and do it yourself?"

There was a pause as the flames seemed to consider the answer. "I want you on my side."

Natalie moved her entire body into the fake fire. Her nervous system had no idea what was happening, and her pulse shot through the roof. "You're an English teacher. Give me a compelling argument." She pushed through the flames. "Excuse me."

Natalie jogged back into her neighborhood without hearing from Redican again. When she reached the edge of the trail, a young boy who couldn't have been older than five walked right up to her.

"Hey little man. Where are your parents?"

The boy started to sniffle and wiped his eyes. "They died."

Natalie's jaw dropped. She felt her heart break. "Oh my gosh, honey. I'm so sorry."

"Bad men came and killed them." The boy ran to Natalie's leg and hugged it. "They killed everybody."

Natalie's instincts told her to call the sheriff right away, but she remembered that her senses could no longer be trusted. She pulled the little boy off her and looked him in the eyes. "Who killed them?"

"The dark souls. I'm all alone now."

Natalie glared at the boy. "That's real sweet, Redican. Sending a little kid to do your dirty work."

The boy began to full-out cry. "I'm scared. I don't know what to do." He ducked under Natalie's arms and hugged her leg again.

Natalie didn't understand.

"I just gave him my memories," a voice in Natalie's brain said. "He's not the only one like me on the other worlds. And there will be more unless Ted stops them."

Natalie wanted to hold the little boy and tell him it would be all right. She thought about hundreds of children having their innocence taken from them because of an inter-dimensional war.

She took the little boy's hand and walked around the corner. "Point taken, Redican. Let the kid have his life back."

The child stopped sniffling and began laughing instead. He ran toward a car where a family was packing up for a weekend trip.

"There you are." The child's mother picked him up off the ground. "Don't run off like that, okay?"

Natalie walked in the opposite direction, toward her house. "Make Ted feel this. I don't want any of it."

The voice continued. "He's too close to Erica. Love blinds him from knowing whom he should really trust."

Natalie went back inside her house and jogged upstairs before anyone else could hear her talking to herself. She tossed off her shoes and picked up her basketball.

Natalie sat on the edge of the bed and dribbled. "As if you can be trusted after playing games with people's lives. Messing with Beth. And Erica. And me."

Natalie intended to keep dribbling the ball, but something inside her made her pull it toward her. Redican took control of her arms and forced her to toss the ball at full speed into a shelf of trophies and other accolades. Her MVP award from the previous hoops season bore the brunt of the impact, the metal girl snapping off the wooden base of the trophy and crashing to the ground. Several other medals and trophies toppled over as well.

"Nobody can be trusted!" The voice had moved into Natalie's room and was getting angrier by the word. "But lives can be saved. Join me, Natalie. Help me to tell Ted the truth."

Natalie wasn't taking any more of this. She screamed. "And what's the truth?! That you're too much of a pansy to do this yourself? You want me to do this willingly." She clenched her fists. "Never gonna happen."

The voice was almost a whisper. "Very well."

Natalie felt a strange feeling come over her. All of the emotion from the conversation vanished, and she stepped into the bathroom to shower off the grime of the run. After she toweled herself dry, she laid out the dress she'd worn to homecoming. Natalie applied makeup to her face as if it were the most natural thing. Time began to blow by in gusts, and before Natalie knew it, she was ready to go do a dance she didn't even want to attend.

When she took one final glance into the mirror to check her makeup, she saw a man behind her in the reflection. It was the puppeteer, Mr. Redican. Natalie squinted her eyes as hard as they could, and when she opened them, the man was gone.

"Get out of my head!"

Natalie locked the bathroom door behind her, hoping to trap Redican inside. She sprung toward her end table to pick up her phone. She needed to tell Ted that Redican had the upper hand, and this might be her last chance to do it. Natalie scrolled to her favorite contacts and was about to hit the image of Ted when she froze in place. Natalie strained every muscle in an effort to push that button, but it was no use. She felt her mouth begin to move without her command.

"Relax, Natalie." She couldn't help but think her voice sounded alien when she wasn't the one in control. "I've finally decided how I'm going to use you to help convince Ted of the right thing to do."

Natalie felt her arm put down the phone as she unlocked the bathroom door. Redican forced her back in front of the mirror to do a final makeup check. She tried to block the man from taking over her thoughts and exerted one last moment of control.

"What? You're going to make him dance with me?"

Natalie watched as her strained face melted into relaxation. Her mouth even turned up into a calm smile.

"No. I'm going to make him kill you."

The grin grew wider as Natalie grabbed her purse and walked out the door.

CHAPTER 40

Ted's face hurt as he smiled for what felt like the millionth time. It's not that he wasn't happy. He had his arm around the waist of Erica LaPlante, who was wearing a beautiful black and purple dress that showed enough skin to keep Ted perpetually excited. When he caught Erica's glance, she had a look on her face that said, "How many more pictures can they take?"

Ted shrugged with his eyes and looked back toward the cavalcade of parents. He couldn't remember the last time his living room had had that many people inside. His folks and the LaPlantes were having a grand old time. Ted was glad to see his mother in good spirits as she nursed her burns with gauze and painkillers. In between shots, the two sets of parents laughed and sighed, discussing how grown up their "babies" had become. Sheriff Norris chatted politely with Mr. Patel and Winny's mom, who Ted always forgot was the sheriff's sister. Jennifer's dad definitely didn't seem as boisterous as the rest of the photographers.

Ted didn't feel like he was in control of his own body, as the parents kept giving them different poses they were required to do. He looked to his left for additional moral support. Jennifer and Dhiraj looked too happy together to even notice they were being photographed. When Jennifer walked over to her dad and her aunt to check a shot on the camera, Dhiraj looked right at Ted.

"Eh?" Dhiraj's dopey grin couldn't help but make Ted laugh. He gestured over to his date, who was wearing a similar style to Erica's, though Jennifer's hemline went a bit lower.

"You did good, Dhiraj." Ted patted his friend on the shoulder.

"You, too." He glanced over at Erica, who had migrated over to Winny and her hulking date, Rico. "These pictures would make 14-year-old Ted super jealous."

Ted laughed. "You're probably right." He watched Erica share a laugh-filled moment with her popular friend. "Would there be a note on the back that says: original Erica's consciousness sold separately?"

Dhiraj pondered the joke for a moment. "If Erica stayed dead in those woods and you didn't have powers, would life be better or worse?"

Ted wondered if his answer should include the fact that they might be wandering into certain doom within the next two hours.

"I'm not complaining." Ted floated a small red candy his way and chomped it out of the air. "It's just different than I expected."

Dhiraj rubbed at his wrists, which still looked red from the handcuffs. "Tell me about it."

Ted gave his parents one last embrace before hopping into the limo.

"Welcome to my palace on four wheels." The limo driver's proud voice filled the vehicle.

Dhiraj and the driver bantered as if they were old friends, though Ted couldn't place the man's accent at first. Greek maybe. Whatever the driver's origin, he was right. The limo was a palace.

The new car smell complemented the plush leather seats beneath them. It took about 30 seconds for Winny to open the minibar, which had been filled with cold soda. Ted had been a reluctant celebrity for the last few months, but there was something about the limo that made him feel like he deserved to be in the papers.

It was a few minutes before Ted got over the awe of his first limo experience. By that time, Winny and Rico were already making out at one end of the vehicle, and the rest were going over the plan on the other.

"Everyone have their comm links tested?" Erica tapped at her own earpiece.

The other three did the same.

"Good." Erica pulled out a drawing that mapped the layout of the dance. "We've got the walkway into the hall, a lobby, the main area and the backstage. You've all got your assignments. It's imperative that you see Redican before he sees you and immediately radio your position over."

Jennifer clears her throat. "And if he sees us first?"

Erica pointed at her head. "Don't let that happen. The second one of us calls his position in, Ted can snatch him up and send him to me."

Ted smiled. "And then you can give him a taste of his own medicine."

She gripped his leg. "Exactly."

They were still a block away from the dance when the limo stopped.

After a minute with no movement, Ted tapped on the partition to get the driver's attention. "Why are we stopped?"

"Sorry, my friend." The limo driver gestured outside as if Ted could see through the tinted glass. "They're blocking us."

Erica hit the controls for the sunroof and poked her head out the top of the limo. She ducked back down inside and looked at Ted. "You should see this."

Ted shifted over to Erica and squeezed into the space beside her. When he looked outside, his jaw dropped. During the jewelry heist earlier that week, the GHA protest sported a little over 100 people. The number of GHAers outside of their prom was closer to a thousand. And all of them were looking right at him.

"Finley." A familiar voice called out from a megaphone. A small part of the crowd parted to reveal Thomas Cobblestone. "Happy junior prom."

Erica shook her head. "That idiot doesn't even realize what he's doing. We need to get to Redican."

Ted looked out at the crowd. They were mostly silent, but he imagined they'd make one heck of a ruckus if that's what Cobblestone wanted.

"I have Agent Vott's number."

Erica snorted. "We are not bringing the DHS into this. We can handle our own problems." Ted wasn't so sure. He cupped his hands around his mouth. "I thought you were supposed to be in prison."

The onlookers booed all around the limo.

Cobblestone was too far away for a clear picture, but it was easy to tell he was smiling on the other side of the megaphone. "Our sponsors have deep pockets, Ted. We're sorry we have to ruin your high school's little dance here... unless you leave town tonight." The word "tonight" got a big rise from the crowd. "We'd be happy to let the rest of your classmates enjoy themselves."

Ted and Erica ducked down into the limo. Winny and Rico continued to kiss as if nothing else could possibly be happening. Dhiraj looked through the sunroof as Erica, Ted and Jennifer plotted.

"He could make a temporary deal with DHS." Jennifer shifted her dress with her hands. "At least so we could get inside."

Erica looked like she wanted to punch somebody. "No deals. If he goes off to fight terrorists somewhere and we need him to handle something cosmic, the world could be totally screwed."

The group of protestors began to chant outside of the limo. The voices joined in unison, shouting "G. H. A.! G. H. A.!"

Ted pulled out his cell phone. "I'm calling Agent Vott. This is ridiculous."

Erica reached for the phone before he could dial. "It's not a good idea, Ted."

"Do you have a better one?"

Dhiraj bent back down into the limo. "Guys, you should get a look at this."

During the argument, Ted hadn't noticed that that the chanting came to a close. When he looked through the sunroof, the crowd had almost completely parted, leaving a limo-shaped opening for them to drive through.

"Back in the car." The limo driver said. "You've only got me for the hour."

Before Ted complied, he looked directly at Cobblestone. Like the other thousand people in attendance, he was staring straight ahead as if in a trance.

"This isn't good." Ted sat down next to Erica. "I think Redican knows we're coming. And he's got an army of brain-dead cultists behind him."

The limo driver pulled up to the front of the venue. As Jennifer rolled down the window, the four of them looked outside to get a better view.

Ted couldn't concentrate on the white and gold exterior of the massive event space, the expertly manicured garden of blue and yellow flowers or the red carpet that was rolled right up to the open glass doors. All he could see were his peers.

Just as the protestors had been staring straight ahead, so were his classmates, and all of them were looking right at the limo. Ted watched as their mouths opened at once and spoke.

"Hello, Mr. Finley."

CHAPTER 41

Erica shivered when all the students spoke in unison. She pushed away Jennifer's shaking hand from the window control and rolled the window up herself. Even Winny and Rico had stopped making out.

"Why are we still in here?" Winny started to look for a door handle, as if she had just realized they weren't in some private make out room. She was about to open one of the doors, when Erica grabbed her hand.

"No!" She motioned to Ted. "Lock the doors."

With a slight twitch of his wrist, all the locks clicked down into place.

Erica released her friend. "We can't go out there yet."

Dhiraj looked through the tinted window as if he could see the onlookers. "At least they were polite."

"For now." Jennifer took his hand.

Ted and the rest of the passengers looked at Erica. She should have known there wouldn't be much surprise in their limo arrival, but she had no way of knowing Redican would be able to control so many minds at once.

Erica gave Ted a sharp look. "Could you move them?"

He took in a long breath. "I've shifted a crowd of 100 people before. Not a thousand. Besides, if I got them up, I'm not sure I could put them down safely."

Dhiraj laughed. "I'm sure nobody would mind if Cobblestone and the

GHAers got a little roughed up."

Jennifer grabbed his shoulder. "No! It's not their fault they got mind-wiped." She looked at Ted. "They shouldn't get sent to the hospital for that."

Ted smirked. "Aw, your first lovers' quarrel."

Without hesitation, they responded in unison. "Shut up." Then Jennifer and Dhiraj smiled at each other.

Erica bent over and racked her brain.

"If we could just distract most of the students, I could get inside and find Redican."

Winny made a scoffing sound that made the others turn in her direction. "If they're here to get you, you're the only one who's gonna be able to distract 'em, you idiot."

Rico was the only one who laughed, eliciting a kiss from his date.

Erica felt an idea forming in her head. "Winny, you're a genius."

Winny blushed. "Aw, thanks. I have my moments."

Erica looked at Ted and hoped. She hoped that he wouldn't turn out like Adam. She hoped that she wouldn't have to kill a person she loved, as she had done with William. She also hoped that having Ted tap into his powers didn't kill him in the first place.

"Alright, Ted." She took his hand. "I'm going to give you a crash course in controlling people's minds."

Ted raised his eyebrows. "I thought you were worried that would make me go crazy and try to end humanity."

She nodded. "Yup. That could happen."

Erica heard all the students move toward the limo with a coordinated footstep forward. Even if they took their time, the limo would be completely surrounded within the next minute.

Redican must be getting bored.

"Guys." Dhiraj pointed toward the window. "I don't think we have much choice."

Ted's fingers tapped on the leather seats.

Erica took his hand to stop the movement. "I'm not going to let you go crazy. I'm here to protect you."

Ted looked into Erica's eyes and swallowed hard. "I trust you."

"Good." She looked deep into his eyes. "Before I tell you how to do this, you need to promise me something. You need to promise you'll never change anybody's mind for good. If you abuse this power even once, you'll give yourself the permission to do it over and over again. Promise me you won't do that."

"Of course."

"You'll be tempted." Erica took his face in her hands. "Just promise, OK?"

Ted nodded. "Alright. I promise I won't abuse it. If I can do it in the first place."

"You can. You will." Erica filled her lungs with air and began. "You know how you can move objects around? You can do the same with memories. You have the ability to make the mind see things that aren't really there."

Erica recognized the face Ted made. It was the same bewildered look he gave her when she tried to explain who she was and where she'd come from.

"How?" he asked.

Erica heard the mob outside take another step toward the limo. "It's like when you asked for me to be fixed, and suddenly I was. You were in my head and saw what was wrong. Try asking for something else."

Ted looked around the limo and focused on Winny and Rico. Erica watched him close his eyes and squint. His body started to shake as he held his breath. When he let out the air with a big huff, everybody in the limo except for Winny looked like a carbon copy of Rico.

"What the heck?!" Winny's head darted around like a puppy's. "There are five Ricos!" She licked her lips. "Not that I'm complaining."

Jennifer and Dhiraj, both of whom looked like Rico from top to bottom, touched each others faces. Jennifer moved her hand down to Dhiraj's arm.

"Nice biceps." She squeezed his arm.

Dhiraj touched her face, which sported a goatee like the rest of the Ricos. "Nice stubble."

The Rico to Winny's left grasped her hand. "Rico is one of a kind, baby."

They kissed, and the other Ricos turned away. Erica watched the Rico to her side, Ted, slump over from fatigue.

201

She picked him back up. "Now change them back."

Ted breathed heavily and nodded. He squinted again and it took only a moment for the image of the fake Ricos to disappear.

Erica put her arm around Ted. "Was it easier the second time? Changing them back?" She could feel Ted's speedy heartbeat through his back.

"Um." He tried to catch his breath. "Sure."

Jennifer laughed and looked at her date. "You were pretty manly-looking, Dhiraj."

"You, too." Dhiraj was about to laugh, but he heard a tapping on the door. It was the sound of dozens of fingers rapping on the windows.

Erica tried to ignore the sound, which now came from all around the limo. "Looks like the crash course is over. Now you just need to do it for a thousand people."

Ted eyes darted from side to side. "Great. Because doing it for six wasn't hard enough."

"We believe in you, Ted." Jennifer forced a compassionate grin. "Always have."

Rico gave Ted and Erica the thumbs-up and Dhiraj showed his flashy smile.

Winny rolled her eyes. "You're a dork. But you're the best chance we've got."

"Thanks for the vote of confidence." His voice shook. "If I can get into their heads, what should I do? Make everybody normal again?"

Erica shook her head. "Redican'll change them right back. And until you're practiced at this, he's going to be stronger than you."

"What're you gonna do?" Dhiraj started to back away from the windows. "Make them all think we're naked or something."

Erica looked at Dhiraj with a grin. "No, I've got something much better in mind."

CHAPTER 42

"I don't know if I like this plan." Dhiraj looked to Jennifer for support.

She gave him a half-smile that seemed to say she didn't have any better ideas.

"I thought you liked being bait." Ted glanced at him before grimacing at the tapping sounds that were growing louder and louder.

"It's different when it's one vs. a hundred."

"More like a thousand." Winny looked pleased by her insight.

Dhiraj glared at her and then turned his attention toward Erica. The plan was a simple bait-and-switch. Ted would find his way into the minds of all the protestors and students long enough to make them believe that Dhiraj was actually Ted. Dhiraj would draw as many people as possible away from the dance, which would give the others the opportunity to get to Redican.

"What if the mob gets to me before you get to Redican?" Dhiraj felt the dread grow to the size of a watermelon in his stomach.

Erica looked back and forth between Dhiraj and Ted. "We're going to do everything we can to make sure that doesn't happen. Ted, if you don't start now—"

"Wait!"

All the passengers, Dhiraj included, looked over at Jennifer. She'd been silent since Erica brought up the plan. "If you're going to make them really believe it...." Jennifer gripped Dhiraj's hand. "He's gonna need an Erica with him. Change me, too."

Dhiraj pulled Jennifer toward him, attempting to whisper quietly enough to not be heard. "No, Jen. You shouldn't–"

"I'm your date, remember?" She adjusted the boutonnière on Dhiraj's lapel. "Where you go, I go."

Dhiraj felt some of the dread dissipate. He didn't want to put her in any kind of danger, but two people might have better odds than one.

"Guys?" Erica moved away from the door as the tapping began to turn into a pounding.

"Both of us." Jennifer put on her game face.

Dhiraj clenched her hand tightly. "Do it."

"I'll try my best." Ted looked at the two of them one last time before shutting his eyes.

Dhiraj watched as Ted scrunched up his face. The pounding got more forceful as Ted started to shake.

"Owww." Ted gripped Erica's hand. "My head is–"

Erica shouted at Ted like a drill sergeant. "Keep going! Just a little bit longer!"

Ted gritted his teeth and let out an anguished noise as if it was the hardest thing he'd ever done. Dhiraj could feel himself changing, even though he knew it was only an optical illusion. He looked at his hands as the color faded from brown to a pale peach. The cracking sound of a breaking window startled Dhiraj and he turned toward Jennifer. Her dark hair was changing to a shade of dirty blond, and her dress changed to black and purple to match Erica's. As another window started to crack on the other side of the car, Dhiraj and Jennifer's transformation was complete. They looked exactly like Ted and Erica.

Ted opened his eyes and let out a hard, exasperated breath, like he'd just run a mile-long sprint. "It's done." He shook his head from left to right as if to rouse himself. "My brain feels like a puddle."

Dhiraj grinned and suddenly felt self-conscious of what his grin looked like with another person's face. "What's next?"

Dhiraj gripped Jennifer's now very Erica-like hand. He thought back to a few months earlier when the recently possessed Erica gave him a kiss on the cheek. He couldn't help but blush at the memory and turned back toward Erica and Ted.

"Your dad's office building—" Ted paused to catch his breath. "It's not too far from here. I can fly you there – far enough that you can get inside and lead the mob there."

Dhiraj wanted to comment that Ted looked about as capable of flying them as he was of winning a bench press competition, but he figured that wouldn't inspire much confidence. "You sure you can do it?"

A hand came smashing through the window closest to Winny and Rico. The brainwashed classmate grabbed at Winny's dress, threatening to rip it from her shoulders. Her shriek was so loud and high-pitched, Dhiraj thought it might break the other windows all on its own.

Ted hit the controls for the sunroof. "We're about to find out."

Erica took Jennifer's hand for a moment. "Good luck."

"You too." Jennifer took hold of Dhiraj's waist.

Before Dhiraj could take one more breath, he felt himself jerk into the air, through the sunroof and about five feet above the top of the limo. There was a moment of silence as Dhiraj looked down at the hundreds of pursuers. He felt Jennifer pinch his side.

"Say something."

Dhiraj was surprised to hear Erica's voice come out of Jen's mouth. He wondered if Ted's voice would be likewise transplanted.

"Hello, boys." Dhiraj assumptions were right. No matter what he said, Ted's voice would come out of his mouth. "If you want me, come and get me!"

With that, Dhiraj and Jennifer started to fly through the air. He felt the wind whipping against his cheeks as his partner in flight pulled herself even closer to him. There was a weightless freedom inside he'd never before experienced. He'd planned on showing Jen a good time, but even he couldn't have expected anything as exhilarating as this.

"This is incredible." Jennifer looked back toward the limo. "It looks like they're coming."

Sure enough, when Dhiraj turned back, he saw the mob pursuing them on foot. When he turned back, Dhiraj and Jennifer were headed straight for the windows of an office building.

"Holy crap!" Dhiraj shielded his eyes with his free arm. The two of them banked at the last second and zipped around the building.

Jennifer laughed loud enough for Dhiraj to hear it over the air blowing by them.

He caught her eye. "I think you've somehow gone crazier."

As they began to descend, Jennifer pulled herself close to Dhiraj's ear. "You wouldn't want it any other way."

He smiled as their feet hit the ground.

It took Dhiraj a second to get his bearings. Once he did, he realized they were just a block away from his dad's office. In the distance, he could hear the sound of dress shoes hitting pavement, like the most formal marathon of all time.

"They're coming." Any trace of Jennifer's previous daredevil joy had gone out of her.

Dhiraj took her hand, wondering if their disguised appearance would change how fast they could run. "This way."

While Treasure was by no means a major city, this street nearly gave the town a skyline. Dhiraj typically walked into his father's office with dreams of owning the block. Now he just wanted to stay alive. When they got to the front door of the tallest building in Treasure, Dhiraj waved a keycard in front of a grey control pad. A light turned from red to green, causing a massive glass door to swing open.

"Do you think they can stop him in time?" Jennifer asked.

Dhiraj looked back, spying the fastest runner in the pack running straight for the building. "I know they will."

Dhiraj shut the door behind them, making a loud clicking sound. He took Jennifer's hand and prayed the door would hold.

CHAPTER 43

Ted watched through one of the holes in the window as Dhiraj and Jennifer drew the onlookers away. Occupying the minds of a thousand people made him feel heavy, like wearing a coat of steel armor. He wasn't sure if he'd be able to do that and fly his friends safely, but aside from almost ramming them into a building, he was impressed with his mental multi-tasking. Ted felt them land on the ground and released his control of their movements.

"That was amazing, Ted!" Erica kissed him on the lips, though his senses seemed more deadened than usual.

He figured that had something to do with being tapped into the senses of so many minds at once.

"Thanks." Ted heard a noise in the front of the limo. With the path of kids cleared, the driver slammed the door behind him as he ran off in the opposite direction. "I guess we get to keep the limo."

Winny opened the door that faced the parking lot. "He's got the right idea." She looked toward Rico and then Erica. "You're a hero now, aren't you?"

Ted knew that Erica had kept her identity secret from everybody but the main gang. He supposed it was impossible to keep secrets from your friends forever.

"I can explain–"

Winny stopped Erica's sentence with a sharp hug. Ted watched Erica sink into it.

"No need." Winny kissed her friend on the cheek. "Text me and Beth about it later."

Erica nodded. Rico scooted around his date and led her out of the limo. When the door closed behind him, it was just Ted and Erica left inside.

"I feel like I'm still in everybody's mind." Ted forced a smile. "It's like watching the TV, laptop and phone at the same time. Times a million."

"I'm sorry, Ted."

"No, it's actually really cool. Exhausting but cool."

"I hope you can still fight." She gestured through another hole in the window. "Not everybody took the bait."

Ted looked toward the venue and saw about 20 students remaining. The reflection from a row of hanging lights glistened against the dresses and suits of the kids who stood between Ted and Redican.

Ted took her hand and opened the door. It only took a few seconds for the guards to realize it was time to take action. When a kid in a grey suit rushed the two of them, Ted used his powers to push him back into three of the other guards. A girl in a pink, poofy dress rushed Erica. Before Ted could use his powers, he watched his protector expertly duck to the ground and sweep the legs out from under the attacker. When another guard rushed at Ted, he attempted to float him up into the air, but Ted's powers failed him. The classmate swung his fist and connected with Ted's face. The sharp sting made his vision go dark for a moment. As Ted bent to the ground in pain, he felt Erica roll her back onto his. He looked up to see her easily handle the boy with a roundhouse kick.

Erica helped Ted to his feet.

"I tried to use.... I couldn't."

She nodded before using a quick backhand to take out another attacker. "You're drained." She looked behind her. "Your hands and feet still work?"

Ted realized that the months of training weren't just about him developing his powers. He needed to be prepared in case his abilities weren't available. Ted got into a fighting stance. "They do."

One of the attackers attempted to punch Erica in the back. When she ducked, Ted leapt over her, planting both of his feet in the assailant's chest. The boy toppled to the ground and Ted turned back toward his trainer.

"Not bad, eh?"

Erica shook her head. "Let's save the gloating for after we win, OK?"

Ted didn't speak again for the rest of the fight. There were about a dozen guards still left standing. Ted took them down as gently as he could; after all, it wasn't their fault they were serving Redican. Erica did the same, and before long, the pair had entered the building. At Erica's direction, they lugged several tables over to the door to barricade themselves inside. They didn't need the 20 guards they'd just faced to come back to haunt them.

For a moment, Ted found himself growing sentimental of the prom that could have been. The table settings and centerpieces were dotted with green and purple flowers. There was equipment set up for a live band to perform a variety of classics and top hits. The checkerboard wooden dance floor would have been big enough to accommodate the entire class. He wondered if the dance he dreamed of might still be possible if they could stop Redican.

"Same plan?" Ted hoped they wouldn't have to split up. With his powers on the fritz, Erica was truly his protector.

"Let's stick together." She grabbed and squeezed his palm quickly before motioning him to follow her.

He wondered if she was the one reading his mind as they started to search the building. Ted attempted to use his powers to see if he could detect Redican or anybody nearby. He felt a familiar blip of recognition that somebody he knew was inside, but it didn't last.

"This is so annoying." Ted kicked at the leg of a soft, comfortable-looking couch. "When you... were like me, did you ever burn out?"

Erica hopped up on the stage and started rifling through the curtains. Without even turning back, she answered. "I didn't live long enough for that to happen."

Ted didn't know quite how to respond to that. He let the conversation drop until Erica motioned in his direction.

"I hear something."

Before Ted could ascend the stage, several pairs of hands grabbed Erica through the curtain. She tried to fight them off, but they wrapped her in the thick velvet to fend off her blows.

She screamed in anger. "Ted!"

Ted reached for her with his powers, but once again nothing happened. By the time he jumped on the stage, Erica had been pulled out of view.

He rushed backstage and ran down a long, dark corridor. Ted could no longer see or hear Erica or the footsteps of the people who'd grabbed her. When he reached the end of the hall, he saw theater lights and sandbags, but no Erica. That's when Ted remembered his comm link and flipped it on.

"Ted!" Erica's voice sounded muffled.

"Erica." Ted ran back in the opposite direction. "Tell me where you are."

"Catwalk." Erica's breath was heavy, as if she were still trying to struggle her way free. "He's here."

"I'm coming." Ted ran back toward the stage and looked for a way to climb up to the catwalk.

He looked up at the hanging stage lights and traced them back down to a black ladder. As he gripped the bottom rung, he heard Erica's voice again.

"They've got Natalie, too."

With that, the comm link went dead and any sounds of the struggle were replaced by a low hum. Ted got up the ladder quicker than he ever thought possible. He was surprised to see how much space there was among the lights above the stage. The catwalk stretched at least 10 feet off the stage and 10 feet behind it. Ted glanced down for a moment. While his recently acquired ability to fly had helped to stave off any fear of heights, his malfunctioning powers made his position 25 feet above the ground very dangerous.

"Theatre techies have a death wish."

He saw several people in the distance and ran toward them. As he got closer, the recognition began to set in.

"No." He shook his head. "I'm dreaming again, I have to be."

Ted didn't see Erica. Natalie wasn't there, either. Even Redican was nowhere to be found. Instead, Ted saw Nigel cracking his knuckles and staring straight at him. By his side was Jason Torello, who looked as big and strong as ever. Even in the dark of the catwalk, Nigel's smile seemed to glisten.

"Did you miss us, old friend?"

CHAPTER 44

As the glass door clicked shut behind Jennifer and Dhiraj, the fastest member of the brainwashed mob slammed face first into the barrier like a daredevil bird. Jennifer shrieked at the sound and the sight of him, the man's body slumping to the ground as his compatriots gathered around him. She watched for a reaction from Dhiraj, who was still cloaked in Ted's appearance.

He let out a soft chuckle. "We really should put some stickers up to keep them from doing that."

Jennifer saw three members of the crowd outside attempt to pull the handle of the glass door at once. It strained at its hinges before locking right back into place.

Jennifer put her hands through her hair and remembered that she was a temporary blonde. "Is that gonna hold?"

Dhiraj smiled. "Of course. Lawyers need more security than most." He took her hand. "We'll be safe as long as we need to be."

Jennifer noticed several of the mob members clear a path in the front. A group of seven of the strongest had ripped a wooden bench out of the ground. Jennifer could barely hear the group screaming through the glass, but she was pretty sure she heard the word "charge." Using the bench as a battering ram, the crowd cracked the mighty door. Jennifer saw Dhiraj's face

213

turn even whiter.

"I'll never look at that bench the same way again." He pulled her away from the commotion. "We better hide."

They rushed away as the gang took another run at the door and left an even larger crack. As Dhiraj pulled Jennifer to a hallway full of elevators, she barely had a moment to note the green, marble walls and massively high ceilings. When Dhiraj pushed the elevator button, the heavy, metal doors opened with a ding and they sped inside. As the door closed, Jennifer heard large chunks of glass crashing down on the lobby floor.

"Your dad is gonna be pissed." Jennifer looked at their reflection in the mirror. "You think I'd be used to seeing hallucinations by now." She noticed Dhiraj glancing down at her exposed legs. "Quit checking out my friend's assets."

Dhiraj blushed and hit the button for the 16th floor. "Is there a way for me to blame this on Ted?"

The elevator lurched up and Jennifer had to grab a hold of Dhiraj to steady herself.

The doors opened and Jennifer planted both feet back on the ground. If it weren't for the lights in the massive fish tank that lined one of the walls, the hall would've been too dark to see a thing. Because of the aquatic illumination, Jen could see a strip of rooms that looked straight out of an upscale furniture catalogue. She wondered if there'd be enough places to hide, given the clear glass walls that made up some of the offices.

"It's nice."

Dhiraj nodded. "I'd hope so. Wouldn't want my dad to spend 80 hours a week somewhere crappy." He pushed all the buttons on the elevator and led Jennifer into the hallway. "That ought keep them busy for a second."

As he tried to tug her forward, Jennifer pulled Dhiraj back toward her. "Close your eyes."

She waited to close hers until he followed her instructions. "I don't know how much longer we'll last, but before anything happens, I want to kiss you. I just want you to know that I'm going to be thinking of you when I do it."

"Same here."

They moved closer in the darkness and their lips connected. Jennifer's body grew warm as she felt his mouth collide with hers. She pulled Dhiraj in tighter and wished they had just a few more minutes. The fear of the mob and the pain she'd been carrying around seemed to wash away like a dry patch of sand being carried out to sea by the tide.

When Jennifer opened her eyes, she didn't see Ted's face any longer. It was Dhiraj staring back at her once again.

"You're back to normal." For a moment, Jennifer wondered if it was her feelings for Dhiraj that changed him.

"You are, too."

Jennifer looked down to see that her dress, hands and legs were once again familiar. While her identity crisis was over, she wondered if the change meant another one had begun.

"If we're changed back, does that mean Ted is in trouble?" Jennifer heard the sound of a door opening.

Dhiraj took Jennifer by the shoulder and crouched down. "If he is, he'll have to handle it on his own. Come on."

They crossed the hall and opened a door adjacent to the fish tank, then scurried in and locked the door behind them. Dhiraj knelt down and put his back against the wall; Jennifer mirrored his position. They lowered their voices to a whisper.

"Should we tell them we're not who they're looking for?" Jennifer took Dhiraj's hand. She noticed it was starting to shake.

"I don't think we should take any chances." Dhiraj turned toward her. "Besides, isn't this romantic?"

Jennifer cupped her mouth to stop the laugh from escaping. "Almost as romantic as a joint funeral."

Jennifer felt Dhiraj squeeze her hand tighter as they huddled against the wall together. The sound of a half-dozen footsteps echoed through the hall-way. Jennifer couldn't help but wonder how much longer their time together would last.

CHAPTER 45

Natalie's abdomen itched against the fabric of her dress, but she wasn't in enough control of her own body to scratch it. She attempted to glare at Mr. Redican, but her efforts to contort her face only resulted in a twitch. Redican had frozen the emotion on her face as a pleasant but vacant smile after she gave him one too many evil eyes. The only thing Natalie did have control over was the words that came out of her mouth, though she had a feeling she should limit those to make sure she didn't lose that ability as well.

"I think you should talk out your plan." Natalie felt weird letting the words tumble out with her face stuck in happy mode. "That way, you can make sure you're gonna get it exactly right."

Redican barely registered her voice. The man held a massive and ancient-looking book in his hands. The tome seemed to glow like it contained some sort of electricity. He was looking down into the ballroom and waiting for something to happen.

He's waiting for Ted. He's nervous.

"I'm not nervous, Ms. Dormer." Redican smiled, as if he was taunting her for his ability to read thoughts. "I'd call it excited."

Is that why you pissed yourself?

Redican looked down at his pants. Natalie let a small chuckle out of her immovable face. Redican's scowl made her realize that he was not in the

217

mood for a joke.

"Don't you realize I could've left you in that fantasy world with Ted for the rest of your life?"

Redican got so close to Natalie, she could smell his breath. It wasn't pleasant.

He continued. "You could've been perfectly happy in your mind while your body was here in a coma. Your parents would spend every day weeping over your broken life."

Redican paced away from Natalie and back. He had a sort of limp as he walked, as if one wrong move might cause him to topple over. Natalie knew he was trying to scare her, but there was no way fear was going to help her out of this. The best way for her to win was to keep a level head.

"At least I'm not in some fantasy land that makes it okay to go around messing with people's minds." Redican was about to shout something back, but Natalie cut him off. "You think it's justified to destroy everybody's lives because some army attacked your homeland on another world in another time. You don't get to play God just because someone played God with you."

Natalie figured she'd gone overboard. She watched Redican tighten his grip on a metal bar of the catwalk as his back heaved up and down with heavy breaths. Within moments, she knew she'd have her right to speak taken away from her. Natalie watched Redican as he took in a long, slow breath. He surprised her when he turned around sporting a sad frown.

"You're right."

Natalie wasn't sure he heard him right. "You agree with me?"

Redican waved his hands and Natalie had complete control over her body again. She took the opportunity to scratch her abdomen at length.

"Controlling hundreds of people." Redican took a few steps toward Natalie with each sentence. "Ruining people's lives. It makes me almost as bad as the dark souls who killed my family."

Natalie took a glance down to the stage. She wondered if she took a jump while he was monologuing if she'd survive the fall.

Natalie turned back toward her captor and gave him part of a smile. "Does that mean you'll let me go?"

Redican pursed his lips and looked at Natalie with apologetic eyes. "If only that would accomplish anything."

Natalie could sense the conversation turning and made a gut decision to try to jump onto one of the tables below. She stepped up onto the top of the railing and prepared to leap.

As quickly as Redican had given Natalie back the control, he took it away once again. She knelt and grabbed the railing, lowering herself back down slowly. Natalie walked back to her previous spot and her eyes focused on the substitute teacher.

"The dark souls took over my world and because it wasn't as high a priority as Earth, the light souls didn't lift a finger. Nearly everybody I knew was either killed or possessed by an evil spirit. Playing nice did nothing but eradicate us, Ms. Dormer."

Natalie tried to say something back, but Redican had now taken everything from her. She had a feeling he wouldn't hear much of what she said regardless.

"We were too giving. We needed to take. If the light souls won't label us as deserving as humanity, they sure as hell better respect what we're willing to do to survive."

Natalie heard the noise of a struggle on the other side of the catwalk and tried to turn her head. It was no use, and she had to rely on her sense of hearing alone. She heard several people restraining a girl from attacking them. It didn't take her long to recognize Erica's voice.

They've got me. They've got her. If they get Ted then we're all screwed.

Natalie thought she saw Redican smirk in her direction after her pessimistic thought. Completely out of her view, she heard Erica say Natalie's name before the struggling stopped. The scuffle was over and the guards took their hands off her without consequence. Natalie realized that Redican had taken over Erica's mind as well. The sub controlled Erica's legs and made her walk over next to Natalie.

Natalie wished that her first thought upon seeing Erica wasn't related to her being Ted's prom date. After all, she had a feeling that prom had been more or less cancelled. Once Natalie had shed the thought, she did her best to communicate with Erica through her eyes. She attempted to convey her desire to toss Redican to his death. Erica's eyes seemed to agree. They looked toward Redican, who was commanding his lackeys to remain in the shadows just in case.

By the time Ted appeared on the other side of the catwalk, Redican had completely disappeared from view. It was as if he simply popped out of existence. Natalie struggled to pull herself free, but Redican remained in control of her mind.

Ted ran over toward their side of the catwalk, but he stopped around 10 feet short. He looked at the two of them like they were ghosts.

Help us, Ted. What are you waiting for?

Natalie looked over at Erica, but that's not who she saw at all. Instead, Erica's body had been replaced by a familiar apparition. Gone was the purple and black dress, replaced by a dark shirt and even darker pants. Erica's new face was that of Nigel's, the man who'd almost stabbed her to death. Natalie tried to pull away and noticed her own body had changed as well. Though the nagging itch on her abdomen remained, the dress was gone, replaced by a similar outfit to the one Erica was now wearing. She looked at the hair on her arms and marveled at her wider, fatter hands. She watched Ted's eyes. Judging by his reaction, Natalie had a feeling that she'd taken on the appearance of someone equally intimidating. Someone who was equally dead.

Natalie watched as Erica's mouth moved through her Nigel-like appearance.

"Did you miss us, old friend?"

Ted's face said it all. It was a combination of fear and confusion. He looked as much ready to run as he was to fight. "I killed you."

Now Natalie felt her own mouth move with a voice that was decidedly that of one of her least favorite people. "Not even death can keep us from missing prom."

As Ted crouched into a ready stance, Natalie felt her body move into a similar pose.

Redican was right. If anybody's gonna kill me tonight, it's gonna be Ted.

If Natalie had any control over her body, she would've thrown up right then. Instead, she felt herself run toward her friend and swing her right fist.

CHAPTER 46

Ted wasn't sure if he could move.

It's got to be another trick.

"You're not real." Ted straightened his spine and looked around the catwalk. "Come out, Mr. Redican. Let's finish this."

The supposed apparition of Jason Torello began to move toward him. Ted stood his ground and stared into the bully's eyes. For something that might be a dream, the way Torello walked toward him sure did seem realistic.

"You're not even gonna put up a fight?" Torello grinned as he got within swinging distance of Ted.

For all that Ted had been through, coming face to face with a school bully still sent shivers down his spine. He attempted to ignore the Torello twin. "If you want to teach me something, Mr. Redican, tell me. You don't need to play games."

Ted could hear Torello's knuckles crack as he balled up his fists.

"If anyone's tryin' to teach you something, it's to never put your guard down." Torello reared his fist back and swung.

Ted blocked the punch and pushed it off to the side. Another fist came flying, and he knocked it away with his wrist.

Torello growled and kept stepping toward Ted. "Do I feel real enough to you yet?"

Ted attempted to fly backward away from the charging brute, but his powers remained weak, only allowing him to get off the ground for a split second. He stumbled, which gave Torello a clean blow at his head. Ted felt the pain ringing in his ears as a bruise began to form. Before he could shake off the punch, Torello let a flurry of kicks fly. Ted used his own leg to block most of them, but the final kick hit his ankle, sending another burst of pain through his body. He scampered back and rubbed at the spot of the kick.

If he were a real dark soul, that would've broken my leg.

Ted wasn't sure where the thought came from, but it multiplied in his brain. If he stopped treating this like a fight with the real Jason Torello, what would happen?

"Had enough, Finley?" Torello bounced on his toes, waiting to send another attack Ted's way.

Ted stood up tall and let his lungs fill with air. He remembered back to his months of training and clenched his fists. "I'm just getting started."

Torello came at Ted with another swing. Instead of attempting to avoid it, Ted gripped his attacker's wrist. It didn't feel at all like he expected. While he saw the dark black hair that covered Torello's arms, he didn't feel the hair when he grabbed ahold of the teen. Torello swung with his other hand, and Ted caught that wrist as well. He felt the same illusion of hair with the same hairless feeling.

"You may be real, but you're not Jason Torello."

As the fake Jason Torello aimed for a headbutt, Ted used the momentum to do a backward roll. At just the right moment, Ted kicked his legs into Torello's chest, sending him flying behind Ted's back. He heard his attacker land with a thud that rattled the metal catwalk.

Ted got back to his feet and walked toward the person who looked like Nigel. It was eerie how much the voice and mannerisms of the British villain had been replicated on another person's body.

Ted got a few feet away and crouched into a ready stance. "Nigel's dead, so, you aren't particularly scary right now."

Nigel smirked. "Let's see if I can change your mind."

Nigel faked a high punch and when Ted went to block it, the man kicked Ted so hard that he flew off the ground, cleared the railing and went plummeting to the dance floor. Ted saw the checkerboards fast approaching and braced for impact. As he was about to make contact with the wood below, his powers finally kicked in. His face was an inch away from the floor when his body stopped.

"I've gotta stop doing this." Ted placed his feet on the ground and used his replenished powers to push himself back up to the catwalk.

Before he had a chance to land, Nigel was on him again with a series of powerful punches.

He's strong like Nigel. Maybe it really is—

Before Ted could finish the thought, the fake Jason Torello grabbed Ted's arms from behind. Nigel took his opportunity for a free shot and landed it right in Ted's stomach. The air shot out of Ted's lungs in a hurry, and if Torello hadn't been holding him up, he might have collapsed to the ground. There was so much pain and so little oxygen, Ted was completely surprised by what happened next. It was instinct – it had to have been.

Jason Torello tried to hold onto Ted, but his arms pulled free. "Hey, what gives?"

Torello began to move backward into the air. Ted blocked Nigel's next punch with his mind, wrenched Nigel's arms behind his back and sent him into the air as well. The lack of support from the Torello twin sent Ted to his knees, but he held his assailants above the ground nevertheless. Ted sped up his recovery process by looking inside himself and manually re-inflating his lungs. He stood and watched the two men hovering above the ground.

"If you were them"—Ted coughed—"you'd block my powers. Who are you?"

He heard a low chuckle and turned toward it. At long last, it was Mr. Redican, who looked like he was about to pass out. His skin was so pale, he almost glowed on the dimly lit catwalk. Ted noticed his substitute teacher gripping a book in his hand. The blue veins leading to his fingers seemed ready to burst.

"That was a fun one, wasn't it?" Redican shook as he walked toward the three of them. "I wasn't sure how that was going to turn out."

Ted felt the anger build up in his chest. "You know, I've never considered trying to rip a person's head off with my powers, but I really have a hankering right about now."

Ted was about to lift Redican above the catwalk as well when his powers seemed to give out once again. Nigel and Jason Torello dropped back to the catwalk with a clang. Ted tried to use his abilities, but the muscles of his body no longer seemed to be in control. He saw Redican concentrating all his attention on Ted. The man's skin became paler with every passing second.

"You'll die if you keep this up." Ted strained to move against the mind control of his enemy. "You're already dying."

Redican shook even more. Ted wondered if his enemy would kick the bucket before things came to blows.

"As long as I take her with me."

Ted looked in the direction Redican spoke. The image of Nigel had completely changed. The black and purple dress gave away Erica's identity almost immediately.

Ted began walking toward her without any control whatsoever. Butterflies multiplied in his stomach. "Let me go, Redican!"

Redican's voice was weaker than it'd been before. "Millions of people are dying on other worlds, but the light souls are only protecting Earth and their way of living."

Ted spied the other person he'd been fighting. Natalie was completely motionless on the other side of the catwalk aisle. He reached Erica and his hands turned her over.

"If you want me to save your people, I'll do it." Ted's hands moved toward Erica's neck. His voice grew sharper. "Leave her out of this!"

"It's okay, Ted." Erica's eyes were filled with tears. "I don't blame you for this."

Ted's hands began to move toward Erica's neck. "No! But I love you."

Erica forced a smile. "You're strong enough to go on without me."

Ted's hands gripped Erica's throat and began to squeeze. "Let me go, Redican!"

"I can't." Redican's voice became raspier with each passing word. "Without her, you can reach – true potential – save – every world."

Ted used all the muscles in his body to try to pull his hands off Erica's neck. He could see her trying to struggle but likewise unable to prevent the inevitable.

Ted felt the tears come out of his eyes and watched them land on Erica's dress. "I'm sorry. I'm sorry."

Redican laughed at Ted's pain. The bellowing laughter echoed through the ballroom. Ted closed his eyes, no longer wanting to see what his hands were doing.

Suddenly there was the sound of breaking glass and metal smashing into bone. The echoing laughter was replaced by the thump of a body against the catwalk railing.

CHAPTER 47

Dhiraj had pictured himself living to the ripe old age of 100. By that time, he would have had time to run dozens of companies, write a few best-selling how-to books and lead hundreds of seminars throughout the world. As the noise of footsteps grew closer, Dhiraj thought he might not even get 20 percent of the way there. The sweet scent of Jennifer's perfume filled Dhiraj's nostrils as he tried to put the potential last moments of his life into loving her.

"I liked you, too." Jennifer shifted her head on Dhiraj's chest.

He pulled his arm tighter around her body. "What do you mean?"

She looked up into his eyes. "I knew that you liked me. For years. I liked you back that whole time."

Through all the fear and worry, Dhiraj felt a burst of joy. He smiled down on her. "I never knew."

She sighed and pulled herself up to a sitting position. "I know. And it sucks." Jennifer's voice broke. "We could've had years together, but we won't because I was stupid."

Dhiraj moved his hand to Jennifer's face. He felt his eyes start to water. "You've been in my life, and I'm grateful for that." Dhiraj helped Jennifer to her feet. "And I'm not ready for it to end."

He tossed his jacket to the ground. Dhiraj started to try to psych himself up.

"It's probably two dozen people on this floor alone." Jennifer tried to stop Dhiraj's warm-up. "The odds are impossible."

Dhiraj smirked. "Never tell me the odds."

Jennifer rolled her eyes. "I think you're a lot more like Butch Cassidy than Han Solo in this situation."

Dhiraj pulled Jennifer toward her for a quick kiss on the lips. "You're a closet nerd? I knew I loved you for a good reason."

She placed her hand on Dhiraj's shoulder. "If we get out of this alive, we can watch all the trilogies you want. What's the plan?"

Dhiraj mapped out a potential path. His father occasionally took the service elevator down to avoid waiting to get to the bottom. The only problem was that the service exit was four floors up. They would need to somehow sneak to the stairs, slip past any brainwashed students, run up four flights and get to the other side of the floor to reach the elevator. If there were any locked doors along the way, they'd be cornered without a doubt.

"Sounds slightly less than impossible." Jennifer did an abbreviated field hockey stretching routine. With a cute hop off the ground, she gave Dhiraj a nod. "I'm ready when you are."

He kissed her on the cheek. "We're going to survive."

She attempted to smile, though it came off more like a farewell. "Keep dreaming big, moneybags."

Dhiraj opened the door and looked down the hallway. The students who'd been patrolling the floor seemed to be gone. Dhiraj wondered why they'd stopped before trying the door to their hiding spot. He waved Jennifer on and they tiptoed toward the floor's only entrance to the stairs. When they turned a corner, Dhiraj froze in his place. There were almost a dozen students milling around right outside the door. Almost immediately, three or four of the students spotted them.

Dhiraj was about to grab Jennifer and run, when nobody gave chase. None of the students even got up from their conversations. In fact, one of them gave Dhiraj a polite wave.

Jennifer and Dhiraj shared a confused look.

"Hey!" a student wearing a frilly, orange gown said. "Do you guys have any idea how we all got here?"

* * *

Ted regained full control over his body shortly after Redican went crashing to the ground. He pulled his hands away from Erica's neck right away. She wasn't moving.

"Erica?" Ted's voice trembled. "Erica?!"

With a heavy gasp, Erica sprung back to life. Her chest heaved up and down to bring in as much air as possible.

"You're alive!" Ted's tremble changed to a giddy shout. "Are you OK?"

"Yeah." Erica's voice was scratchy, as if she'd been screaming for hours. "Good thing you strangle like a girl."

Ted laughed. He assumed that Natalie had come to and saved the day just as she had in their previous incident in the caves. When he glanced back at her, he noticed she was still on the ground, struggling to get to her feet.

What the...?

With some trepidation, he looked over at Redican. He was passed out cold on the floor of the catwalk. Standing above him with a busted stage light was none other than Erica's friend Beth. She'd changed out of the hospital gown Ted had last seen her in. The typically dainty girl was wearing a little black dress that matched her tiny black purse. It was unlikely that her weapon of choice was a planned part of the ensemble.

"You can make me commit all the crimes in the world." Beth let the stage light drop to the side of her former teacher. "But nobody's gonna make me miss prom."

Ted could tell that Redican was still breathing by the motion of his back. After helping both Erica and Natalie to their feet, Ted pulled the powerful book away from Redican's tightly gripped fingers. As he did, Ted felt a burst of power go through him that was almost more disruptive than the one he felt that morning at Page's Diner. Millions of thoughts went through his mind at the same time, as if he'd had a chance to peer into the brains of every person in Treasure. He almost fell to the ground, but Natalie caught him before he could join Redican below them.

"Easy there." Natalie hoisted his arm around her neck. "I guess that punch of mine finally caught up with you."

Erica politely smiled. "Actually it was the book. It's full of immense–"

Natalie coughed to interrupt Erica. "Duh. I'm not an idiot. You alright, Ted?"

After a few more seconds of the room spinning, Ted felt like he was once again on solid ground.

"That was a rush. I just saw what pretty much everyone in town is thinking." He looked at the three women around him and laughed. "A lot of people think mostly about sex."

The ladies gave him a cockeyed glance before joining in on the joke.

Beth moved over to Erica and gave her a half-hug. She looked over at Redican. "What are we gonna do about him?"

Ted watched as Erica rubbed Beth's back. He supposed it was a good that the two of them had stayed friends after her identity change. "Before he wakes up–"

"If he wakes up." Natalie scoffed.

Erica wrinkled her nose. "I'm gonna keep him from hurting anyone."

She knelt down beside Redican and put her hands on his temples. Ted watched in awe as a tiny burst of blue electricity shot between Erica's hands and went through his skull. Redican's body shook for a few seconds before resuming its barely alive status.

Ted looked over at the others. While Erica's display of power didn't seem to make much of an impact on Natalie, Beth's jaw was practically on the floor.

"What did you do?"

Erica stood up. Her voice was hard, as if she'd just gotten some bad news. "Two things." She looked at Natalie. "I turned an enemy into a friend." Erica moved her eyes back to Ted. "And I found out some new information."

Before Ted could process what Erica had said, he heard a voice echoing through the ballroom.

"Ted!"

Ted touched Erica's shoulder. "I'll be right back." He was about to jump down to the dance floor when he stopped himself. "I don't think I said this today, but you look great."

Erica took Ted's hand, pulled him closer to her and kissed him. Ted wasn't sure what he would have done if he'd been forced to kill her.

She gave him one more kiss on the cheek. "Thanks."

Ted floated down below. Dhiraj was the leader of the pack. It looked like he was the grand marshal of a parade as dozens of teens came in behind him.

"They're all friendly again." Dhiraj grinned from ear to ear. "I figure we have a couple more hours to party. Jen's trying to find the band."

Jennifer walked through the front door with four scraggly-looking 20-somethings. "I found the band. And we've got an hour and 45 minutes left!"

The students began to cheer and dance, as if they hadn't spent most of their evening trying to hunt down Ted and his friends. Ted decided not to let it bog him down. After all, this was prom, and he'd be damned if he wouldn't get at least one dance with the girl of his dreams.

* * *

Natalie stood by the refreshments table as she sipped on her third glass of punch. Her nerves still felt on edge from the events of the last couple days. It wasn't every weekend you were kidnapped, framed for arson, taken through a magical fantasy world with your ex-boyfriend and forced to attack said ex-boyfriend. She was glad to see that most of the students around her were having a good time, but she wasn't sure if she could let herself do the same.

Dhiraj and Jennifer jumped into view, taking her out of her thoughts.

"Natalie, you've gotta get out there." Dhiraj looked punch-drunk with joy.

"It's like brainwashing made the band at least 30% better." Jennifer had the same kind of smile on her face.

"So, you guys are finishing each other's thoughts now." Natalie looked to the side. "That's not entirely vomit-inducing or anything."

Dhiraj and Jennifer forced Natalie to put down her punch and join them on the dance floor. While being surrounded by gyrating classmates seemed unpleasant and a little smelly at first, she tried to let the upbeat music take her for the next three songs. Even though it wasn't her choice to attend, she was glad she came. When the music turned slow, she watched Jennifer put her arms around Dhiraj's neck. She wondered if her friend had ever felt as happy as he had in that very moment. Natalie couldn't help but wonder if she'd ever get back to the jubilation she'd experienced at the homecoming dance with Ted.

A familiar voice caused her to turn around. "May I have this dance?"

Natalie thought her mind was playing tricks on her. It would only be the millionth time that had happened in the last 48 hours. But with Redican on his way to a holding cell, Natalie figured it actually was Ted asking her to dance.

"Where's Erica?"

Ted gestured toward a pack of other dancers. "Somewhere over there. I asked if I could have a dance with you."

Natalie frowned. "And if I say no?"

Ted took her hand and pulled her in between a few other couples. When his hands locked around the back of her waist, she instinctively threw her hands around his neck. It had been a while since they had been as physically close as they were just then. Natalie felt a shiver and looked away.

"Hell of a weekend," he said.

Natalie could feel Ted's eyes attempting to meet hers. She resisted for a moment before giving in.

"It was looking pretty bad there for a second." Natalie looked down and back up into Ted's eyes.

His stare was unwavering. "You know, you were right to not want to help me." He loosened his grip on her back to let her pull away a bit if she wanted. "You're gonna be a big star someday, and being involved in all of this is too dangerous."

Natalie moved in closer and put her head on Ted's chest. She could hear his heart start to beat faster as she did so. "I care about you, Ted. It's why I spied for you. It's why I'm going to keep putting myself in danger for you."

Natalie felt Ted's hands tighten around her back. He sniffled. "I care about you, too."

A minute went by before either of them spoke again. Natalie let herself stay in the moment as long as possible, swaying back and forth with her friend as the music came to its final few bars.

"What are you gonna do about the war?" Natalie pulled herself off of Ted's chest to look him in the eye. "And the GHA?"

After the brainwashing passed, the protestors had reformed a mob outside the venue.

"I don't know." Ted looked up to the lights. "There are people here I can help. But maybe there are people on other worlds who need me, too. Then again, the light souls gave me this power, so I can't just ignore what they're asking me to do."

Natalie parted her lips and let out a big smile. "You're freakin' Super Ted. You can do whatever the hell you want."

Ted looked back at Natalie. Even though what she'd said was meant partially as a joke, it seemed to make something click. He grinned right back at her.

"You're right." He nodded, more to himself than to Natalie. "You're right."

As the song ended, Ted backed away and gave a ridiculous bow. Natalie clapped and shook her head. Ted wrapped his arms around her in a big hug.

Natalie felt warm as she squeezed her friend. "I'm glad you're still an idiot."

"I'm glad I am, too," he said.

CHAPTER 48

Erica looked around the crowd of happy students. When she was human, there were occasional dances in her village, but she'd never been old enough to participate in the events' more intimate embraces. Though she'd crossed over into a few teenage lives, she'd never had the opportunity to be part of a prom. When the band came on the microphone and said this would be the last dance, she had a moment of panic.

Where is he?

Ted appeared before her as if it was magic. He put his arms around Erica's waist without saying a word.

Have you been reading my thoughts?

"Maybe." Ted looked as sly and confident as Erica had seen him. "I can stop if you want me to."

It's actually kind of fun. I get to make you look like a crazy person.

Ted chuckled, forming two cute dimples on his cheeks. She wrapped her arms around him as the music began to play.

"Mind if we have a conversation out loud?" Ted pulled Erica closer.

She bit her lip. "Fine. We'll talk like normal people."

Ted let his face relax into a calm smile. "So, you're letting me test out the mental stuff. What's next for training?"

As much as she'd been trying to enjoy the night, Erica's mind had been pondering the exact same question.

"We take things slow." Erica's eyes narrowed. "I need you to know that I'm nervous about this, Ted. Having all this power... it changes most people."

Ted leaned down and kissed Erica on the neck. "Are you saying I'm like most people?"

As he kissed her again, Erica felt a tingling sensation trickle down the length of her body. "Mmm." Erica let out a small breath. "I just want you to be careful. If things get bad, I don't want you to get all unethical on me."

Ted pulled back from Erica's neck. He had a look on his face that Erica couldn't read. It looked like understanding mixed with apology.

"I promise I'll use my head."

Erica squinted. "Alright." She figured tonight wasn't the night to press him on his facial expressions. "Good." Erica pulled Ted closer. "I wish we could dance like this all night."

Ted let out a smiling sigh. "Me too."

A few minutes later, the gang gathered at the entrance to wait for their limo. To their surprise, the driver had already gotten the broken windows patched up and was wearing a grin. As the seven of them walked toward the limo, a group of protestors quickly formed a wall to keep them from moving ahead. In their midst was Thomas Cobblestone, who was close enough to stow the megaphone.

"You know, Finley, that was quite a trick you pulled today." Cobblestone had a growl in his voice that seemed to rile up the protestors around him. "Messing with our minds to make us think that you saved the day in the end. It's one more reason that you should go home. And now!"

The protestors grew from a group of a dozen to several dozen in a matter of moments. Erica looked at Ted. He was staring directly at Cobblestone.

She took his shoulder. "It's OK. We'll get through eventually."

Ted's nostrils flared. "Do you know how easy it would be?" He looked at Erica. "I could wipe all of their minds and that would be the end of it."

Erica's heart dropped.

Have I already lost him?

"He's not worth it." She made an effort to rub the tension from the back of Ted's neck.

He moved forward to escape from her hand. "He put my mother in the hospital and tried to screw with my friend's reputation." Ted began to breathe faster. "You can't tell me he doesn't deserve it."

Erica had a vision of Adam just before she brought the building down on top of him. He'd looked just as angry as Ted. If he turned, she wasn't sure she'd be able to do the same thing twice. She might just have to let the world burn.

"Please." Erica took Ted's hand. "It would be the start of something you wouldn't be able to stop."

Ted turned back to Erica, the anger wiped from his face. "I know." He gestured beyond the crowd. "That's why I had to choose something else."

Sirens blared as at least a dozen black SUVs pulled into the parking lot. The vehicles unloaded to reveal over 50 agents in black suits. Erica recognized Agents Vott and Harding right away. She also noticed a YNN news van that had pulled in along with the DHS.

"Listen up, everybody." Agent Vott's voice carried surprisingly well among the hundred-plus protestors on hand. "We have the authority to publicly arrest you on national television."

Cobblestone looked like he was about to pitch a fit. "On whose authority?!"

Vott looked like he was hoping someone would ask that question. "The President of the United States of America." He went back to addressing the entire crowd. "If you'd like to be placed in handcuffs and broadcast before millions of people, including all your friends and family, please remain where you are. An agent will attend to you shortly."

Erica wondered if Agent Vott had done this before. Suburban life was all about reputation, and it didn't take long for about 90 percent of the protesters to dissipate.

"Man, I wish I'd filmed that." Dhiraj put his arms around Erica and Ted's shoulders. "I could put it on the TedFinley.com home page."

When two agents came to Cobblestone's side, he struggled against them and attempted to walk toward Erica and Ted. The robust government agents put a halt to that in a hurry.

Cobblestone strained against the grip of the agents. "I'll be out in a day."

Vott went back to his Cheshire grin. "That's funny. I hear we're aiming to hold you folks without bail."

Cobblestone growled and pointed at Ted. "This isn't the last you've seen of me, alien!"

As the hubbub died down, it became clear to Erica what had happened.

Agent Harding stopped over to shake Ted's hand and made it even more apparent. "See you this summer, kid. Have a good prom night, you guys."

After they'd gotten into the limo, Erica let all the emotions hit her at once. She wasn't sure if she wanted to cry or shout. "Why didn't you ask me first?"

Ted looked calm, which infuriated her even more.

"First of all, it's on a trial basis. I'm going to work with the government during the summer. On natural disasters and stuff. In return, they're going to shut the GHA down."

Erica looked around the limo. She was hoping for some moral support, but pretty much everyone was too tired to react to Ted's news.

"What if there's an attack?"

Ted nodded. "If something happens I'm allowed to come back. No questions asked."

Erica crossed her arms and looked away from Ted. Away from everybody. "Sounds like you've got everything figured out."

Erica wasn't completely sure why was she was so angry. It would've been much worse if Ted had brainwashed Cobblestone. She wondered if it had anything to do with the fact that she'd feel lost and purposeless without him.

Ted sat beside her. "I think this'll be good for my training. I'll be able to use my powers in a pressure situation without relying on you guys. I can test out my mind stuff by searching for people in danger. It's a win-win."

Erica didn't want to have tears in her eyes when she looked back at Ted, but it was the only option. "What about us?"

"Nothing's going to change." Ted took both of her hands in his. She noticed he had tears in his eyes as well. "You're still my girlfriend. You're still my protector. You can even come visit me at nearby disasters."

His soothing words helped, but she still felt devastated. "I'm just blindsided is all."

Erica let herself fall into Ted's arms. He wrapped himself around her. "We have two months left until summer. Let's make the most of it, OK?"

She nodded. In the short time she'd been back on Earth, Erica had been attacked multiple times, but it wasn't until this very moment she felt vulnerable.

The next two months flew by without much incident.

Ted agreed to focus on his new mental powers for now. When senior year began, they'd crack the spine on the other four books. Erica was proud that he continued to grow stronger, even outside of his powers, but she couldn't help but count down the days until she'd need to stay goodbye for an entire season.

After Ted bid adieu to his parents in person and his sister via video chat, a black SUV took the gang to a private airfield where Ted would take a government-chartered plane to Washington. From there, he would go wherever help was needed most. The vehicle drove right up to the runway and even Erica was impressed by the size of the plane.

Dhiraj was the first to put it into words. "It could carry a tank if it had to."

Agent Vott slammed the front door and beamed with pride. "It has."

Erica looked around at the high barbed-wire fences and the guards with earpieces. She felt like she was in another world – a world in which she wasn't sure she belonged.

After the agents loaded his luggage, Ted began to say his goodbyes. First, he shared a hug with both Jennifer and Dhiraj. "You'll keep the business afloat?"

"Afloat?" Dhiraj laughed. "It'll grow by at least 20% while you're gone."

Ted smirked. "Jen, please keep him from going crazy without me."

Jennifer ran her hand through the back of Dhiraj's hair. "I can only do so much."

Natalie was next. When they hugged, Erica couldn't stop herself from feeling jealousy. She tried her best to squelch it.

To Erica's surprise, Natalie started to cry.

"What's wrong?" Ted appeared to tighten his grip around her.

"I don't know." Natalie sniffled and wiped her eyes. "Be safe. Don't fall in a sinkhole or anything."

Ted pulled back and kissed Natalie on the cheek. Erica started to rhythmically tap her hand on her hip.

"I promise I'll be safe." Ted pulled back from the hug and focused his attention on Erica.

She tried to hide the fact that she'd been dreading this moment since the night in the limo. "You'll let me know if you're within driving distance?"

"I'll fly to your house and pick you up if I am."

Erica ran toward Ted and kissed him deeply. She wanted to get as much of the smell and taste of him into her mind as she could, as if it would somehow help her survive three months without seeing him. Ted kissed her back, and she felt a few of his tears run down her cheek.

Though they embraced for several minutes, it felt like five seconds in Erica's mind. Before she knew it, he was waving goodbye as the door to the aircraft closed for departure. Erica had the strange feeling that he wouldn't be the same Ted when he returned.

She felt a hand on her back. It was Natalie's. The cheerleader put her arm around the basketball star and they watched together as the plane flew away.

"Good riddance." Everyone looked at Dhiraj, who burst out laughing.

The others responded with chuckles and tears in equal measure.

He let out a big sigh. "What do we do now?"

"We wait for something bad to happen." Erica wiped away the last of the moisture from her face. "Then we stop it."

Natalie kept her arm around Erica's shoulder and gave her a squeeze on the back. "It almost sounds like you want something bad to happen."

Erica looked up in the sky and watched as Ted's plane disappeared behind a cloud. "I have a feeling that we won't have much of a choice."

The four of them piled back into the SUV and headed home.

Epilogue

The samurai sat in a meditative state in the middle of the damp cave. He could hear the droplets of water land on the rock below.

Whap. Whap. Whap. Plop.

The difference in sound clued the warrior into the presence of other men in the cave. After a full night without food and water, he knew the exercise was about to begin. The samurai stayed in his meditation as long as he could. After all, this fight wasn't going to last very long.

He used all of his senses to plot his next move. The sound of the water dripping on the cave floor and the men's footsteps told him the number of people coming his way. The feeling of the moisture in the air and on the ground informed him that the fighter who made the least movement had the strongest chance of victory. A faint scent of cologne told him that at least one of his attackers didn't plan on breaking a sweat. He let his eyes open to see how well his other senses had informed him.

Sure enough, there were five attackers and one of them looked like he'd rather be anywhere but here. Two men with beards looked ready to prove themselves and a wide brute with a scar on his face appeared to be out for vengeance.

The samurai readied himself by getting to his feet. Instead of waiting for his attackers to surround him, he went straight for the man with the scar.

Before his opponent could get his bearings, the samurai peppered his body with six kicks in rapid succession. As the man fell, the samurai used the body as a springboard to leap into one of the two bearded men. The warrior repurposed the man closest to him as a shield, absorbing blows from one bearded man into the other. He used his strength to pick up the now-pummeled assailant and toss him into the other. There were just two attackers remaining, and they were huddled together in the corner. The samurai ran toward them, and they started to flee. Before they could get very far, the warrior had grabbed the hair of one and slammed him into a rock face. The fifth man – the one wearing the cologne – stopped in his tracks.

"This isn't a date." The samurai bent to the ground and swept the legs out from under his last attacker. He looked toward one of the cave walls. "Is this the best you can send?"

Lights turned on throughout the cave, and the dark cavern became illuminated in a hurry. The cave wall turned clear and three men with clipboards took down some notes. A fourth man spoke into a microphone.

"Thank you, everyone. Yoshi, the council would like to see you."

The samurai nodded, walking up to a nondescript part of the cave. He reached for part of the rock. The stone turned in his hand and a doorway made itself apparent.

The man with the cologne called out. "How do you always know where the door is?"

Yoshi considered smiling, but he knew his attacker didn't deserve it. "Some rocks don't belong."

With that, he left.

The five-man council sat around Yoshi in higher chairs than were necessary. Their beards were long and white, as if that would convey wisdom. Yoshi wondered if the council members realized how ridiculous they looked.

One member of the council stroked his beard. "Your skills are top-notch as always."

Yoshi felt the urge to rip the man's facial hair clear off his face. "But not strong enough to be made the living soul."

Another man whose voice shuddered with each syllable spoke up immediately. "The light souls work in mysterious ways. We are here to serve them and nothing more."

Yoshi wanted to pound the walls, throttle the old men and leave this place forever. "I once again ask for permission to leave and join the living soul."

The man with the shuddering voice spoke up again. "The answer remains no. Your place is here. If the war comes, we need you here to fight for our world."

Yoshi repressed his urge for violence and bowed to the members of the council.

The following morning, when the cologne-scented man came to wake Yoshi for his daily training session, the samurai was nowhere to be found. None of the guards had seen or heard him exit. It was as if he'd vanished out of existence.

Hundreds of miles away, Yoshi laughed as he accepted a cup of tea from an attractive, blonde flight attendant. "Thank you. I hope my English isn't completely terrible. It's been a long time since speaking it."

The woman laughed. "Honey, you have better English than most of the people I know. What brings you to the States?"

Yoshi sipped the tea. It was the perfect temperature. He wondered if it was a good omen. "Business. I'm here to collect something that belongs to me."

The flight attendant was intrigued, as if she'd heard the latest celebrity gossip story. "And what's that?"

Yoshi grinned up at the woman as she leaned in closer.

"My birthright."

CO-AUTHORS' NOTE

When this book first came out into the world, we had a lot of preconceptions about how YA and superhero books were supposed to be. That's why it was about 15,000 (boring) words longer, had a cover that didn't fit the genre, and only ended up getting out to a few hundred people.

What we've learned is that there are no hard and fast rules. What's most important is that you do everything you can as an author to entertain. It's about you wonderful people, not us. If you only wanted 400,000-word novels that could double as assault weapons, then that's what we and our carpel tunnel syndrome would have to put out.

Hopefully, you'll like this trimmed length and sped up pacing just fine. I think we also made Natalie one inch taller in this version.

Thanks so much for reading. If you like this, then enjoy the special sneak preview for book #3, The Candidate on the following pages.

Go out there and break the rules! Except the really, really illegal ones.

Sincerely,
Bryan & Casey

PS: Reviews help authors keep writing. Please feel free to leave one!

EXCERPT FROM BOOK 3: THE CANDIDATE

Ted flew in through the front door of the hospital and landed in a puddle. At least, he thought it was a puddle, until he realized the entire ground floor of the building was now a six-inch-high wading pool. Vott and Harding had equipped him with waterproof boots, but the patients who remained inside weren't as lucky. Ted saw a nurse trudge through the water with a patient who didn't even have shoes on.

"How many patients are left?" Ted put his shoulder under the man's other arm.

The nurse's voice was hoarse. "At least 20."

"Vott, Harding. You guys still there?"

"Yeah. Ted, you better–"

"I need somewhere in a three-mile radius where I can send about 20 injured people."

Vott didn't hesitate. Ted heard him tapping away on a nearby keyboard.

"There's a building we have secured and boarded up. You couldn't get in through the front."

Ted looked back to see the patients splashing their way to his position. "Roof access?"

Vott made an affirmative noise. "What are you planning?"

"I'm gonna make a bubble."

Ted gathered all the patients and nurses in the lobby of the hospital emergency room. On the night of the prom, Ted floated the disguised Dhiraj and Jennifer through the air to lure the brainwashed mob away from their limo. Now, he was going to do the same with way more people, all while trying to protect them from the harsh effects of the storm. Ted explained his plan, but most of the looks he received back were dubious.

The building uttered another large creaking noise and the ground seemed to move beneath them. A male patient in his 40s began crying, and an intern did her best to comfort him.

Ted straightened his spine. "Look, guys. I need to get you off the streets and somewhere safe. I don't know if this is going to work, but I'm here to help. Anybody who wants to take a chance with me, step forward."

Everyone in the lobby, from the patients to the doctors, stepped forward or did their best injured-version of the act.

Ted nodded. "Good. Everybody outside."

As they complied, Ted concentrated on blocking all wind and rain from coming into contact with the patients. It wasn't perfect and a few raindrops fell through, but to the naked eye, it looked like there was a clear glass box around the entire group.

"Paint me a picture, Vott."

Off in the distance, through the raging storm, Ted could see a red flare fly high into the sky.

Ted locked onto all the patients, doctors and nurses and shifted them up two feet to ensure he had control. All of them moved as he intended, though even that small movement felt like he was lifting 100-pound dumbbells.

Ted tightened his face and muscles. "See you guys soon." With a hearty grunt, Ted lifted the entire group high into the air.

The group reached the same height as the top of the building, and Ted floated himself high into the air beside them to get a better view of the destination.

"Ready another flare."

"Alright, but it's the last one we've got."

Ted grumbled. "Next time, send your people to Costco to get 'em in bulk."

As he pushed the patients away from the hospital, the hardest part was keeping himself steady in the storm. The wind and rain beat against his face so hard, he could hardly feel it anymore.

"Flare. Now!"

Ted thought the wind might rip the clothes from his body before Vott could comply. Thankfully, the red flare shot into the sky and Ted used all his energy to push the group to the rooftop as fast as possible. In the distance, Ted could barely see as they moved into position above the roof.

"Are they directly above?"

"Yes. Lower them. I'll let you know when to let go."

As Ted agreed, he heard something in his mind. Thoughts of fear and pain wafted through that he hadn't noticed before. He was reading the mind of a little girl – a girl who was still inside the hospital.

"Alright, you can let them go. Get out of there, Ted. The worst of the storm is coming your way."

Ted looked up at the clouds and saw a tint of orange begin to paint the sky. He shook his head. "Can't do it. There's someone still inside."

Ted zipped back down to ground level and went back in through the front. The rising water level on the ground had doubled through the almost deserted building.

"Ted, this is an order. Get out of there now!"

With his first step, Ted felt the liquid sloshing over the top of his water-proof boots. His socks were soaked.

"Are you gonna help me, or do I have to take out my earpiece like they do in the movies?"

Vott mumbled something to himself. "I'll help, but act quick."

The shuddering of the hospital had grown louder and Ted watched as several ceiling tiles and beams dropped to the ground. He searched his mind to find the girl. The girl's thoughts grew louder and louder until he walked into a room with several beds. There she was, standing on top of a pile of sheets in an effort to get away from the water.

"Hey, honey. I'm Ted."

The girl shivered and stared. "I'm Sophie."

"Good to meet you. Can I get you out of here, Sophie?"

The girl breathed so hard and fast, Ted feared she might hyperventilate.

But through all that, the girl nodded her assent.

Ted wrapped his arm around her waist and flew the two of them out of the room. As he did, he heard a pipe burst in the distance and a flood of new water came pouring in. The water level was now up to Ted's knees. Sophie cried out and buried her head in Ted's chest.

"It's ok. We'll get out of—"

A beam came crashing down from the ceiling and hit Ted right in the back of the skull. He lost his hold of the girl and they both tumbled into the water. Ted's face made impact with the flood first. His eyes stung with whatever was floating around in the water. When he came back up for air, Sophie was nowhere to be seen. Ted felt his pulse race.

"Sophie?!"

He dove under the water. Ted looked in every direction but he couldn't see the girl. He felt his breath grow heavy. As Ted left the water, he saw something he never would've expected. In the middle of the crumbling building and the water, there was a blue portal hovering a few inches off the ground. Amidst the chaos, the shimmering light from whatever it was remained calm and steady. Sophie was right beside it, and though the water was up to her midsection, she waded toward the gateway.

"Sophie, no!"

Before Ted could stop her, the girl had disappeared through the blue portal. Ted ran toward the phenomenon, but it closed with a sound that reminded him of a classic video game. As he reached for where the portal had been, another series of beams fell to the ground and surrounded him.

"Ted, are you out of the building?"

Before Ted could respond, the rest of the hospital came down on top of him.

About the Authors

Bryan Cohen

Bryan Cohen is an author, a podcaster, and a coach. He's published over 40 books, which have been downloaded over half a million times. His books include How to Write a Sizzling Synopsis and five novels in The Viral Superhero Series. He's the co-host of The Sell More Books Show and the head writer at Best Page Forward, a book description writing service.

You can find out more about Bryan at http://www.bryancohen.com

Bryan is a graduate of the University of North Carolina at Chapel Hill. In 2013, Bryan appeared on an episode of the nationally televised "Who Wants to Be a Millionaire." He did just fine. Bryan lives with his wife and their Netflix account in Chicago.

Casey Lane

Casey Lane loves fairy tales, superheroes, and magic of all kinds. As the author of the Fairy Tales Forever series, Casey is grateful for the opportunity to spice up classic tales with some kickass heroines.

Get the free novella "Snow White's Revenge" by joining Casey's list at: http://bit.ly/caseylanelist

Check out "Cinderella Dreams of Fire," the first book in Casey's new series right here: http://bit.ly/cindydreams

Made in the USA
Monee, IL
26 February 2020